Placeholders

James Roseman

VERVE BOOKS

First published in 2024 by VERVE Books Ltd,
Harpenden, UK

vervebooks.co.uk
@VERVE_Books

A CIP catalogue record for this book is available from the British Library.

ISBN
978-0-85730-857-3 (Paperback)
978-0-85730-858-0 (Ebook)

2 4 6 8 10 9 7 5 3 1

Typeset 11.2 Adobe Garamond Pro
by Avocet Typeset, Bideford, Devon, EX39 2BP
Printed and bound in Great Britain by
CPI Group (UK) Ltd, Croydon CR0 4YY

MIX
Paper | Supporting
responsible forestry
FSC® C171272

For Sarah

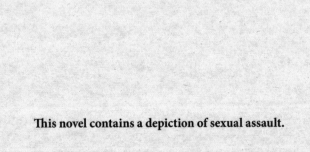
This novel contains a depiction of sexual assault.

1

Aaron passes into and out of circles of light cast from the street lamps above. There's a stabbing pain in his right side that he's been ignoring for at least three blocks, a steak knife tucked neatly between his ninth and tenth rib. The rubber soles of his high-tops slap the concrete as he runs. He's at the point now where he can actually feel himself perspiring, the sweat pooling under his arms and across his back. None of it matters; he's nearly there. That's all that counts. She'll understand. He can make up a story that is believable enough to make her forgive him. That is the power of words. They erase the things they purport to describe.

But there is truth, it is a thing that exists, and the truth in this case is devastatingly simple. Mornings come without warning when Aaron finds it impossible to do anything but stare at his alarm clock and watch time pass, guilt and dread churning like oil in his stomach. Sometimes he cries uncontrollably, violent sobs that leave an ache in the hollow of his chest for days. Sometimes he doesn't cry at all. It started after Moe died, of course. Everything like that started with Moe. He tries not to think about it. Last night, he had a dream that he and his brother were bicycling along their hometown boardwalk. Seagulls and whirring bike gears. Tyres sticking and unsticking themselves to the pavement. The sounds and smells of summer ocean waves crashing against the sea wall beneath them, shooting up and spraying them with mist.

Moe's smiling face. The sun beating down on them. It all felt so real.

Aaron woke in the cobweb remnants of the dream surprised to find himself not in his childhood home but in the basement bedroom of his apartment, his home of the past five years. He spent the morning horizontal beneath the duvet, watching the minute hand go round in circles, praying for an aneurysm or a carbon monoxide leak. It is a miracle he managed to escape his house at all, albeit an hour late, evidence in some capacity of how much he wants to be there with her. This is, of course, going to be much too difficult for Aaron to explain. The truth so often is.

The steak knife twists and Aaron stops in a circle of light, panting, hands on his knees, a throbbing in his side. The restaurant is only a few blocks more. It is possible that she's left already. Maybe she never came. Aaron takes a deep breath and tries not to think about it. He focuses instead on something else, something like a week ago, the last time he saw her face.

When the bartender finally did come over, Aaron ordered two tequila sodas. He didn't ask what the girl beside him wanted, he just ordered. He hoped this would make him look decisive.

'Why the soda?' she asked.

'No soda!' he yelled to the bartender.

'Two shots, then?' the bartender asked.

'Four shots.'

A wave of dancers crashed against the bar, pushing her into him, then ebbed back towards the dance floor. She stayed close.

'I don't even know your name,' he said.

The bartender dropped off the shots. They took them one after the other.

'Camilla,' she said. 'My name is Camilla.'

There was a nasal lilt to her voice, an accent Aaron was only then able to disentangle from the enormous noise around them.

'Where are you from?'

'Ireland,' she said, then frowned. 'Is it obvious?'

Aaron didn't often come to places like this. It was hot and loud and dark. Circles of coloured light sling-shotted from one wall to another. Jake had said it would be fun to get out and that Aaron should lighten the fuck up sometimes. Aaron couldn't really talk Jake out of things like that. They came together, Jake got separated, and Aaron got drunk. These events happened in rapid succession. He soon found himself on the dance floor with someone much too beautiful to be real. His head felt like it was full of water sloshing from one side to the other. Every time she took a step, he stepped where her foot had just been. He thought about how he would tell this story to Jake later even as it was playing out in real time in front of him. She smiled, her face illuminated by a passing green light, and that voice in his head went quiet. Now they were at the bar so he must have done something right. People did this all the time. They bought women drinks in hot, loud places and charmed them without wondering which version of themselves to affect.

'Let me guess,' Camilla said. 'You're Irish too. You've a great-great-grand-uncle who was born in Cork, or actually – come to think of it – maybe it was Donegal.'

'I'm not Irish,' Aaron said.

'You might be the only one here who isn't.' Her laugh was genuine, as was the smile that followed it.

'What brought you here? Have you got family in Boston or something?'

'I've always been a bit obsessed with America,' she said. 'I burned out our VHS tape of *Forrest Gump* I watched it so much as a kid.'

She put a hand on his arm as she talked. The gesture was casual and warm. She must glide through her entire life with this ease, he thought. He imagined sitting with her on a train somewhere, sunshine through the window, her head resting on his shoulder.

'…Da would get me on the table and he'd start a line and I'd finish it, that's how well I knew it.'

Aaron nodded, unsure of what to say to keep her talking. Then came a tap on her shoulder from a blonde in a sequined dress, leaning forward to whisper something into her ear.

'Right so,' Camilla said and patted Aaron's chest. 'Thanks for the drinks.'

'Any time,' he said, but she'd already left.

Aaron found Jake singing in a bathroom stall with some suit who was holding out his phone. Jake snorted something off its screen. Music pounded through the door. The man in the suit was named Percy. The stall smelled strongly of patchouli and piss.

'This is Aaron, this is the guy I was telling you about,' Jake said.

'That's fucking – that's crazy, man, isn't it? You were just talking about him and now he's here. What is that, serendipity? Coincidence? What do you call that?'

'Here,' Jake said, holding out Percy's phone. 'Have some of this.'

'What is it?' Aaron asked.

'Do you care?'

'Not really, no.'

There was a rip of fire up his nostril and then clumps of baking soda bitterness at the back of his throat. He sniffled a few times. There was a sensation like water dripping out of his nose. He waited for something to happen.

'They want us spinning like hamsters in our wheels, churning out profits,' Percy said. He took a bag of off-white powder from the inside pocket of his blazer and balanced the phone in one hand and tapped out a line with the other, all while bopping his head along to the music. 'And we're approaching the endgame. What's unemployment at? What's the average Fortune 500 CEO make?'

'It's fucked,' Jake agreed.

'It's absolutely fucked,' Percy said. He straightened out the line with a metal credit card. 'And the worst part is that it's intentional. Have you heard of the Rothschilds? George Soros?'

'What is this, coke?' Aaron asked.

'Ket,' Percy said, evening out the lines. 'Did you know that I work at a bank?'

'What did he say?' Aaron asked Jake. 'I can't hear a fucking thing.'

'A bank,' Percy shouted. 'I said, I work at a bank! Get some of this into you, it'll fix your hearing.'

This time felt more like snorting tiny shards of glass. Aaron wiped at his nose with the back of his hand and it came away with a paintbrush of watery red across it. The blood beaded on the skin. Aaron hadn't always done drugs in bathrooms with strangers. He'd been one of those kids who took notes during the drug awareness seminars in high school, convinced that so much as a joint could render his future comprehensively fucked. But that was before. Before he lived with Jake. Before Moe died. Before he stopped speaking to his parents. Coke – or something like it – was now an expected staple of their nights out. Aaron stared at the blood streaked across the back of his hand. Oblivion was, at its heart, another form of absolution.

'Oh fuck.' Percy had two baggies in his hands and he was looking between them. 'Fuck me, man, this one's the ketamine.'

They returned to the dance floor and treaded water in the ocean of bodies. The bass was overwhelming. Aaron closed his eyes and let his arms hang loose at his sides and felt his heartbeat slow down and speed up to match the underlying rhythm of the beat. He was covered in sweat and his mouth was dry. Percy returned with three drinks in hand.

'I've got an expense account,' he shouted. 'Fuck 'em, right? I'll say I was out with prospective clients; they won't give a shit. Fuck 'em!'

This was how people behaved. Aaron knew Percy, or at least people like Percy, but only in the abstract. Individuals who participated in just the right amount of social discourse to fit into these circles, using phrases like 'change from the inside' in defence of their careers, then enacting that change by charging thirteen-dollar whiskey sodas to a bank that made $82 billion last year. Aaron didn't like Percy. He wanted to grab him by the front of his shirt and scream in his face, ask him how he'd like to live on a hundred bucks a week. But maybe he was just a less successful Percy. Wasn't he too given every opportunity? And didn't he decide to flop face-first instead of making some leap towards greatness? Greatness? Avarice. Something, surely, if not greatness.

'Those fucks drive around in their fancy cars and live in their fancy apartments,' Percy said. 'My boss made three mil last year overseeing derivatives, can you believe that? He wasn't even the one selling them. If I were a ditch digger at least there'd be some holes in the ground.'

'You've never dug a hole in your fucking life,' Jake shouted.

Percy nodded and bopped his head to the music. 'They all go out in Seaport, but this is more my scene. These are my people. Real, salt-of-the-earth, normal people.' His jaw swivelled back and forth as he ground his teeth. 'Have you guys ever been to Gstaad?'

Jake nudged Aaron's shoulder and pointed to someone at the bar through a split in the crowd. 'She keeps making eyes at you.'

There was a brunette deep in conversation with her friend. The crowd merged together and Aaron lost sight of her.

'In Thailand they have these brothels where you select the women through a one-way mirror,' Percy shouted at no one in particular. 'It's disgusting, but in a way it's more direct, isn't it? I mean, isn't the transaction basically the same?'

Aaron wanted to point out how the social intricacies of dating and international sex trafficking had a subtle but significant difference that Percy may have overlooked but then the crowd opened up and the brunette from the bar walked over to them. Aaron finished his drink in four burning gulps and shoved his empty plastic cup into Percy's hands. The woman led Aaron away by the hand as his head began to swim.

'Dance with me,' she said, so he put all his effort into sticking one foot in front of the other.

There were rules to this. People talked about alcohol tolerance like it was strength, some physiological attribute that could be trained intentionally over time, as if at a certain point four beers didn't make a dent. To Aaron it was more like driving a fifty-year-old shitbox in a Nor'easter. You could practise downshifting in the snow and turning against the drift and get better at it with time. There was a knack to it. It wasn't that you didn't get drunk, you just got better at being drunk, the core mechanical operation of driving a body that was out of commission.

He stepped where her foot had just been. She put her arms around his neck and it felt nice, but then he thought about Camilla at the bar and her hand on his arm and he squirrelled out of her embrace in what he hoped looked like an elaborate dance move. Her face reflected her confusion, and then the image clicked.

'Camilla,' he said.

'You forgot my name, didn't you?'

'No, I just–'

'You absolutely forgot my name,' she said. 'You're lucky you're drunk.'

Aaron explained the shitbox and the Nor'easter, the downshifting in the snow. She waved away the words and pulled him down by the neck, kissing him. Aaron wondered if his heart was going to explode, it was beating so fast.

'My name isn't Camilla, it's Róisín.'

'I don't understand.'

'I don't like giving my name out to strangers.'

Aaron smiled.

'What?' she asked.

'We're not strangers, then,' he said.

'No,' she said, returning the smile. 'I suppose not.'

They spent the rest of the night alternating between dancing and drinking. Aaron felt something like the lifting of a weight and imagined a knot in his stomach loosening just enough to sneak a finger between the gaps in the rope. This was something very near real life, a simulacrum of emotional connection, of loneliness corrected. Róisín danced, illuminated by the passing colours. She looked truly beautiful. Aaron could have watched her for the rest of his life.

At one thirty, the lights came on and the music stopped and the exit doors opened. They stood for a moment in the stark reality, blinking and waiting for it all to come into focus. Róisín tapped a spot below her nostril.

'You're bleeding,' she said.

Aaron found a paper napkin in his pocket and pressed it against his face. 'I get nosebleeds,' he said, nodding.

Conversation bubbled up from the crowd surrounding them. There was a lurch and then they were caught in a flow of sweaty people emptying out onto the sidewalk beside the club. The air was sudden and cold. They stood beneath a street light and the crowd dissolved around them. Róisín saw Sofia, her blonde friend in the red sequined dress, and called her over. There was a punch on Aaron's arm and he was reunited with Jake, who was soaked in sweat and bleeding a little from his nose, and with Percy, who looked much younger in the yellow light.

'Let's get a taxi back to my place,' he said, so they did.

Róisín held Aaron's hand as they got into the car. That's how easily it started.

2

The waiter leads Róisín to a table, pulls out a chair, waits for her to sit and then pushes in the chair. Light jazz plays from hidden speakers. The walls are crammed with framed sepia photographs and memorabilia. Róisín removes her phone from her handbag and types out a message then presses send. She returns the phone to her bag. The waiter sets down a basket of bread.

'How are we doing tonight?' he asks. 'Have you dined with us before?'

'No,' Róisín says.

'First time, that's awesome. Welcome. Would you like me to run you through how the menu works, or will I wait for the rest of your party to arrive?'

'He must be running late,' she says.

The waiter offers a wide smile and nods before leaving. She takes a roll from the basket and pulls it apart. She puts a piece of warm dough onto her tongue and sucks on it until it turns tasteless in her mouth. Across the restaurant, a man takes a sip from his wine glass and nods to a waiter to pour more.

'Excellent choice,' the waiter says, smiling widely. 'A truly excellent choice.'

The man at the table sets down his wine glass and shrugs at his wife as if to say, 'But what do I know?' Róisín feels an acute longing in the space behind her heart. All she's ever wanted is someone to shrug at her from across the table, someone who also feels they're playing pretend, the two of them children in grown-up clothing both in on the big joke of it all.

There's a candle in the centre of the table, a tealight in a red glass holder. She peers above the lip to check if it's real. It is. Her phone buzzes in her bag. It's Sofia.

so???

Róisín types out a message.

not here yet. 10 demerits.

Her phone vibrates in her hand as another message appears.

poor form. bad start.

She is unsure what to expect of this reunion. The last time she spoke to Aaron they were in his bed, naked, and he was apologising.

Percy had taken them from the club to a luxury complex in Seaport overlooking the harbour. His gaff was a two-bed with in-unit laundry and a six-burner double-oven Viking cooking range with a built-in heating shelf. Rent cost $6,890 per month. He told them all of this on the lift ride up to the twenty-third floor.

'Are you two fucking?' Percy asked Róisín. 'Is he, like, your boyfriend or something?'

'Not yet,' Róisín said, yawning.

She felt Aaron tense beneath his coat. There was a simple beauty in his transparency. When she'd kissed him that first time on the dance floor, he'd kissed her back like he'd been wanting to do it all night, holding nothing back. And the way he'd spun out of her grip out of loyalty before realising she was the woman from the bar. His open want for her was pleasantly blatant.

'Hm,' Percy said. He bit his thumbnail and nodded towards Jake and Sofia. 'And what about you two?'

Sofia shook her head. 'I don't believe in monogamy.'

Róisín knew Sofia from the café they worked at. Sofia joined and got herself promoted from barista to 'social media manager' in only a few weeks, a dubious title that involved fewer hours and higher pay. Róisín would have minded if Sofia didn't spend so much of her free time in the café anyway, which made the shifts more bearable. Róisín enjoyed the company of people whose motives and opinions were clear to her.

They passed the same artwork three times before arriving at a heavy door. The apartment was spotless. There was a chandelier hanging over a glass dining table with gold legs, a low grey sectional pushed up against floor-to-ceiling windows, a white fur area rug. No plants or pets or photographs. The walls were bare except for a framed *Wall Street* poster, the bottom corner of which, he was eager to point out, had been signed by both Michael Douglas and Charlie Sheen. It had cost him $5,000.

'The furniture is all Scandinavian. Very expensive. My girlfriend is a Swedish model. Was a Swedish model. She still is a Swedish model, I mean, she's just not my girlfriend anymore. Wine, anyone?'

Sofia watched him carefully. He wouldn't stand a chance.

'What do you do when you go into your office or whatever and sit down?' Jake asked. 'What is it that you actually do?'

Percy sat back and looked around like he was taking it all in for the first time. The muted green walls. The moulding. The granite countertops and trendy, retro-style appliances. 'The first thing I do when I get to the office is close my blinds and jerk off.'

'Right so,' Róisín said, stepping out to the balcony for a smoke.

There wasn't a nuanced explanation for people like Percy. His driving force was to accrue wealth, a preoccupation that took up so much of his thinking that he didn't quite know what to do now that he had it. He wanted a life of sex and money, not as side-effects of a rich and interesting life, but because he thought it important to have them. He was simple in that way. The door slid shut again and then there was Aaron beside her.

He let out a short, low whistle. 'That's a nice view.'

The water of the harbour reflected the stale yellow light from the lamps across the street in rippling waves. The black, punched-out silhouettes of boats bobbed in the water. The air smelled like the sea.

Róisín held up her cigarette packet. 'Did you want one?'

'No, thanks.' Aaron picked at something on the golden railing attached to the balcony parapet. He glanced from her to the railing and back. 'I only met him tonight,' he offered, rubbing his neck. 'It's not like I know him.'

'Okay,' she said.

'He's not a friend, I mean. I don't want you to go off me by association.'

'There was a risk,' she said, which made him smile. She took a drag from her cigarette and pushed the smoke out of her open mouth. 'You don't have to wait out here for me, you know. I'm fine.'

'Oh,' he said. He turned towards the sliding glass door, and then back. 'I don't really want to go back in there quite yet, if it's all the same.'

There was a silence, accented only by the whipping wind and the shuffling sound of sails from the boats below.

'Do you live in a place like this?' she asked.

Aaron shook his head and laughed.

'What, is that such a ridiculous question?'

'If you saw where I live, you'd understand. The entirety of

my apartment could probably fit on that half of the balcony. I mean, Jesus, is that a fire pit?'

'So your rent isn't seven grand a month?' she asked.

'Close,' Aaron said. 'Very close.' He tapped his palm against the railing and let it drop by his side. 'What about you, do you live in a place like this?'

Róisín smoked her cigarette and shook her head. 'I do not.'

'No Viking stovetop? No Scandinavian furniture?' Aaron unrolled the cuffs of his button-down and pulled his sleeves to his wrists, crossing his arms. He had a kind face. His hair, tousled by the wind, came over his forehead in a curl.

'You must be freezing,' she said. 'You don't have to stand out here for me.'

'I'm fine,' he said, shivering. 'I'm used to it.'

'You're a local, then, or what?'

'There's a tiny beach town about forty-five minutes north of here. That's where I grew up.' He leant forward over the railing and then back onto his feet. 'Where in Southern Ireland are you from?'

'There is no Southern Ireland. There's Northern Ireland and there's Ireland.'

'Where in Ireland are you from?'

'Do you know where Wicklow is?'

Aaron shook his head.

'Do you know where Dublin is?'

'No,' he said.

'Why'd you ask me where I'm from if you don't know where anything is?'

He smiled. 'I just like hearing you speak.'

Róisín felt the heat in her cheeks. She flicked her cigarette away and watched the red dot get carried by the wind before extinguishing. When she looked at him, Aaron was quick to look away. His eyes were on some spectrum between grey and blue. She felt a sudden urge to tell him that she thought he was beautiful. 'Tell me something about yourself.'

Aaron sucked on the inside of his cheek, thinking. Then he faced her, smiling. 'I'm afraid of flying.'

'A metal tube in the sky, I don't blame you.'

'I don't actually mind being up there in the clouds. And I don't get nervous taking off either, it's just the landing.'

'Sure yeah, it feels like you're going to crash.'

'Exactly,' he said. 'Tell me why you moved here. And don't say *Forrest Gump*.'

'What, you don't believe in the power of Tom Hanks?'

'It'd be a more compelling argument if you hadn't missed Mississippi by a few thousand miles.'

'Forrest is from Alabama.' She took a deep breath in through her nose and out through her mouth, searching for the right words. There was common ground between them, she could feel that already, but in practical terms the two of them were effectively strangers. What would his reaction be, she wondered, if she told him the truth? *I wasted years of my life in an emotionally manipulative relationship and only found the courage to leave him while in a foreign country.* No, that wouldn't do. 'I guess I wanted to do something exciting with my life and moving away was the easiest thing.'

'And have you got a big family?'

'A brother and a sister. You?'

'A brother,' Aaron said. 'Moe.'

'And what's Moe do?'

He opened his mouth to say something and then closed it instead. 'Any aunts or uncles?'

'A few,' Róisín said. 'What's Moe do?'

'How many?'

'I don't know. Like at least twenty. What's Moe do?'

'Jesus, twenty. Twenty's a lot. How many cousins do you have, like a hundred?'

'Why won't you answer the question?'

Aaron sucked on the inside of his cheek. 'Moe is at Harvard. He wants to be a doctor.'

'Ah,' Róisín said. 'So you're the stupid one, then?'

He laughed. He had a nice laugh. 'You've no idea.'

'Well, it must be nice having your family so close.'

'Sure,' he said. He unbuttoned one of his cuffs and started to roll up the sleeve, changed his mind and rolled it back down again. 'I don't get along with my parents, to be honest.'

'Families can be tough,' Róisín said. She took a quiet step towards Aaron, hoping he wouldn't notice.

'My mom used to tell Moe and me that when an octopus gives birth it sits on the eggs and when they hatch the children eat the mother from the inside out. She'd make a point of telling us this whenever one of us asked for a ride to a friend's house or pocket money for the movies.'

'Sure, isn't that all mothers, though?'

Aaron moved towards her. 'Is your mom like that?'

'No,' Róisín admitted. 'No, my mam is lovely.'

They were only inches apart now, both leaning against the railing. Róisín felt the static charge in her skin as she got closer.

'We can switch mothers if you'd like,' Aaron said.

'Sounds like I'd be getting the raw end of that deal,' Róisín said. Then she kissed him.

When they went back in, Percy and Jake and Sofia were in much higher spirits. There was a baggie on the table and Percy encouraged them both to help themselves. Aaron didn't respond. He sat down and waved away the offer, glancing from

Percy to Róisín and back. Such beautiful transparency. Under normal circumstances he'd have helped himself, and that was a useful thing to know. Because Róisín was there, these weren't normal circumstances, and that knowledge was useful in a different way. People so often showed you exactly who they were.

They went from Percy's to Sofia's and then back to Aaron's, where they'd tugged at each other's clothes as soon as they got into the bedroom. Then, naked, what often happened behind closed doors almost did.

'Do you not find me attractive?' she asked him.

'It's not that, I swear, it's not that at all. I don't know what it is.'

'I'm only joking,' she said and put her hand on his arm. 'It's kind of sweet, honestly.'

Aaron sat on the edge of the bed with his face in his hands. 'Will you let me take you out to dinner?' he asked from behind his fingers.

Róisín laughed.

'Are you laughing at me?' he asked.

'I'm not, I'm not,' she said. 'I don't know how you made that jump. Is that the going rate of erections these days?'

'I'm such an idiot,' Aaron said.

'What's your erection worth?' she asked, poking him in the ribs. 'Eh, mopey? A burger and some chips? A packet of crisps?'

He smiled from behind his hands and turned to face her. 'No, I was thinking something nice.'

'Well then,' she said, raising her eyebrows. 'High expectations.'

They fell asleep wrapped in each other's arms and, when the heat became stifling, she pushed him off and rolled over.

Róisín tugs at the sleeve of her blouse. She spent her day off this week scouring thrift shops with Sofia for something casual but chic and, most importantly, cheap. She checks her phone. Aaron is now twenty-eight minutes late. *If it gets to thirty*, she tells herself, *I'm leaving.* The waiter asks if she'd like to start with a cocktail while she waits and gives a half-frown when she says, 'No, thank you, I'm sure he'll be here soon.'

It's another twenty minutes before Aaron arrives in jeans and a wrinkled long-sleeve T-shirt patched with sweat. His hair is flat on one side and the back of it sticks up like a jagged wave. He takes off his jacket and the full extent of the sweat patches becomes apparent. It is immediately clear to Róisín how much more thought she has put into this night than he has.

Aaron doesn't apologise as he sits. He pulls the napkin out from the metal ring and pats his forehead with it as he looks around. His eyes are red and puffy. 'Fancy,' he says.

'You say that as if you're surprised.'

'What's the matter?'

'Nothing,' Róisín says and breathes out through her nose. 'You seem surprised, is all. Haven't you been here before?'

'No,' Aaron says, shaking his head. He plucks a roll from the basket and takes a bite out of it. 'I asked Jake for a recommendation, and Jake asked Percy.'

'Oh.' Róisín looks down at her lap. Her phone buzzes inside her bag and she ignores it. She feels her face growing warm.

The waiter reappears at the table, wide smile in place. 'Welcome, sir. I understand this is your first time dining with us tonight?'

Aaron looks from the waiter to Róisín, somewhat alarmed at the man's sudden presence. 'It is,' he says.

'If you'd like, I'd be happy to run you through how our menu works here–'

'I'm guessing I pick something from this list and you bring it to the table, something like that?' he says.

The waiter smiles wider. 'Exactly right, sir. Why don't I give you a few minutes to read it over and I'll be right back to take your order.'

Aaron scans the menu. 'I'm starving,' he says.

'I think I'd like to go home,' Róisín says quietly.

He wipes his forehead with the napkin and rubs the back of his neck. 'What?'

Róisín stands, feels light-headed and puts a hand onto the table to steady herself. She knocks over her glass of water. 'Sorry,' she says.

'What's going on?' Aaron asks.

Róisín slips on her coat and takes her bag from the seat beside her. The world loses some of its colour and the blood rushing in her ears sounds like television static. The waiting room jazz seems to warble in the background. Aaron stands and reaches to put a hand on her shoulder, stops, and instead digs both of his hands into his pockets.

'I'm really sorry,' he says. 'I fucked the whole thing up.'

She wonders what he hopes to accomplish with this observation. She's upset he cared so little, but she's more upset for allowing herself to care so much. She was joking when she implied his suggestion of a meal was compensation for them not having sex, but now it seems obvious in retrospect that he's only here because he thinks he owes her something. She feels used and tired. She leaves the restaurant and listens out as she walks down the sidewalk. The door to the restaurant does not open behind her.

In the first few months after moving, Róisín developed homesickness like a disease of the heart. She walked to work alone, spoke only to customers and returned home again alone. All her life, she had been told by people she trusted that she was a pleasant person with a warm personality. What explanation was there for this? Three years gone and her only friend was Sofia. Róisín grew up without silence in a house too small for the family living inside it. And now this quiet life. She has become accustomed to the taste of her own saliva. The burn as tears form. The heat on her cheeks as they fall. Still she stays. There is a fundamental difference between being the child who moved to America and being the child who moved to America and came back a few years later, who wound up in the same place she'd always been.

She looks at the alien lamp lights and the cars on the wrong side of the road and wonders if this will ever feel like a place she belongs. There are restaurants and bars full of people who know and love each other and she watches them from outside the glass as she walks by. She passes a couple holding hands and attempts a smile, first at the woman and then at her partner. Both look at their shoes as they pass.

3

The communal coffee pot is found in the break room, half full. Its contents are somehow both too watery and too bitter, a paradoxical combination Aaron considers as he stares into the depths of the murky brown liquid in his insulated disposable cup. People type in sporadic bursts on keyboards which are much louder than they need to be. Phones ring, unanswered, and are then picked up with a customary, 'How the hell are ya?' And then, 'Can I put you on hold for a sec?' The copy machine beeps and whines and grinds as paper goes in and paper comes out. The noise blends together in a cacophony of office doldrums, waves in an ocean of mediocrity. This is productivity at work. Aaron takes another sip and grimaces. He rubs his thumb on a brown spot near one of his buttons. It doesn't come off. A poster on the wall encourages Aaron to *Do Your Part!* He watches the second hand of the clock rotate around the white circle until it's gone five times and then he forces himself to walk back to his desk.

There's a paper plate with a slice of deflated cake on it that has appeared beside his keyboard. He looks around the other cubicles but there's nobody there. The office chair squeaks as he sits on it. The back is loose and, when he sits, he falls backwards momentarily and gasps as he reaches his hands out to steady himself. The mechanism catches and he's fine. He sits upright. It's nice to feel something.

Aaron pulls himself into his desk and adjusts the keyboard so that it sits comfortably under his hands. He unlocks his computer. There are four new emails in his inbox. Someone has messaged him on a popular social media website. A banner promises him that there are hot new singles in his area. His cursor hovers over the lurid image of a woman in a bikini leaning forward and looking into his eyes. He closes the window of the web browser.

There's a plastic fork resting on the paper plate. The cake has begun to sag. Aaron presses his tongue against the inside of the top row of his teeth. He hasn't spoken to anyone in person since arriving. He takes a sip of coffee. It's already gone lukewarm. He sets the cup back down next to the plate. The red light on his phone lights up and then the ringing begins. Aaron lifts the plastic phone to his ear. There's static on the other end, then the sound of heavy breathing.

'Is this Shipping?' the caller says.

'No,' Aaron says. 'This is Data Entry.'

The caller coughs and asks him to speak up.

'Data. Entry.'

'Fucking bullshit. Goddamn fuckwits,' the caller says and hangs up.

Aaron considers the plastic receiver in his hand and then places it back onto its base. He opens the first of the four unanswered emails. There's a fifty-percent-off sale at a popular department store. His cursor hovers over the *delete* key. He weighs the pros and cons of deleting this promotional material. He presses archive instead. The second email is a mass memo from corporate that he's been added to as part of a mailing list. There are twenty replies in the chain so far so he has to scroll for quite a while to find the original message.

Remove please.

Why was I added to this?

REMOVE ME

What email list is this?

spam spam spam spam spam

Hidden among them is a reply which says simply, **Why am I even here?** Aaron stops scrolling and reads the original message. It was sent by someone in Human Resources named Heather. He clicks on her email address and a window opens displaying her company badge photograph. She's pretty in an ordinary kind of way. He pictures Róisín's face. He taps the screen of his cell phone. There are no new texts. He opens their messaging thread and reads the four unanswered messages he's sent since their botched date. He wonders yet again if he should have gone after her. He helped the waiter soak up the spilt water with napkins instead. There was a not insignificant part of him that was glad when she walked away. *Someone like that*, he thought then, *deserves a lot more than someone like me*. There's a knock on the wall of his cubicle and then Marge appears, taking up all the space.

'Howdy,' she says cheerfully. 'How are we this morning?'

'We are good,' Aaron says.

Marge stands there, smiling, and Aaron wonders if there's something he can do for her so that she'll go away and bother someone else instead of bothering him.

'Is there something I can do for you?' he asks.

'No, no,' she says. 'Just wanted to see if you'd had a chance to try the cake I brought in.'

'The cake,' Aaron repeats.

Marge smiles cheerfully and points to the plate beside his coffee. 'For Barbara's birthday.'

It's hardly ten thirty, Aaron thinks. 'Ah, right, the cake. Thanks.'

Marge nods, waiting. 'So did you like it?'

'I, uh, haven't tried it yet.'

Marge tilts her head, smiling so fucking wide it hurts to look at. He can see that she has no intention of leaving until he tries this cake. He lifts the plastic fork and cuts a piece from the bottom of the three layers. He spears it and brings it to his mouth. It dissolves almost instantly on his tongue, disintegrating into a merciless paste of processed flavours. He can't even tell if it's supposed to be chocolate.

'Yum,' he says.

'You didn't even get any of the frosting!' Marge says and laughs. Loudly.

'Right,' Aaron says. He cuts another bite, mostly frosting, and the bottom tine of the plastic fork snaps off. He uses the tip of his index finger to dollop a blob of cake onto the broken fork. The frosting tastes like granulated sugar and canola oil. He swallows. 'It's great,' he says.

'It's from Costco!' Marge says.

'Wow.'

'You'd never have guessed, right?'

'No, Marge, I never would have guessed.'

'And guess what else.'

Aaron stabs the cake with his fork and slides it away. 'What else.'

'No, no, go on, guess.'

Aaron shrugs. 'I don't know.'

'Guess,' she insists. She's really not going to let this go.

'Something about the frosting, maybe?'

She looks around and then leans in to whisper, 'It's not even real buttercream!'

'No,' he says.

Marge won't stop fucking smiling. She nods cheerfully. Her face looks absolutely diabolical in the sterile blue fluorescent lighting. 'It's Costco!'

'Costco,' Aaron repeats.

They stare at one another for an awkward moment. Aaron thumbs at the computer monitor behind him. 'Well, I'd better…'

'Of course, of course,' Marge says. She squints at his monitor screen and her face wavers. She hurries away.

Aaron swivels his office chair to face his monitor. There, in full screen, is the office profile page for Heather from Human Resources. Her photo takes up half the screen. Aaron feels the heat in his face. He closes the page immediately. He breathes in through his nose and out through his mouth. There is only a little bit of coffee left in his cup. He swallows it and stands.

At eleven o'clock he has a project meeting. He was added to this team by his manager in the hopes that he will 'bring more enthusiasm' to his everyday work. He wanted to explain at the time that she was confusing his lack of bringing enthusiasm with his lack of having enthusiasm. He is selling his time at an hourly rate, he wanted to say. There is nothing in his contract about being happy about it. Instead, he nodded glumly and said, 'Whatever you think is best.'

The meeting room is large enough to fit twenty people. Aaron is the only one attending in person. He turns on the lights and fumbles around with the remote control until the television screen turns on. It takes a minute to set it up so by the time the meeting floats into focus someone is already in the middle of speaking.

'And I see we have someone from Data Entry,' the speaker says. 'Nice of you to join us.'

Aaron gives a tight-lipped smile and nod. The television screen is split into neat video-conferencing squares like you'd see on a game show, but a sort of local-access game show where even the contestants don't want to be there. He sees his manager in one of the squares on the screen. She's clenching her jaw and typing something furiously on her keyboard. Those are quite obviously pillows that she's leaning against. He wonders if anyone else notices but then he sees at least two other squares in which people are also leaning on pillows. There was a memo that got sent out last month reminding the Data Entry department that **working from home was not permitted due to the sensitive nature of their work.** It had bounced to the top of his email inbox all morning every time someone replied saying something like, **Please remove me from this list.**

A ding and then an instant message on the screen of Aaron's work laptop. The message is from his manager.

Please be sure to prioritise coming to meetings on time.

Then another ding.

:)

The speaker stops speaking, clears his throat and then asks for anyone who isn't muted to please mute themselves because 'those dings are pretty distracting'. There's a flurry of activity as all of the faces in all of the squares scramble to check if they were the one unmuted, each looking relieved as they realise that they were not. Aaron searches the remote control for a mute button. Another ding from his laptop.

'Okay, people, seriously?' the speaker says.

The instant message is from his manager.

Please mute your computer.

Another ding.

:)

The speaker clicks a button on his computer and a large notification window comes up on the television screen indicating that Aaron has been involuntarily muted for the remainder of the meeting.

'As I was saying…' the speaker continues.

The project involves a new system of data which will replace an old system of data. The speaker invites one of the software engineers to lead the team through a high-level design of the project. The engineer looks like an undergraduate. Aaron types her name into the company directory as she talks. Wendy from Engineering. She joined the company two months ago. He can see that she graduated less than six months ago. He wonders what she did with her last four months of freedom. She looks kind and severe and actually quite intimidating. The people in the squares look more confused the more she talks, particularly the ones propped up on pillows.

'Any questions?' she asks.

She's left the architectural diagram shared on the screen. Aaron looks at it and is hit with nostalgia for his core computer science lectures in the old halls of his university. He had a professor named Professor Hescott who refused to use PowerPoint in favour of a chalkboard and who was, easily, the best professor he'd ever had. He wonders if Professor Hescott even knew his name. He'd been one of the only professors to meet students during the university's prospective student open day. He was warm and kind and shook Aaron's hand with an earnest appreciation, as if he were selling the university to Aaron rather than the other way around, as if Aaron didn't need to sell a better version of himself to be let in. The world seemed possible back then. Now, before he knows what he's doing, Aaron is raising his hand.

'Have you considered the throughput for user events coming off that data stream? Is the system designed to scale horizontally to handle bursts in traffic?'

The squares are silent. Wendy stares into her camera, out

of the television screen and into Aaron's eyes, saying nothing. Finally, the project lead unmutes himself.

'Data Entry,' he says. 'You're on mute.'

Aaron fumbles with the remote control. The project lead thanks Wendy for taking the time to give them Engineering's perspective on the project. The people in the squares unmute themselves and applaud. One by one the squares go black as they disconnect. Aaron's laptop dings.

Did you have a question?

It's from his manager. Another ding.

:)

He starts typing a message and then feels an overwhelming wave of raw emotion, like he could just about throw his chair through the fucking window and jump. He swallows, hard, and types a simple message before clicking send.

All good. :)

When he gets back to his desk, he opens a web browser and types in the name of a popular job-searching website. The browser displays a star to the right of the URL, indicating that Aaron has previously bookmarked this page for easier navigation to it in the future. There is a notification from someone named Marion O'Toole.

'Just accepted the promotion of my dreams!' it says. 'Seattle, here I come! #Microsoft'

The modal displaying this message also displays a tooltip which indicates that Aaron might remember Marion O'Toole from university. He does not. And then, in a flash, he does. There was the spring semester of sophomore year before he got kicked out that he was a teaching assistant. Marion offered to bring a carton of thirty light beers to his room in return for an A on her final project. Marion was on the women's volleyball team. The thought of thirty beers in his room was a nice one.

The thought of Marion in his room was even nicer. Aaron said yes. Nobody ever found out and, the day after grades were posted, Marion dropped off the promised case of beer. He let her into his room and felt his heart in his throat. Then David, her boyfriend, came in to pick her up. David high-fived Aaron just before they shut the door and left together. Jake had gone home by then. Aaron watched *Moneyball* alone on his laptop and drank six beers and then vomited in the urinal of the communal bathroom.

He closes the web browser and stares at his empty coffee cup until it's time for lunch.

Aaron's tray contains a ham and cheese baguette which is tightly wrapped in plastic. There's a plastic container with some wilted lettuce and a cherry tomato, as well as some bits of raw onion. There's a translucent plastic cup of water too. The cutlery is plastic and is itself wrapped in plastic. Aaron wonders if the tray is plastic too and the table as well. He tries to unwrap his ham and cheese baguette but it's too hot to touch. He sets it aside. Jake is telling him a story that he has told before, many times, in fact. Aaron doesn't mind it when Jake does this because he knows where to laugh and how to set up the jokes with questions like, 'And then what happened?' The narrative tension of the story depends on the listener's expectation that Jake will not urinate into the sink of the university dean's office, but the punchline of the story is that he does. Aaron laughs. His ham and cheese baguette has cooled to a temperature he can handle. He unwraps the sandwich and bites into it. It tastes like plastic. There's a poster on the wall behind Jake's left ear that reminds Aaron in block letters that, *Nothing Is Someone Else's Problem!*

On the far wall near the lunch line, another poster.

This Is What It Means To Be Part Of A Team.
'Isn't that fucking great?' Jake says, still laughing.

After lunch, Aaron goes into the break room to get another cup of coffee. The coffee pot is empty. He returns to his desk with a small translucent cup of water instead. Another paper plate has appeared next to his keyboard. It has a slightly larger piece of cake on it. He feels a tap on his shoulder.

'I got you one with extra frosting,' Marge says cheerfully.

Aaron sits down on his chair. Someone calls Marge away. Aaron feels like crying. Instead, he opens his email inbox. There are three new messages. The first is the same corporate chain as this morning, now with ten new replies.

> I do not remember ever being added to this list.
>
> guys don't respond to the message we're all getting notified!!1!
>
> spam spam spam spam spam
>
> What do you mean 'guys'? Let's do better. Here's a link to our guidelines on inclusive language.

The second new message is a group email which includes everyone working on the data system overhaul project. Wendy from Engineering has sent across her diagram outlining the engineering architecture of her solution. Aaron opens the attachment and drags on a corner of the window until it takes up most of the screen. There is a delicate beauty in Wendy's design. The lines interact in strict ninety-degree angles. Everything has a place. Everything has a purpose. Aaron closes the window. The phone on his desk rings.

'Hello?' he says.

The line is dead. He hangs up the phone. As he puts down the receiver, it rings again.

'Is someone there?' he says into the phone. 'Is anybody there?'

'Shipping?' someone says.

'No, Data Entry.'

'Shipping,' the man says, more insistent this time.

Before Aaron can say anything, the man hangs up. Aaron sets the receiver back onto its base. There's a sound like a slug keeling over and he sees that the slice of cake has collapsed in on itself. He watches it melt until the digital clock on the bottom right of his computer monitor indicates that fifteen minutes have passed.

When Aaron joined the company, they set him up at a desk that looked out over the courtyard in the centre of the business park. There was this great big tree that Aaron's window had a beautiful view of. He used to think it looked like a cartoon, that's how perfectly it was shaped. The last week of September rolled around and it was like the whole thing burst into fire. Bright yellow. Little specks of red. It was about a year after his brother Moe had died. He'd moved out and had just started ignoring phone calls from his parents. The volume on everything was turned down to a whisper; back then he was always asking people to repeat themselves. He was unable to focus, unable to sleep. He drank more than he'd ever drunk before in his life. By mid-October, Aaron was up to two bottles of wine most nights. Jake still refers to this period as Aaron 'at his most fun' and often brings it up when Aaron turns down an offer to snort another line of cocaine on a Tuesday night.

'What happened to fun Aaron?' he'll say. 'Remember him?'

One morning Aaron woke up and thought, *This is the rest of my life, this is all there is.* And then he thought of the tree in the courtyard and its brilliant leaves waiting for him and it was all only just bearable. He and Jake drove through a downpour to get to work that day and when Aaron was punched in and settled at his desk with a cup of coffee, he looked hopefully out of the window. The tree was bare. All of its leaves had blown off in the storm. He laughed at first, he couldn't help himself, and then he rushed for the bathroom. He locked himself in a stall and wept. It was the first time he had cried since Moe's death. He couldn't explain it.

A year ago, they reorganised the layout of the Data Entry floor and, as a part of that change, his desk was moved from the window to the centre pit. They constructed cubicles soon after that. They didn't call them cubicles at the time, of course, they sent out some mass email about 'partial wall enclosures for the purpose of increased productivity' that were to be erected. One morning, they were. The great big tree was cut down the following spring to make room for picnic benches nobody used. Marge started using the phrase 'work family' regularly.

Aaron clicks through a few tasks and sips from his plastic cup of water. He waits for the keys to stop clacking, for the phones to stop ringing, for the copy machine to shut down, for the casual conversations to wither away. Soon he is alone and it is time to leave. He puts on his canvas jacket slowly, mechanically, and makes his way to the parking lot where Jake is waiting for him. Tonight they will drink. Tomorrow they will work. And on. Aaron does his part. Aaron is part of a team. Nothing, Aaron knows, is someone else's problem.

There is a semi-truck ahead of them on the freeway. Jake upshifts and the car grinds before it catches, then they're both pushed back against their seats as they switch lanes and speed past the truck. Before they've overtaken it, a sports car comes flying out of nowhere. In the moment before it overtakes them, Aaron looks at the cars at either side of him and thinks, *I am part of a system.* And then, like anything else, the moment passes.

4

The group of students looks somewhere between the ages of twelve and twenty. They approach the counter of the café in a clump and talk over each other as they order so it becomes impossible to determine which girl wants which type of latté with which type of syrup. Someone asks for oat milk and now the rest want to change their orders from dairy to oat milk too. There is a girl at the end standing apart from the others. She patiently waits until the counter is clear to approach and orders quietly while looking at her feet. Róisín compliments her earrings and the girl blushes. She drops a folded dollar bill into the tip jar.

The bell above the door rings as a middle-aged man enters the front of the café. He stops at the counter and waves to get Róisín's attention.

'Black coffee, when you get a minute,' he says. 'Bring it to the back.'

Róisín nods and sets to work. The man's name is Charles Bosworth, though he insists that everyone who works in his café calls him Charlie.

Charlie interviewed Róisín for the barista position in the back room of the café. Róisín spent most of the time answering questions about Ireland and how she's been settling into Boston. He wrote some of her answers down on a piece of paper fixed to a clipboard. He asked her how old she was and she told him. This was one of the things he did not write down. Charlie didn't mind that Róisín couldn't fill out a W-2. He offered to pay her in envelopes of cash and didn't ask many questions about her situation. Then, just before he offered her the job, he asked if she had a boyfriend. Róisín wasn't sure what she was expected to say. She looked from Charlie to the framed photograph of his wife that sat on his desk then laughed it off and changed the topic.

Róisín pulls a shot of espresso and tops it with boiling water. She knows that when Charlie asks for 'a black coffee' he means an americano, though she'd never correct him. She sets the cup on the counter and opens the swing gate to step out from behind it. She picks up the cup and walks in careful, measured steps to avoid spilling.

Once, while sharing a pint of ice cream and a bottle of wine, Sofia admitted to Róisín that Charlie had put his hand on her breast while she was closing up.

'It was only for a second,' she said, then dipped her spoon back into the pint. 'It was just an accident.'

An 'accident', as Róisín understood it, connoted something unintentional, like slipping in the rain or dropping a plate. A fifty-something man groping the breast of the twenty-something barista he hired only weeks prior did not fit comfortably into this definition. It seemed incredibly intentional.

'You're making such a big deal out of it. He had his hand on my shoulder and it just happened, I guess,' she said, shrugging.

Shortly after Sofia admitted this incident to Róisín, she was promoted to manage and oversee the social media presence of the café and never brought it up again. Charlie explained in a mass email that Sofia had shown *initiative* in her first few weeks and that he hoped her work would bolster the popularity of the café among students in the local high school. He signed the email, 'Boz'.

Róisín knocks twice before opening the door. Charlie

looks up from his laptop and gestures at an empty spot on his otherwise cluttered desk. She sets down his coffee. He lets out a huff of air through his nose and points to the screen. The door drifts shut behind her.

'Do you know anything about this?' he asks.

'Could you turn the screen around?'

'It's stuck,' he says. 'Just come back here, it'll only take a second.'

Róisín steps behind the desk and Charlie rolls his chair to the right to make room. She can smell his sweat mixed with his cologne. The spreadsheet document he's working on is supposed to be tracking profit and loss but he's mixed up the formulae for some of the cells and now the whole thing is full of reference errors.

'You need to copy what's in these cells into these ones and you'll be sorted.'

'Right, okay,' he says, leaning back and crossing his arms. He huffs again. 'I'm not sure I know how to do that.'

The room feels smaller than it was when she walked in. The silence pulls the walls closer around them.

'Like this,' Róisín says. She types a few things on his keyboard and the errors disappear.

Charlie points at the screen. 'How'd you do that?'

Róisín explains about the formulae and the references when she feels his hand on her lower back. She freezes.

'Go on,' he says, leaning towards the screen.

The hand slides lower, squeezes, kneading her roughly, then lets go. Róisín stands and crosses her arms over her chest.

'Thanks for that, sweetheart,' Charlie says. 'I don't know what I'd do without you.'

Róisín leaves the back room and sets her apron on the counter before leaving the café through the side door. Her breaths come ragged and shallow. She can't get enough air into her lungs. She fishes a cigarette out from its packet but her hands are trembling and it slips between her fingers and bounces down the steps. The world goes blurry as she bends to pick it up. When she touches her eyes, she finds that she is crying.

There's a piece of concrete the size of a baseball. It's dusted in powder and bits of rock like it broke off the bottom step somewhat recently. Róisín smokes her cigarette and stares at the piece of concrete. She'd like to lift it up and take it into the back room where Charlie is sitting and hit him in the head with it. She imagines the surprised look on his face when he sees the thing hurling down upon him at the last moment, just before contact. There is no satisfaction in this image. She flicks the cigarette away even though it's only half-finished, balls her hands into fists and presses them against her eyes until it all popcorns into green-and-white static and the tears stop. She wants to go inside and slap her hands on the counter and yell out, 'Everyone, guess what the owner just did to me!'

Neither of these fantasies are practical options. What Róisín will do is simple: she will return to the counter and finish her shift, pretending none of this ever happened. She knows that she is outside only waiting for the feeling in her stomach to pass and to come to terms with this. The tears will stop eventually. Her chest feels hollow.

'Róisín,' a voice calls out.

She's quick to wipe her eyes with the heel of her hand. She takes a deep breath through her nose to steady herself before looking up. There, at the end of the alley leading to the back of the café, is Aaron.

'Róisín?' he calls out again. 'You okay?'

'What are you doing here?'

'You weren't responding to my texts,' he says. He's got a crumpled bouquet of flowers gripped in his right hand.

'What are those?'

'Flowers,' he says. 'In American culture, sometimes men buy flowers for women. This is seen as a romantic gesture. They often accompany an apology. Are you okay?'

'Go on, then,' Róisín says.

'Right. Well, I'm, uh, I'm so sorry,' he says, handing over the bouquet.

The plastic crinkles as she takes it. She fights the urge to smell them, to rub the petals between her index finger and thumb. This is the first time someone has ever bought her flowers.

'Did you even want to see me again?' she asks.

'Obviously.'

'It's not obvious, though, is it? When you show up an hour late to a dinner you invited me to. It's not obvious at all, actually. I felt really stupid,' she says. 'Can you understand how that made me feel stupid?'

'Yes,' he says. 'I can understand how that made you feel stupid.'

'Don't do that.'

'I'm serious. I can, yeah, of course I can.'

There's a tickle on her skin where one of the daffodils has come loose. She adjusts the flowers in the crook of her arm. Aaron smiles when he sees her do it. There is a simple and refreshing plainness to the way he wears his open heart. She has to remind herself she's mad at him.

'What was so important you couldn't even text me you were going to be late?' she asks.

He shrugs, his eyes fixed on the ground. 'Some days I really struggle to get up.'

'Everybody does.'

'No, I don't mean that it's difficult to get up, I mean I physically can't. Well not physically, obviously physically I can get up. This isn't coming out right.' He takes a deep breath and rubs the back of his neck. '"Episodes" might be a better word for what they are. I feel like I'm stuck in bed and all that I can do is watch the minute hand on my alarm clock spin around the white. It's like I'm rooted in place, I don't know how to explain it.'

'I don't understand,' Róisín says softly.

Aaron looks up at her then. His eyes are glossy and she understands that she will forgive him. 'I get sad sometimes,' he says.

Such beautiful transparency. The plastic crinkles in her arms. The last time she had this feeling was with Brian, who came into the Dublin café years ago demanding she remake his macchiato over and over, taking a sip of her third attempt and smiling. She should have been furious but all she felt was the pride of satisfying a man so discerning. He came back the next day and the day after and so on, until he finally told – not asked, told – her to join him for dinner. She had this feeling then. She cannot trust this feeling. Whatever commanded Brian's attention commanded it fully, and the things he left behind he abandoned completely. He shattered her with sentences and pieced the fragments back together in whatever form suited him best. He often told her she was fragile. She must be, she thought then, otherwise she wouldn't be so breakable.

Róisín used to dress in the clothes Brian wanted her to wear. She ate the things he wanted her to eat. She said the things he wanted her to say and, more importantly, avoided saying the things he didn't. He had the power to make a room feel small enough to hug the people inside of it or, with a breath of silence, pull the air out to make it feel cavernous, like Róisín was never meant to be there at all. He paid for them to fly to Boston. He gave her a diamond ring. He wanted her to say yes. But there, looking down at him beside the Charles River, she found inside of herself her voice, extant but long asleep. Brian flew back to Ireland alone. Róisín has been in Boston ever since. She is careful with the men she allows into her life because men are so often dangerous or boring or, worse, both. Still, she cannot deny the existence of this feeling.

'The flowers are a nice touch,' Róisín says finally.

Aaron takes another deep breath. 'I was hoping you'd let me take you out for a drink.'

'Why?'

'Because I want to make up for before.'

'You've sufficiently apologised. You don't owe me anything.'

He rubs his neck and stares at the ground.

'Quit your moping.'

'Sorry.' His hand comes down by his side. 'I like you,' he blurts out. He shakes his head. 'Jesus, did I actually just say that out loud?'

'So you like me, then, is that it?' she asks, smiling. 'Like me or like like me?'

'I like like you, Róisín,' he says, sighing. 'And I want to get to know you better.'

She looks from the flowers to Aaron. 'I hate lying,' she says.

'Okay.'

'For this to work, I need honesty, always.'

Aaron nods.

'Always,' she repeats.

'Always.'

She sighs. 'One drink. And you're buying.'

5

The bar is called Rudy's and it is a mainstay of both Aaron's neighbourhood and his life. Those who know Rudy by name – meaning, firstly, that they know his real name is Morris and, secondly, not to call him that – are welcome through the back door at any hour. The beer is warm and metallic and cheap. It is the sort of place that attracts degenerates and burnouts, which is why Aaron loves it so much. He often surrounds himself with people he considers fuckups so that he might feel functional by comparison.

Aaron chooses a seat at a table by the window. He hangs his canvas jacket on the back of the chair and orders a beer and a glass of red wine at the bar. Rudy fills the order without making conversation. This is another reason Aaron loves it here. He brings the drinks to the table and slides his phone out of his jacket pocket. He types a message out and sends it, then puts the phone face-down on the table.

He went to Róisín's café with a bouquet of flowers. He imagined her smile, her laugh, her small mouth pressed against his. Instead, she stood on the back steps with her arms crossed and asked for an explanation. He said something more honest than intended and she responded in kind. Aaron checks his phone but there are no new notifications since the last time he checked. He takes a small sip from his glass of beer and sets it on the table. He thinks that maybe this tardiness is an intentional form of soft revenge but he already knows, even from his short time knowing her, that this isn't something that Róisín is capable of doing.

As if in response to the thought, the door to the bar opens and she walks in. Aaron stands to greet her. They fumble between a hug and a kiss on the cheek.

Róisín looks around. 'This is not what I expected when you said we were meeting in Cambridge.'

'It's not all Harvard and MIT,' he smiles.

'Evidently not.'

'I wanted to bring you somewhere I go all the time. I thought it'd be more personal than pretending I go to places I don't just to impress you,' Aaron says. He rubs his neck. 'If you don't like it, though, we can go somewhere else. It is a bit of a dive.'

'It is,' she says, sitting. 'But I don't mind a bit of dinge.'

They clink their glasses and drink from them.

Aaron asks Róisín about growing up in Ireland. Róisín asks Aaron about growing up in Boston. She wants to know if he's ever eaten at an Olive Garden or shopped at a Home Depot. She's heard of these things in sitcoms and movies.

'We grew up hearing about Target and Walmart. There's nothing comparable to them.'

This is a joke on Aaron. She's fascinated by this breed of soulless corporations because they're unique to the largely unrestricted American markets that facilitate their existence. To ask about them calls attention to this disparity between the priorities of American and European governments. It's a put-down. But then her face lights up as she tells him about the first time she went to a Costco and got a hot dog there – 'It was just like a movie!' – and maybe it really is earnest fascination. When the drinks are finished, Aaron buys them another round.

Rudy glances at their table and hands Aaron his order.

'Don't fuck this up,' he says.

The bar hums along. The drinkers drink. The talkers talk. They get back onto the topic of family. Róisín reaches for his hand and holds it. Aaron would have thought and re-thought that motion until the moment had passed, yet here she is, reaching for his hand because she wants to hold it and thinking nothing more of it than that.

'I'm glad I gave you another chance,' she says.

'Me too,' Aaron says.

The door opens and a breeze cuts through the comfortable warmth of the bar. Sunshine streams through the windows.

'It's hard to believe it ever snows here,' Róisín says. 'I don't know if I'll ever get used to how cold it can get.'

'Do you not get winters like we do back home?'

'No. I used to write to Santa to bring us snow,' Róisín says. 'I bet you got a white Christmas every year, didn't you?'

'No, not really,' Aaron says.

'You're just saying that to make me feel better. Go on, brag a little.'

'I, uh, well. I wouldn't know.'

'Go on,' she says. 'I'd say you had the tree and the snow and the eggnog. My dream, and you had it every year. Didn't you?'

'I'm Jewish,' he says. He watches her eyes for some hint of how this news has landed.

'Oh.' She takes a sip of wine. 'And are you very religious?'

'We didn't grow up keeping kosher or anything, but we'd go to services and all that. My brother was the more religious of the two of us. Are you?'

'No religion in our house at all,' she says.

'Really? I would have expected—'

'What, because I'm Irish?'

Aaron feels his cheeks flush.

'Religion was never a big part of our lives growing up,' she says. 'If you never had a tree or presents or any of that, what did you do for Christmas, then?'

'What did you do for Hanukkah?' he asks, sharper than he intends.

Róisín tilts her head. She sets her glass back onto the table between them. 'Does it bother you that I'm not Jewish?'

'No,' he says. He breathes out of his nose. 'I'm sorry. We got Chinese food and went to the movies.'

'Chinese food and movies. You're joking.'

'They're the only places that are open,' he says, and she laughs. 'What's it like at yours?'

'Oh, you know, we gather in a little circle before Mass to celebrate the birth of our Lord and Saviour and then we pray about it,' she says, then smiles. 'No, we open presents and have a big feed. Mam cooks a dry roast and hands-down the best mash you've ever tasted.'

'Did you tell me you haven't been home since you moved?'

Róisín nods.

'Do you not go home for Christmas at least, or what?'

'It's a visa issue,' she says. She drains the dregs of her wine and then takes Aaron's empty glass. 'I'll get us another round.'

After their drinks, they decide they're hungry and Aaron suggests a place for burgers near Harvard Square. They walk there together, arm in arm. The restaurant is busy and the tables are packed in tight. The air is thick with the smell of hot grease. Aaron's shoulders rub against the shoulders of the man sitting at the table beside them. Aaron bites his nails and looks around. Conversations from the people surrounding them overlap into a buzz of background noise.

'Is this all right?' he asks, and she nods.

It's too loud to think properly. A waitress comes over with menus and takes their orders and Aaron alternates between drinking from his plastic cup of water and biting his nails. Róisín is telling him a story he can't follow about a place this place reminds her of.

'Would you have burger spots like this back home?' he asks.

'In Dublin, sure.'

'You're not from Dublin?'

'Not the city, no,' she says. 'I'm from Wicklow. I've told you that.'

'Ah,' he says.

The man at the table next to them reaches for ketchup, pushing his shoulder into Aaron's. Róisín says something he can't hear. He leans forward and asks her to repeat it, holding his hand up to his ear.

'I said, my brother lives in Dublin – maybe that's what you were thinking of.'

'Ah, yeah. That's it, probably.'

Their food arrives. Aaron hunches over his plate and digs in. Róisín takes a bite and sets her burger down. She takes a sip of water.

'It's really good,' she says.

He smiles and nods. The man at the table next to them laughs at something his friend says and pushes into Aaron again. Aaron finishes his burger in three more neat bites then folds its wrapper into squares. Róisín sets her burger down and looks at her plate. She hates it, obviously, and he's an idiot for bringing her here of all places. It's a greasy spoon filled with students who won't pipe the fuck down for even a minute. Róisín is the type of woman who men take to Italian restaurants in the North End or something. Aaron bites at his nail but there's no nail left so he bites at the skin on its side.

'Have I done something to annoy you?' Róisín asks.

'No,' he says. 'Why would you think that?'

'You've hardly said a word since we got here.'

'No, yeah. You're right. Sorry.'

She dabs at her mouth with her paper napkin and breathes out through her nose. She picks up the burger and the patty slips out between the bun and lands on her plate. She sets the bun down beside it.

'Sorry,' she says quietly and moves to swab up the specks of liquid that have splashed onto the table.

'It's okay.'

Aaron removes two bills from the inside of his wallet and calls the waitress over. She gives him a slip of paper and he gives her the bills, then tells her to keep the change. He stands up and walks to the door. He holds it open for Róisín as they walk back into the night.

'I'm sorry if I've done anything to upset you,' she says. She looks down at her shoes as she says it.

Aaron does something very brave and takes her by the hand. He tilts his head and bends forward so he can catch her eye-line. 'I have this thing with noise,' he says. He feels his cheeks flush. 'I get distracted in places like that, and especially with the guy next to me bumping into me. I got a little self-conscious in case you didn't like it. I know it's not the nicest place. I'm sorry for being busy in my head.'

'I did like it,' she says.

He moves his hand around her waist and pulls her into him for a kiss. Her nose presses cold against his cheek. When he pulls away, he sees she's smiling. She was sad and now, because of him, she's happy again.

'I know a communist pub just down the road, back towards Central. What do you think?'

Aaron lives in the bottom section of a duplex. His room is larger than Jake's but is in the basement. He leads Róisín up the driveway, around the back of the house and then down the brick steps to the door.

'Don't expect much,' he says.

'I've been here before, you know.'

'Yeah, but we were drunker last time.'

Róisín asks for a glass of water and heads for the bedroom while he locks up. Aaron walks up the steps to the kitchen. Jake is on the couch with a beer, playing a video game.

'Have a good night?' Jake calls out to him.

'Yeah,' Aaron says. He takes a glass from the cupboard and fills it in the sink.

'What'd you get up to?'

'Rudy's then Charlie's and then to People's Republik,' he says. 'She's downstairs, actually.'

'Is she? Attaboy,' Jake says. He doesn't turn from the screen. 'How many of these fucking Guild quests have I got to do? They're fucking endless, man.'

Aaron brings the water downstairs. He opens the bedroom door and finds Róisín with the duvet pulled up to her chin, her clothes discarded in a pile on the floor.

'Stop,' she commands. 'You've much too much on.'

He sets the glass of water down on the bedside table and reaches for the light switch.

'Stop,' she says, and then she smiles. 'I didn't get a good look at you last time.'

Róisín scoots to the edge of the mattress, bringing the duvet with her. Aaron bends forward to kiss her and pulls her up off the bed. The duvet falls away.

'This doesn't seem fair,' she whispers. She helps him unbutton his shirt, their mouths pressed together. She presses her palms against his chest, his shoulders, his arms. She kisses his neck and slips a hand beneath his waistband, holding him in her hand. 'Burger and some chips,' she says.

'What's that?'

'The going rate.'

After they have sex, he holds her. He traces aimless circles onto her back with his fingertips. Her skin is soft and smooth. She's the image of a marble statue. She feels slight and soft against his chest. He kisses her forehead. She looks up at him. For the first time in a long time, Aaron feels that he is exactly where he is supposed to be.

'I was worried you were off me back at the burger place,' Róisín says. 'Then I thought maybe you were worried about bumping into your brother or something.'

Aaron's hand stops tracing. 'What do you mean?'

'I don't mean anything by it. I just remember you saying he went to college there, is all. Studying medicine, wasn't it? He got all the brains, isn't that right?'

Aaron clears his throat.

'You all right?' she asks. 'Your heart is beating really fast.'

He nods and swallows hard.

Róisín sits up and Aaron looks away, reaching for the light switch. She puts a hand on his cheek. 'Look at me,' she says. 'What's wrong?'

'Nothing,' he says.

'Don't cry,' she whispers. The tears stripe down his cheek. She wipes them away with her thumb. 'He doesn't go to Harvard, does he?'

Aaron shakes his head. 'No,' he says. His voice is thick and gummy. He tries to clear his throat but it feels like something's stuck. He opens his mouth to say more but nothing comes and he closes it instead. Then he makes a sound like a whimper and Róisín holds him as he cries.

6

The map interface displayed on the screen of Róisín's phone shows a blue dot representing her current location and a red pin representing her destination. The blue dot overlaps the red pin completely, indicating that she has arrived. She looks from the screen of her phone up the side of the tall wooden building she is standing beside. A crowd has started to congregate on the outside steps.

Aaron stands in a button-down shirt and khakis and running shoes, leant against the fence out front of the synagogue. He rubs the back of his neck and removes the phone from his pocket to check it. He bites his thumbnail, looking around. This is Aaron as he is without her. He sees her and his face erupts into a terrifically contagious smile. He removes his earbuds and coils the cord around his index finger before pocketing them. He wraps her in a hug and kisses her cheek. Róisín feels a tightness between her shoulder blades release like a rock that's been fished out of a shoe after a long day, a constant irritation noticed only by the relief of its absence.

'This is really weird, isn't it? It is, you know it is. It's okay, you can tell me it's weird.'

'No,' Róisín says, looking back up at the building. 'Maybe.'

'Good weird, though, right?'

'Yeah, sure, good weird,' she says.

'But still weird.'

'Maybe still weird.'

She reaches for his hand, and he takes it. They walk up the stairs to the synagogue together. There's a wicker basket of head coverings to their left and a pile of pamphlets for various Jewish organisations and activities on a table to their right. There are rows of pews visible through the doors ahead of them and, at the end of the room, a pulpit. Aaron takes a head covering and smooths it out with his thumbs before putting it on. Róisín reaches tentatively towards the basket.

'Only the men,' Aaron says.

They sit in the last row. The sanctuary feels enormous from here. There's an ornately decorated wall in front of the pulpit. The rest of the room is made from wood and smells like mothballs. The floorboards groan as families stream into the main hall through the aisles. The men wear suits. The women wear dresses. The children wear suits and dresses. Fathers shake hands and pat shoulders and nod solemnly. Mothers smile. The children stand very still. Nobody stops as they pass, or seems to notice the two of them sitting there at all.

Everything was fine until Charlie showed up for work. One moment she was making a cortado and the next she looked up and there he was, face scrunched up in concentration as he pulled open the front door. Then he smiled – he actually smiled at her – as he passed the counter on his way to the back office. The customer had to remind her to charge him for the coffee. She tossed her apron on the counter and told Sofia to cover for her.

something weird happened to me.

She stared at the message, her thumb hovering over the send button. She held the delete key and watched it disappear, character by character. She typed something else.

fancy seeing the irish girl with the killer collarbones again?

Three dots appeared. The recipient of the message was typing. Róisín held her phone in both hands watching the animation repeat. Each breath became fuller; she felt that much more herself again. The animation stopped. Her phone buzzed as the message arrived.

100%

Róisín considered what to write next when Aaron's face appeared, taking up the whole screen. She hesitated before swiping right on a floating icon to answer the call.

'Hello?' she said.

'I thought that this might be easier than texting back and forth,' he said.

'Probably easier,' she said. She pressed the phone screen against her cheek and held her elbow with her other hand. 'Are you free tonight?'

'Tonight?' he said. 'Oh, uh, well...'

'Have you already got plans?'

He didn't speak for a moment. Róisín heard cars pass him by and then the intermittent beeps of a pedestrian crosswalk. If it were something routine, he'd say it, so then it must not be routine. There was only one thing Róisín could imagine he would hesitate to say. She wondered if they'd broached the topic of exclusivity yet. She felt stupid for thinking it was implied. She felt stupid for texting, stupid for picking up the phone, stupid for relying on someone who she had only known for a few weeks to make her feel better in a sudden moment of crisis.

'It's fine,' she said. 'I actually have to go back in–'

'I do have plans,' he said. 'But I don't want you to think differently of me when you hear what they are.'

'It's all right,' Róisín said. 'It's fine. We never said–'

'I'm going to services. Like, Jewish services. It's our New Year tonight, it's one of, like, three times a year I go.'

'Oh,' she said.

There was another pause. Róisín pictured Aaron standing at a crosswalk biting his nails or rubbing the back of his neck, anxious to hear the words she was deciding between. The realisation of that power was reassuring to Róisín. His day, his week, maybe his month, would be impacted by the next words she chose.

When they undressed to sleep together a few nights ago, Róisín saw Aaron's body in the light for the first time. They stood in his bedroom together, lit by the soft light of his bedside lamp. She ran her hands over his skin, feeling his warmth, and then she slid off his boxers. There, on the inner thigh of his left leg, were five or so circular scars, the width of cigarettes. His eyes were closed, a smile on his lips. He didn't notice her noticing. She ran her thumb over the scars of his left leg while she kissed his neck. He wrapped her in his arms and whispered in her ear. Who could ever hurt a man like this, she thought to herself then. He who loves with ease.

Then he told her about his brother. Moe came back from a teenage trip to Israel with newfound devotion and piety. He volunteered for the Israel Defense Forces without telling Aaron and, when his application was accepted, he went. After he was killed, Aaron stopped speaking to his parents. It's been over five years without contact. They live forty-five minutes away. Everyone carries inside themselves a locked room containing some central trauma they believe defines their life. Aaron had only known Róisín a few weeks and he unlocked that door for her.

'I don't think any differently of you,' she said finally.

'You don't?'

'No.'

He sighed. 'And you don't think it's hypocritical?'

'No,' she said again. 'No, of course not.'

'You wouldn't want to…' Aaron started. He sounded like he was speaking through a nervous smile. She could perfectly imagine his face when he said, 'No, forget it.'

'Go on.'

'You wouldn't want to go with me, would you?'

Róisín smiled. 'If you'd have me. I would, yeah. You might have to teach me how to behave, but I'd love to.'

Aaron bites at his thumb and glances around the room and at his shoes. Róisín gestures towards a man a few rows in front of them who's holding a shawl in his hands, whispering and kissing its corners before draping it over his shoulders.

'It's called a tallis,' Aaron says. 'You start wearing them when you get bar mitzvahed.'

He's less nervous when he explains things.

'Do only the men wear them?' she asks.

'Yeah, only the men.'

'And the women, do they get to do anything in this religion of yours?'

Aaron laughs. 'Just the honour of having Jewish sons,' he says.

This is how Róisín imagines church might feel. It is because of her parents that Róisín can only imagine, rather than remember, what going to church is like. Róisín's mother Sinéad grew up among twelve siblings, a nice big Catholic family. And Sinéad fell in love with Henry, who was thin and serious and proud and, like the rest of his family, a Protestant. Sinéad's siblings were unable or else unwilling to differentiate *a* Protestant from *the* Protestants. They didn't speak to Sinéad for the better part of twenty years. Of her thirty cousins, Róisín has only met four. Sinéad and Henry raised their children with an inherited disdain for religion on the whole and it is true that, even here, in a room so thick with religious admiration, she can't see the point.

'Here we go, the main event,' Aaron says.

The rabbi ascends the pulpit and turns towards the crowd. 'We will begin on page 384,' he says. Then he starts to sing. The sanctuary comes alive with the voices of fathers, mothers and children, all joining his. Aaron does not sing along. He does not recite the prayers. He holds the prayer book between his hands and turns the page when the rabbi says to turn the page, stands when the rabbi says to stand and sits when the rabbi says to sit. He wears an expression of vague annoyance, like a man tasked with watering plants that don't belong to him. This is a very private side of Aaron's life. Whenever he has spoken about religion or faith, he has always done so with dismissive derision, and yet here he is in earnest service to some higher calling. She wants him to smile at her and let her in on the joke. He only stares ahead.

The rabbi removes something from the ark and hands it to the man beside him.

'That's the Torah,' Aaron says, and Róisín nods as if that word means something to her.

The man holding the Torah walks in procession with a few other people down one aisle and then the procession loops around the back of the room by way of another aisle. The Torah is brought back to the pulpit and placed on a stand and then the rabbi indicates that everyone can sit. A bald man in a green button-down shirt with the sleeves rolled up takes his place at the Torah. Then begins a sort of orchestrated reading as congregants cycle through to say a prayer and then stand aside while the man in the green shirt reads from the scroll. After this, the rabbi gives a sermon about judgement. Another man ascends the pulpit with a bone horn that's about two feet long.

'That's called the shofar. That's why we're here – this is one of the few times they blow it,' Aaron says. He opens his mouth to say something else and then closes it instead.

The man's cheeks puff out, his face goes red and there's a stuttered noise like an out-of-tune trumpet. The rabbi calls out in what Róisín can only assume is Hebrew and the man responds with more out-of-tune trumpet blasts. There's an archaic element to the whole procedure. It reminds Róisín of a school trip she took in primary school to the Viking village in Wexford, all of those people dressed up in traditional clothes hanging around fires and huts. People pretending to be people. Performative actions recited out of obligation. Rote memorisation. It's all so meaningless when it's boiled down, isn't it? The type of behaviour that lies in distinct opposition to progress.

'This is Moe's favourite part,' Aaron says. 'Was Moe's favourite part.'

The rabbi calls out a final instruction and the shofar-blower responds with one long, sustained note that warbles before falling off. The congregation claps. Someone ascends the pulpit and starts talking about Israeli bonds and the importance of raising a family with Jewish values.

'We can go now,' Aaron says.

They slip out of the row and back into the entrance hall. Aaron returns his head covering to the basket where he got it from before they leave the building. He stops on the steps and looks back up at the synagogue.

'That was the last conversation I had with Moe,' he says. 'He was about to be transferred to Jerusalem just before Rosh Hashanah and he kept going on about how excited he was. Supposedly you can hear the shofars on the streets, everyone blowing one.'

Róisín nods as he speaks. It is clear to her that, without religion, Moe would still be alive. She wants to ask Aaron if he sees this clearly too. She has spent so much of her life convinced of the archaic divisions religion invites that it is surprising to be confronted by someone who still believes in its virtues, at least in whatever capacity Aaron does believe. It is charming and it is troubling and it is all intensely personal.

They walk down the sidewalk together, the synagogue behind them. They pass a man on the street with an outstretched paper cup and Róisín digs through her purse for spare change to give him. The coins make a soft noise when they hit the bottom of the cup.

7

It's the morning after the night before. The stale bedroom air smells like a nosebleed. The inside of Aaron's mouth tastes like a missing tooth. There are ants beneath his skin hurrying in busy clumps, unable to agree which way they are going but going all the same, to and from his fingertips and toes. Every individual muscle is sore at a cellular level. His jaw feels loose. He is hungover. He is extremely hungover. There is something comforting about waking up feeling like the victim of a car crash and finding Róisín beside him in the rubble of his sheets, herself all smeared mascara and morning breath.

'I feel like death,' she says, eyes closed.

He rolls over, facing her, and as he does his arm naturally goes up over her shoulder. They share an inoffensive kiss, there would be no mistaking it for the prelude to anything, but in that routine affection is steady comfort. There is nowhere he would rather be. There is no one whose life he would exchange for his own in this moment. *Maybe this is love*, Aaron thinks. These temporary moments, these fleeting things. This absence of wanting. It certainly has the feel of something similar.

They dress quickly and now the two of them are walking – stumbling, really – down the road, squinting through the abject sunlight. The word somnambulation comes to mind, but at the moment Aaron's brain is too foggy to remember why. He explains to Róisín that eating breakfast in a boxcar diner hungover is something of a rite of passage for those who are committed to living in New England.

'Who said I was committed?' she mumbles behind her sunglasses.

Kelly's is a classic Airstream diner with a charmingly rusted exterior complete with a bright pink-and-blue neon sign on top. It is hot and pleasantly buzzing with conversation and the smell of fried things and coffee. It is, like most of the places Aaron prefers, void of tourists and students. This is not a simulated prop, this is the thing itself, this is the authentic diner others are pretending to be. Places like this always make Aaron feel like he's a part of something.

They put their coats on the hanger with everyone else's and squeeze past the other customers to two hard vinyl seats at the counter. The menus are plastic and outfitted with metal fasteners at the corners. A waitress slides two over and tells them she'll be with them soon.

'I feel like if I don't get a hash brown in the next ten minutes there is a very real chance that I'm going to die,' Róisín says.

'Why did we order shots?'

'Percy. Sofia should have stopped him.'

Aaron taps on the plastic menu and yawns. 'They've got Bloody Marys, did you see that? Probably make us feel better than anything else.'

Róisín hunches over the counter and puts her head in the crook of her elbow. Aaron reaches out and, with a tentative touch, places his hand between her shoulder blades.

The waitress slaps down two plastic cups and fills them with ice water from a large pitcher. 'If you're going to be sick, do it outside. I already mopped up once today.'

Róisín sits up straight. 'Sorry,' she says.

They read the menu and settle quickly on two specials with the works: fried eggs, pancakes, waffles, home fries, sausage patties, toast and bacon.

'And two Bloody Marys,' Aaron adds.

The entrance to the cocktail bar was a door at the side of an empty industrial building by the harbour, unidentifiable except for the line of people outside.

'Percy's picked out a very Percy bar for us,' Aaron said.

'It won't be that bad.'

Aaron wasn't looking forward to tonight. He could tell when Róisín suggested it that she was hoping he'd say yes, so he did. It was as simple for him to understand the things that made her happy as it was difficult for him to put himself in the way of those things.

'It'll buy us some time before we have to do it again at least,' Róisín said. 'Sofia's been into me non-stop at work about a double date since they started going out. It's actually doing my head in.'

There was a murmur through the crowd and then it shuffled forward a few feet before stopping again. Aaron checked the time on his cell phone. They'd been waiting for twenty minutes. Another ten passed and then there was Percy and Sofia emerging from a black car, all white smiles and expensive clothes. Percy pulled Aaron out of the line and they walked in front of Sofia and Róisín towards the entrance. Percy led them up to the man at the door and then, after a quick exchange, past him. He waved them through one at a time and stole one last glance at the long line before ducking into the door. Aaron wondered if there was anything Percy enjoyed more than the view from above other people.

'This place is very prestigious,' Percy said to Aaron as they walked down the tight spiral staircase.

'Sure,' Aaron said.

'Extremely fucking exclusive.'

'Uh-huh.'

The bar was located in a cave-like basement. They were met at the bottom of the stairs by a man in a vest and a skinny tie who led them across the concrete floor to what seemed to be a load-bearing pillar. Some type of grainy jazz backed by a lo-fi beat pumped out of unseen speakers all around them. Aaron waited to be led to a table or a booth but the man in the vest told them he would be right back with some water and left them standing around the pillar.

'Sometimes celebrities come in here,' Percy said.

'Oh yeah?' Róisín asked. 'Like who?'

'And they have a cocktail that costs $500.'

The waiter soon returned and asked what they'd like to drink. Percy and Sofia ordered cocktails Aaron had never heard of. He asked the waiter for a menu.

'We don't do menus,' the waiter said.

'Oh, right,' Aaron said.

'Just tell them what you like, flavour-wise,' Percy said. 'They'll do the rest.'

'Uh, well, I guess I like tequila.'

'Tequila,' the waiter repeated slowly. He nodded blankly and turned towards Róisín.

'Something sweet and strong,' she said. 'Anything but whiskey.'

She was, as always, at ease. Aaron squeezed her hand and she squeezed his back. She was smiling. She was having a good time. Aaron felt a knot relax between his shoulder blades. Maybe this wasn't so bad.

The music got loud but not quite loud enough to drown out Percy as he dived into a story about work. If he made his revenue target, he'd be eligible for a fifty-thousand-dollar bonus, but the projections weren't looking promising with the amount of time he had left in the year. Róisín nodded along politely and asked him if this meant he would have to start working weekends.

'Start?' Percy said, then laughed.

The waiter returned with a tray of cocktails. He placed each on a shelf built into the pillar and announced their names and ingredients with the grandiose tone of someone introducing royalty.

'For the lady, an Aviation. London dry gin, Maraschino liqueur, crème de violette. For the gentleman, an Oaxaca Old Fashioned. Reposado tequila, mezcal, Angostura and agave nectar.'

Sofia took pictures of each drink and typed captions into her phone. Róisín smiled politely. Percy motioned for the waiter to come closer, stuck something in his hand and then patted him on the shoulder.

'What was that?' Aaron asked him.

'Don't worry about it,' Percy said.

Aaron took a sip of his cocktail. It tasted the way he imagined a bar of soap might if it were blended with charred firewood. Róisín took a sip of hers and set the glass back down on the shelf. Soon the waiter returned and led them towards an empty booth along the wall.

'I apologise for the inconvenience,' the waiter said.

'The royal treatment,' Sofia said, smiling.

'They shouldn't have had us standing in the first place,' Percy said. 'Number of fucking times I've come in here with a client.'

'Percy knows everybody,' Sofia explained. 'He said that he can get us into anywhere we want in London.'

'London?' Róisín asked.

'Didn't I tell you? We're going in, like, a week.'

'To London,' Róisín repeated. She looked from Sofia to Percy. 'Boy, you move quick.'

Percy didn't respond. He was looking around the room, scanning the other booths, which Aaron noticed were full of similarly dressed people who were themselves also looking around the room. He wondered if this class of people ever enjoyed the things they did as much as they enjoyed being seen doing them.

'It's just London,' Percy said.

'He goes there all the time with work so this time he's bringing me along. We're flying first class,' Sofia said.

Percy drained the rest of his cocktail. He leant out of his seat, hand raised and snapping, trying to get the attention of the waiter.

'That's fun, I love London,' Róisín said.

'Yeah,' Aaron said. 'That's exciting.'

He wondered if Róisín was disappointed she wasn't with someone who more closely resembled Percy. No, even at his most self-deprecating, he knew she didn't want that. Maybe instead he was wondering if she wished she were with someone whose bank account more closely resembled Percy's, who could give her first-class trips to London and be more concerned with getting another drink than the cost of it.

'It's work,' Percy said, shrugging and gesturing towards Aaron. 'You know what that's like.'

'Not really, no.'

'I thought you worked in tech or something.'

The waiter turned a corner and disappeared behind the bar.

'Son of a bitch,' Percy said under his breath.

'I've never been to London before,' Sofia said.

Percy turned to her, confused. 'Why not?'

'What do you mean "why not?"?' Róisín said pointedly. 'That's not any type of question.'

Percy stayed focused on Sofia. 'You said your father was a businessman.'

Sofia traced the rim of her cocktail glass with the tip of her index finger. 'Yeah, a failed one,' she said softly.

'As in,' Percy said, waiting for her to continue.

'Maybe we should talk about something else,' offered Aaron.

'He ran a few sandwich shops that went out of business and never really got back on his feet.'

Percy leaned against the back of the seat and tilted his head. He moved closer to Sofia. 'I never knew that,' he said. 'I always thought you were born bougie.'

'He never asks me any personal questions,' Sofia said to the table, half-joking.

'What does your father do?' Aaron asked Percy, but then the waiter returned.

'Were you looking to get another round of drinks?' he asked.

Percy recited an order, pointing to each person at the table as he named another exotic-sounding cocktail. The waiter nodded and left. 'My father was a travelling salesman,' he said.

'Really?' Sofia asked.

Percy nodded. They shared a look and then a smile and then Percy kissed Sofia's cheek. 'Never knew that, did you?'

She shook her head. 'No.'

'I'd kind of assumed your father would have been an earl or something,' Róisín said.

The waiter returned with the next round of drinks. Aaron didn't bother listening to the names or ingredients this time. He focused instead on visualising how little liquid would be left in the glass if he were to reach in with his fingers and fish out its softball-sized ice cube. A place without menus had no prices to calculate. He brought the glass to his lips and drank. There was a soft, sweet foam and then the stark coldness of the liquid beneath it. He set down the glass, an aftertaste of cucumber on his lips. Róisín sipped her cocktail and leant against him. He kissed her forehead and she smiled. He wanted to be like her, doing things to do them and thinking nothing more of it than that.

'Two or three times a week, he'd cart out his leather luggage into the hall and take off for a trip. Leather duffel. Leather roller bag. Leather fucking everything. Was he nice, like, as a person? Maybe. Serious? I don't know. But I can tell you what his aftershave smelled like. I can tell you the sound his Allen Edmonds made on the hardwood floors. Smells and sounds of him leaving. That's what sticks.' Percy took a sip from his glass and set it down. He looked past Aaron, in a space entirely his own. 'He'd call sometimes and tell me to get out our map to find him by asking questions. Are you west of Omaha? Are you north of San Francisco? That kind of shit. Can you see mountains? It was a game. When I found him, I'd put a red pin on the city. I'd try my best to get it in under twenty.'

Róisín yawned, nuzzling her head against Aaron's shoulder. He felt his face grow hot. Percy hunched forward over the table.

'You know, I used to think he actually had his meetings or whatever up there. Like, I thought they flew over the city and he just had his meeting right up there, in the plane. Kids are fucking stupid, aren't they? I thought he went up in the sky, flew in circles and only came down when he got home. I don't know where I thought all of those fucking magnets on the refrigerator came from.'

'That's sweet,' Sofia said.

The spell broke. Percy sat upright and started looking for the waiter again. They ordered another round of cocktails. Sofia stood to go to the bathroom, looking at Róisín expectantly, and suddenly Aaron and Percy were in the booth alone.

'This is a good time,' Aaron said.

'Uh-huh.'

'How long have you and Sofia been…' Aaron started.

'Fucking?' Percy said, scanning the booths along the wall of the room.

'I was going to say dating.'

Percy stooped over the table and slipped a hand into the inside pocket of his blazer. He held up a small baggie of off-white powder and raised his eyebrows. He removed a sleek ring of house keys from his pocket and dug the tip of one into the baggie, raising the pea-sized clump of powder up to his left nostril and covertly turning his head towards the wall before sniffing, bringing the key back down clean. Aaron didn't say anything. Then he was holding the baggie in one hand and the key in the other, passed under the table, and Percy was grinning like an insane person at him from across the table.

'I feel like we shouldn't be doing this here,' Aaron said.

Percy didn't respond. He knew he didn't have to. Aaron dipped the key into the bag and snorted a bump of his own. They passed the baggie and the key back and forth beneath the table for another round before Sofia and Róisín returned, excitedly whispering to one another. They made eyes as they sat down, the words of an unfinished thought hanging in the air between them. Sofia faced Aaron and said something.

'What?' he asked, leaning forward.

'I said it's your turn.'

Aaron waited for some kind of elaboration, confused. When she didn't go on, he turned to Róisín, who laughed. 'It's your turn to tell us what your dad does.'

'Seems like that's the topic of tonight,' Sofia said.

'He mostly cooks, I'd say. He always loved to cook.'

'Is he retired?'

Aaron nodded. Róisín put her hand in his and squeezed. He could feel her watching his face carefully.

'He and my brother used to cook together all the time. That was their big thing. They'd cook and I'd garden with my mom.'

'Where'd you grow up, fucking Amish country?' Percy asked, laughing. 'I never knew you were a Mennonite.'

Aaron felt the air vibrating around him. There was a warmth, a comfort, and he felt himself slipping one notch below consciousness. A flat sheen appeared on everything he looked at. Róisín nudged his shoulder lightly. Sofia was asking him something else. Aaron asked her to repeat herself.

'What does your brother do? Does he live in Boston?' she asked.

'Oh, he's dead,' Aaron said.

There was a definitive mood shift. Sofia was staring at him now, her mouth open. This was clearly the wrong thing to say.

'I'm so sorry,' she said.

'I don't know how it happened,' he explained. Maybe if he explained they would feel better about it. 'You just get notified, basically. He died on active service in the Israeli military. They didn't give us any other information. Sometimes I wonder if he suffered or what. I remember asking the Israeli rep – the person who came to the door, whatever they're called. I was screaming at him, actually, my Dad had to pretty actively hold me back. There was concern, I think, that I might do something physical I would regret. I wanted to know if Moe got shot or if he got blown up or what. Did he die on a mission? I don't know. I'll never know. But there's a difference, that's all I'm trying to say.' He felt the blood in his throat. He was shouting now. 'There's a difference if he was ambushed or attacked or what. There's a difference if he expected it. You know? There's a difference.'

Aaron finished the rest of his drink and turned away from the table to scan the room. All of these beautiful people, also all looking around the room. Such wasted time they spend wondering about the thoughts of other people. Aaron became aware of the sudden silence at their table. He looked from Percy to Sofia to Róisín, all looking down, distraught.

'What?' he asked Róisín.

She tapped her nostril. 'You're bleeding,' she said.

When the plates land on the counter, overflowing with food, Róisín laughs. 'It's like the movies,' she says. 'You really don't know the meaning of the words "portion control", do you?'

The Bloody Marys come next. Aaron stares at the glass of cloudy red liquid dotted with black pepper, the chunky ice cubes, the condensation dripping down its side like honey. His mouth is dry. His legs hurt. He's got an awful fucking headache. Aaron pushes the straw out of the way with his finger, lifts the glass to his lips then sets it down half full. He feels visceral relief flood through his body, like a dried-out sponge thrown back into the ocean that's rehydrating so quickly it's audible.

'I don't know how you can drink that,' Róisín says.

'It helps,' he says. 'Trust me.'

She leans forward and takes a tepid sip from her straw. She shudders, shaking her head. 'That is properly disgusting,' she says.

They eat in contented silence. For the first time since they've met, Aaron feels no pretence, no hesitation. This could be any day at all. This could be every day from now on. He can't stop smiling. After he finishes his Bloody Mary, he slides Róisín's in front of him. She watches him take the straw out of the cup and place it next to his plate.

8

Róisín wipes the sweat from her forehead with the back of her hand. The sun is high, the sky cloudless. The air is still with flat heat. There is no ocean here, no harbour breeze. She's never been so far outside of Boston. They're in an area Aaron kept offhandedly referring to as 'Western Mass' during the long drive out as if it meant something. She spots a herd of Americans holding hot dogs ambling by and then, past them, a glimpse of Aaron's hand as he waves her over to a bulletin board.

'See, I think we got mixed up here,' he's saying. His face is covered in sweat and scrunched into a smile. A dark-coloured patch covers most of the back of his grey T-shirt. He's pointing at a cartoon depiction of a parking lot on the east side of the fairgrounds, then to the centre of a group of buildings. 'We're here. I'm almost positive,' he says.

Plastic megaphonic speakers churn out carousel music. The sounds of laughter and conversation from the crowd surrounding them fold into the background noise of amusement rides and barkers cajoling children to shoot tin cans with a BB gun for a dollar a go. Róisín can hardly believe all of this is real. She wipes her forehead again.

'Do you think we could go somewhere a little cooler?' she asks. 'Just for a little while? I know we only just got here.'

'It's not usually this hot. Three weeks from now it'll be dead fall, I swear. Leaves, pumpkins, the whole thing.' Aaron turns back to the map and leans in, humming in concentration, studying the lines and shadows. His head jerks towards and away from the small, smudged legend in the bottom right-hand corner. 'If that's the McDonald's Super Slide, then this must be the Coca-Cola Circus Tent,' he says to himself.

The carousel music crinkles as it cuts out. 'The butter-carving contest begins in five minutes,' a voice announces. 'Attention. If you are a butter carver, please report to the blue entrance on the western side of the Mallary Complex. We extend our gratitude to Costco for sponsoring this year's tractor pull.'

There's a ping like a quarter off a tin roof behind them. A stack of cans crashes down. The kid holding the BB gun cheers. The attendant takes out a hooked stick and pulls down a teddy bear.

Aaron taps a building on the left side of the map. 'I think this might actually be the only place with air conditioning,' he says.

'I don't mean to be a pain,' Róisín says. 'I can bear it for a bit, just forget that I said anything.'

Aaron cuts the distance between them. He rests his hands on her hips. Now she's smiling too, how could she help it with him beaming down at her like this?

'Don't kiss me,' she says. 'You're absolutely soaked.'

'What did the pot say to the kettle?' he says, which makes her laugh.

They pass a concession stand. Róisín watches the man in a paper hat behind the counter shovel popcorn into a gallon bucket and place it into the outstretched arms of a seven-year-old, the child's hands grasping the air in anticipation. Aaron is telling her something about the fair – or exposition, whatever it's called – but she can't focus with all the excitement around her.

'It's like being in a movie,' she says, interrupting.

Aaron grins. 'I knew you'd like this.'

'I do,' she says. She puts a hand in his and he takes it.

It's easy to be at ease around Aaron. There's the transparency, for one. The nail-biting, the rubbing of his neck, the avoidant eye contact. Or else the smiling, the handholding, the kisses on the cheek. The way wrinkles appear at the corners of his eyes when he's grinning as wide as he can.

They stop at a stand selling deep-fried things and Aaron orders fried butter, fried Kool-Aid and a fried Oreo. 'And two beers,' he says.

'Could I get a water?' Róisín asks.

'And a water,' Aaron calls out.

Instead of beer, she'd meant. There's something in the back of her mind that niggles every time she sees Aaron drink. It isn't that she has a problem with it. He drinks more than her, sure, but who doesn't? She doesn't have the right to have a problem. Still, she has to admit, she stepped into the car park today and hoped, amid the loudness of the sunshine and the humid layered air, for something pure about the day.

They take refuge on a shaded bench and eat. Róisín lets Aaron finish the fried butter in exchange for the Oreo. He eats the Kool-Aid in three neat bites.

'Would you have come here as a kid?' she asks.

Aaron shakes his head, chewing. He takes a swill of beer and swallows. 'My mother would rather be deep-fried than spend an afternoon at a state fair.'

Róisín looks around and allows herself to picture her family here, even though it hurts. They would love this kind of thing. Her father would be hunched over the display text on each of the vintage tractors, unsatisfied until he'd read them all, then spend the rest of the trip regurgitating the information as if he'd known it all his life. Her mother would be pushing everyone to get a treat so that she could steal a bite. Her brother, of course, would be nowhere to be found, busy trying to experience every ride in the fairground. They would be happy.

Sometime last week, Róisín and Aaron were in Kelly's when she told him that she'd be closing up the café alone while Sofia was out of town. It was part of a larger story, something about how Charlie had been really annoying about it, telling her at the last minute. It wasn't even the point of what she was talking about. Aaron listened carefully, the way he always did, and, picking at his pancakes, asked her if it was okay to call her when she finished her shift.

'Why?' she asked.

She was afraid she'd suggested something about Charlie accidentally. She wasn't sure how Aaron would react or how she wanted him to react. The word for the incident was assault, a word that felt to Róisín at once too strong and not strong enough to describe how she now felt in the café every time she saw him and he acted as if nothing were wrong. At least when Sofia was around she could distract herself. There was a buffer. When the café was slow or empty, Róisín spent her time behind the counter listening for the opening of the back office, sweating when she heard something that sounded like the creak of the door. When she did see Charlie, she was quick to look somewhere else, to do something with her hands.

'It'd make me feel better knowing that you're getting home safe,' Aaron said.

So that was it. Gentle concern. Easy affection. She was still unaccustomed to this sacrificial charity which she so regularly received from him in which some amount of time and effort could be exchanged in order to solve her discomfort. It was that simple to him.

'You really don't have to do that,' she said. 'I'll be fine.'

'Okay,' he said, and left it at that.

The next night, he called just as she was locking the door. He made it sound as natural as he could, telling her she was on his mind and that he wanted to say hello. He even acted surprised when she told him she was closing up and had a few minutes to talk on the walk to the T station. He called the next night and the night after that. It didn't matter if she was ending up at her apartment or his, he always called. Their conversations had become so reliable he would start winding down whatever anecdote Róisín was into as she got to the station, saying something like, 'No point standing outside, go on and catch your train,' before hanging up. She'd start watching the clock around six, checking her phone whenever she felt a phantom buzz in her pocket. She felt her heart flutter when his name flashed up on the screen.

Last night, he called as usual.

'Have you ever been to a state fair?' he asked.

She didn't even know what a state fair was.

'You're going to love it.'

He picked her up at seven this morning in Jake's car and they spent the first two hours of the drive listening to all of the American boy bands Róisín grew up with. They stopped for gas and Róisín spent twenty dollars on candy and beef jerky, all the brands she'd seen but never tried. They turned the music up as high as it would go. They rolled the windows down and sang along together. It felt like living someone else's life.

A cheer rises from a circle of people across the way. They're standing next to a giant blow-up soldier holding a rifle the size of a bus. She can see someone in the centre now, a teenager, as he does chin-ups.

'What's that about?' Róisín asks, pointing.

She watches carefully as Aaron drinks half of one of the plastic cups of beer in one go and smacks his lips, satisfied. Then he responds.

'What?' he asks. 'The townies doing pull-ups?'

'What's a townie?'

'Not so loud,' Aaron says, laughing. 'It's not the nicest thing.'

There's a particularly scrawny teenager hanging from the metal bar. He struggles to pull his chin up over the line. A broad man in a tan uniform beside him calls out a number, counting. 'Come on, son,' he says. 'You can do it. Dig deep.'

The teenager pulls so hard he is shaking. He makes it halfway up before his grip gives out and he drops into a heap on the asphalt. His friend pushes him aside and jumps onto the bar.

'They're recruiting for the military,' Aaron says. He finishes his beer and puts the second plastic cup into the empty first. He notices her watching him do it. 'Sorry, did you want this?' he asks.

'No, no,' she is quick to say. She holds up her bottle of water and, as if to reiterate the point, unscrews the cap and takes a small sip. The inside of her mouth is coated in butter. Her lips taste like salt. She watches carefully as Aaron drinks from the plastic cup of beer. It's soon empty.

The crowd stops and turns, everyone looking up towards the sky, and then she hears the mechanical roar from miles above. Aaron scoots closer to her on the bench and puts his arm around her shoulders, pointing up.

'See it?' he asks.

'Yes,' she says, even though she doesn't.

And then she can make out the plane against the canvas of blue. It's no larger than a speck at this distance but the noise is enormous. As they watch, she leans into Aaron's chest. *This is surely some kind of American life*, she thinks. The plane flies overhead. The kids in the group all cheer. Then it zooms past, gone as quickly as it arrived, and they watch it recede into the distance.

9

It's a few weeks later that Aaron receives a text.

thinking of you. what are you up to tonight?

He stares at the blurry screen and wills the double-image text to realign over itself so he can read it. The music is loud and obnoxious. Percy is shouting about how government welfare leads to dependency on tax-funded handouts. Jake is shouting back that Percy should grab a hold of his neck and pull his head out of his ass. Aaron squints through the fog and lights; his eyes are stinging. He imagines Róisín in bed with one of her books and a cup of tea.

'Did you hear what he said?' Jake says, grabbing Aaron roughly by the arm. 'Would you get off your phone a minute. Jesus Christ, you are so fucking pussy-whipped.'

'So whipped,' Percy repeats, laughing.

Jake lifts his plastic cup to his lips and tilts his head back until it's empty. He looks expectantly at Percy, who follows suit, and then at Aaron, who doesn't.

'I don't want to get completely shit-faced on a Thursday night,' he says.

'The thing is, though,' Jake says, gently lifting Aaron's cup to his mouth, 'that you probably are going to get completely shit-faced on a Thursday night.' Aaron downs the rest of his drink in one go. Jake slaps him on the back. 'Attaboy.'

Percy pats the breast pocket of his blazer – he's always wearing that fucking blazer – and nods towards the bathroom.

Jake flashes a wild grin and throws his arm around Aaron and the three of them fight their way through shoulders and elbows to get there.

'He's always wearing that fucking blazer,' Aaron shouts.

They step into a bathroom stall and lock it. A phone is procured. Lines are drawn and straightened. The screen is passed around. Aaron doesn't say yes but he doesn't say no either, and Jake is right in that there doesn't wind up being a meaningful difference between those two things. He wipes his nose with the back of his hand and waits for something to happen.

'This close,' Percy is saying, 'This fucking close to that bonus. Fifty-fucking-thousand bucks if I hit target by the end of the year. This fucking close, man.'

'That's just the bonus?' Jake asks.

Aaron has his phone out again.

thinking of you. what are you up to tonight?

He is thinking about what to write back. Jake swipes the phone out of his hand and starts reading out their messaging conversation.

'"I can't stop smiling",' Jake reads out. '"Me neither, everyone on the bus must think I'm some kind of lunatic".'

Percy's laughing like a jackal.

'You are so fucking whipped,' Jake says and tosses the phone back at him.

'Whipped,' Percy repeats and hiccups.

Someone bangs on the stall door. Percy snorts a particularly thick line before shouting at them to 'cop on and fuck off'. The banging doesn't stop.

Jake whips open the door and there's some guy with spiky hair and a gold chain who's all eyebrows and teeth.

'The door's locked, right, which means it's fucking occupied, doesn't it?' Jake yells at him. He slams it shut in the guy's face and locks it and all three of them burst out laughing.

Aaron feels the bass in his chest. He's covered in sweat. His mouth is dry. Percy is showing them pictures of a boat on his phone. He either wants to buy this boat or else he's bought this boat already; the chronology of what he's saying is unclear. Maybe time itself is unsticking and what Percy is saying is otherwise perfectly cogent. Aaron closes his eyes and lets his arms hang loose at his sides. It feels like hot air. He's entered some liminal space where gravity is optional. This isn't Earth he's landed on. He pictures Róisín in bed but now he imagines that the book's been put on the bedside table and the tea's gone cold.

Jake shakes his shoulder. 'Aaron,' he's shouting. 'Aaron! Percy asked you something.'

'He's a bit fucking deaf, isn't he?' Percy says. 'I asked if you went to Tufts. There's a new guy on the team who graduated, like, four years ago. I wondered if you knew him.'

'What?'

Percy cups his hands around his mouth and repeats himself at full volume.

'I went there. Yeah. Well, kind of,' Aaron says.

'Kind of? What does "kind of" mean? Tufts is fine. You should be proud. It's not Cornell, obviously, but, like, not everybody can get into Cornell.'

'I started there, but I–'

'He got thrown out,' Jake says and laughs. 'He punched the president's son in the face at a party and the guy fell through a fucking window.'

'He didn't fall through a window, it was a glass coffee table,' Aaron says.

'A window,' Percy repeats, his eyes wide.

'The son almost died, actually,' Jake says. He's grinning.

'He did not almost die,' Aaron says. 'He spent, like, a week or two in the hospital, max.'

'That's so cool,' Percy says to himself. 'That would never happen at Cornell.'

Someone bumps into Percy's shoulder and his drink jumps from his hand onto the dance floor. 'What the fuck?' the guy yells.

Aaron finds it difficult to discern the shapes in front of him as they take form in the snapshot flashes of the strobe light above them. Someone with spiky hair and a gold chain has his hands on Percy's blazer. Percy is pushing him back. Spiky hair has his hand cocked back. Jake is pulling Percy out of the way. Spiky hair is throwing a punch. The crowd around Aaron explodes into sudden, drunken violence. Percy gets thrown to the floor. Aaron takes a step back from the unfolding chaos, turns around and gets punched in the face.

They were sitting at the counter in Kelly's Diner this morning. It had become a popular breakfast spot for the two of them on mornings after she stayed over. Their regular waitress, a woman named Darlene, came over with menus. Róisín ordered pancakes. Aaron ordered eggs.

'You like those sunny side up, don't you?' Darlene said.

Aaron said yes and, when she left to fill their order, he grinned at Róisín. He held up his hand with his index finger just barely touching his thumb and said, 'We are this close to becoming regulars.'

They ate and then, on a whim, Aaron ordered a slice of apple pie with cheddar cheese. Darlene smiled when he ordered it, as if it were code for something, which he supposed it was when it came down to it. She asked him if he wanted the cheese hot or cold and he said melted.

'Cheese on pie,' Róisín said, shaking her head. 'You are absolutely mental.'

'It's a thing, I swear,' Aaron said. 'Try it.'

'Oh, I don't know,' Róisín said and laughed. 'This might be pushing it.'

'You've heard of Yankees before, right?'

'Yeah, like Americans.'

'Exactly,' Aaron said. He cut a bite of the pie with his fork. 'Everywhere else in the world, a Yankee is an American. In the States, a Yankee is someone from the northeast. In the northeast, a Yankee is anyone from, like, Vermont. And in Vermont, you know who they call Yankees?'

'Who?'

'People who eat their apple pie with cheddar cheese.'

Róisín tried it. After two bites, she slid the plate away from Aaron and towards herself. 'You've had enough,' she said. They fought over the final bites.

'You want the bill?' the waitress asked. 'Or some coffee?'

Neither of them wanted coffee, but neither of them wanted to leave either.

'Two coffees,' Aaron said.

He told Róisín that this was the kind of meal he would have gotten during his first two years of university. The campus began at the end of the street they were on now. It used to take him twenty minutes to walk here from where he lived during his sophomore year.

'I never went to university,' Róisín said. She bit her lower lip and fidgeted with the handle of the mug. 'I figure I should tell you that now in case it matters to you.'

'Why would that matter to me?'

'I don't know,' she said. 'It matters to some people.'

The waitress returned with two mugs and a pot of coffee. She set the mugs on the counter and filled them, then slid over a basket of creamers and a sugar shaker.

'Why haven't you ever gone home for Christmas?' he asked her.

She took a packet of sugar from the basket, tore it open and poured half of its contents into her mug. She picked up a creamer and held it. 'We don't have these, you know, they're a distinctly American thing,' she said. 'There must be something in them the EU doesn't want us eating.'

'Yeah, maybe,' Aaron said.

She fidgeted with the foil wrapper. 'I haven't gone home for Christmas because I don't actually have a visa to live here.'

'What does that mean?'

'It means that I don't know what would happen if I left.'

'Oh,' Aaron said.

They sat for a few minutes in silence, surrounded by the buzz of the diner. He reached for her hand and she let him take it. His phone vibrated; the preview of a message from Jake slid into view on the top half of the lock screen. Róisín saw it and encouraged him to respond, told him that his friends would think she was keeping him in if he kept saying no to their invitations to socialise. Besides, when was the last time he'd been out? So he picked up the phone and opened the thread to reply to the message.

Aaron reads the screen through his left eye, his right covered by a plastic bag filled with ice.

   thinking of you. what are you up to tonight?

His nose has stopped bleeding, at least. He leans over the kitchen sink and unplugs the balled-up tissue in one nostril, then the other. A thick strand of mucus and blood spills out. A dull ache has set in between his eyes.

'I had him on the ropes,' Percy is saying.

'On the ropes. You were on the fucking floor is what you mean,' Jake says.

'Was not.'

They're back at Percy's apartment, recovering. There's a baggie on the coffee table and an empty one next to it. Tinny music plays out of a smartphone that's been placed in a cup. The empty beer bottles have started to gather in a crowd on the granite kitchen counter.

'We're going back out, by the way, for sure,' Jake says. He's sprawled out over one of Percy's armchairs with his head back, pinching the bridge of his nose.

'I know this place in Seaport that's open I could get us into,' Percy says.

Jake snaps and points at him. 'Attaboy,' he says.

This is all that there is. This is all that there ever will be. Percy will always have a place for them to go and Jake will always want to go there. There will always be more bags, more drinks, more fights. He pictures Róisín in bed, lit by the flat glow of her table lamp. He imagines her face pressed up against the pillow. He types something onto the keyboard of his phone.

night's just ending. you asleep?

He sends the message and tucks the phone into his pocket. Percy is telling them about a time he was in London this past summer.

'I was staying in the Kimpton Fitzroy when I got the call that Mom had cancer and I remember hanging up and thinking,

"Shit, this is a really fucking nice hotel." They were out of regular rooms and upgraded me to a suite and everything. And besides, what was I supposed to do? Like, she has cancer, okay, and in a week, when I'm back, she's still going to have fucking cancer. Plus, the company had paid for the week and the hotel gave me an unbelievable deal on the weekend. There was this Spanish girl I had met at a pub and we already had a date planned.'

'Spanish,' Jake repeats in wonder.

'Massive tits,' Percy says. 'And Mom's in remission, anyway, so I was right after all.'

'What's Spanish for tits?' Jake asks.

Aaron nods along to the rest of the story while opening a ride-sharing application on his phone. He selects his address from a list of recent locations. His phone buzzes. He switches back to the messaging application and opens his conversation with Róisín.

not asleep yet.

He imagines her naked, touching herself, letting that little involuntary moan she makes escape between her lips like a whisper. He types out a message and presses send.

i could always come over to tuck you in.

Three dots appear as she types and his phone buzzes as the message arrives. He squints the letters into focus.

that's a nice thought.

He switches back to the ride-sharing application and cancels his order. A modal appears warning him that he will be charged a service fee if he does this and he accepts the terms without reading them. He selects Róisín's address from the list of recent destinations and taps a button to order the ride. He gets his coat and makes an excuse and Percy and Jake yell at him as he shuts the apartment door behind him.

It's five minutes later and he's in the backseat of someone's Prius. It smells like pine-scented air freshener and cigarette smoke. He asks the driver twice in a row if it's been a busy night while rereading the last little bit of his conversation with Róisín.

Her apartment is on the third floor of a narrow building between a Chinese restaurant and a laundromat. He stands out front, breathing. He presses the buzzer button and holds it.

'Hello?' the staticky voice says.

'It's Aaron,' he says.

The line goes silent. The door buzzes as it unlocks and Aaron steps inside. When he gets up to her floor, he's out of breath. He feels a tickle on his upper lip and touches it. His fingertips come away red. The apartment door opens and there's Róisín, oversized shirt and messy hair, yawning and smiling. And then she sees him and her face falls.

'Sorry,' he mumbles. 'Sorry, I'm all fucked up.'

'Jesus.' She pulls him into the apartment. 'Jesus, what happened? Are you okay?'

She sits him down in the kitchen and cleans him up as he tries to explain but the words keep getting jumbled somewhere between his brain and his mouth. Róisín has to ask him to repeat himself three times before she gives up. He won't stop grabbing at her body. She holds his hands and asks if he wants her to call a cab for him or if he wants to sleep it off here.

'Neither,' he says, and he pulls her into him. He gets his mouth on hers and his hands under her nightshirt.

'Aaron,' she says, pulling herself away. 'Why are you here?'

'You invited me over,' he starts, then stops.

'I thought that was just a bit of banter.'

'Oh,' he says.

'Did you just come over here for sex?'

He opens his mouth and closes it instead. This isn't how this is supposed to go. He shakes his head. 'No, no.'

Róisín holds her elbow against her body and looks towards the door. 'I don't think I want to do that,' she says.

'No, yeah.' He rubs his neck. 'Of course.'

'Do you…' she starts. 'No, never mind. It's none of my business.'

'Go on.'

'You're high right now, aren't you?'

Aaron hesitates, then nods.

'And do you do that often?'

He rubs his neck. 'Occasionally.'

'Occasionally,' she repeats. 'Like at that cocktail bar.'

Aaron opens his mouth and closes it. He nods.

'And were you high that first night you met me?'

That first night. It feels like months ago but it was only a matter of weeks. He's in no fit state to do the math. After the night club and Percy's, they went to Sofia's apartment first so Róisín could put her in bed before they went back to Aaron's. Sofia lived in a brick building near Boston University that bordered Storrow Drive. He drank a glass of water in the kitchen while Róisín got Sofia sorted. He felt the hangover beginning at the back of his head and rifled through the drawers for something to drink, settling on three pulls from a dusty bottle of crème de menthe before stashing it back beneath the sink. He drank his water. The cars buzzing past outside sounded like flies trapped in a jar. He opened the kitchen window and the flies went free, filling the room with a grainy hum. The speed had run its course, so had the cocaine. The alcohol was burning strong. The ketamine had kicked but left behind some senseless connection to the universe, like everything was meant to be. And then Róisín walked into the kitchen and Aaron thought for the first time that everything was going to be okay. She kissed him and he kissed her back and then she asked him why his breath was so minty.

Now Aaron pulls his canvas jacket back over his shoulders. He stumbles and catches himself against the wall, then stands.

'Will I take that as a yes?' she says.

He nods, biting at his nail. 'I guess I won't hear from you again,' he says to the door.

'Quit your moping,' she says softly.

He forces his hand down by his side and faces her.

'I just need time to think, is all,' she says.

'Right.' Aaron opens the apartment door and considers the stairwell, standing in the doorway. 'I feel like that's something people say before they never talk again, is all.'

'I don't know what to tell you,' Róisín sighs. 'I really didn't expect this from you.'

'Right. Yeah,' he says. 'That's fair.'

The door closes behind him. He takes the stairs one step at a time and with each feels his heart drop a little lower. There is Aaron and then there is the version of Aaron that Róisín has constructed in her head and, until now, he was hopeful that they were the same. Now he sees that he has bridged some gap between fantasy and reality and that this revelation has irrevocably changed her impression of him. His phone buzzes: a message from Jake that includes a blurry picture of him and Percy in a mass of bodies somewhere, faces painted in blue light.

where r u fucker??1?

Aaron stands on the inside of the main door to the apartment building and looks out through the smeared glass. He feels the emptiness in his chest grow. A man jogs past on the sidewalk, his coat fluttering behind him, a brown paper bag clutched firmly in his hand. The tenants upstairs are throwing some sort of party. Somewhere in the world, someone says a prayer.

10

There is a rush in the morning before work begins and another around the time that school lets out but in between there is a beautiful calm during which the café is occupied only by Róisín's favourite type of customer. The quiet readers. The gazing writers. The feverish students. There's an acoustic cover of a popular rock song playing over the speakers.

The bell rings as Sofia comes in. She waves to Róisín and takes her usual seat, the one closest to the counter, removing her laptop, water bottle and earbuds from her tote bag and laying them out in a neat grid on the table. Her drink is a flat white and Róisín enjoys the practice of its precision. The portafilter must be rotated under the grinder to ensure an even coverage in the basket. A wedge is placed onto the grinds and spun a few times to flatten them. She steams the milk, taps the jug against the counter to break up the bubbles, then tamps and pulls the shot. These individual actions are so minuscule they can be thought to be meaningless but to Róisín they are the one thing she can collectively do better than any other thing. She draws a symmetrical leaf with the foam and goes around the counter to set the cup and saucer on Sofia's table.

She waits behind the counter for the next customer to come in. This is how she spent the previous day and the day before that and so on, a trail of time defined by absence of activity rather than activity itself. These were days spent not texting and not calling, doing anything and everything to leave it alone for at least a little while longer. It is unclear to Róisín what she is hoping to accomplish by this hiatus in communication. She told Aaron almost two weeks ago that this was 'time to think' and yet so much of this time has been spent deliberately doing the opposite. The problem is twofold: first, that everything is better when Aaron is around; and second, that everything might be safer when he isn't.

'Róisín,' Sofia calls to her. She snaps her fingers. 'Your phone is ringing.'

She steps out the side door before she reaches for the buzzing phone in her pocket. She leaves her hand there, unsure of whether she should take it out. It feels counterintuitive, even childish, to answer Aaron's call for the sole purpose of informing him that, despite speaking to him now, she is staying the tack of not speaking to him. On the other hand, to leave his call unanswered feels needlessly cruel. The phone goes silent in her hand then rings again. Róisín takes a deep breath and removes the phone from her pocket. She is surprised by the face on its screen. She swipes her thumb across the screen and puts the phone up to her ear.

'Darragh?' she says.

The first thing she hears is the ambient buzz of a pub in the background. It sounds like the place their parents would have brought them to as children back when dinners consisted of Ribena and cheese and onion crisps. Then as teenagers, sneaking pints in the back. And finally as adults, drinking alongside their parents, nodding along as they complained about the noise from the kids and teenagers they themselves had been only a few years earlier. Darragh lives in Dublin full-time now. It's certain the pub she's hearing isn't the one they grew up in but the stab of homesickness hurts the same as if it were.

'Another pint,' Darragh is saying to someone. 'G'wan, it's your feckin' round.'

'Darragh,' someone says. 'Darragh, your phone.'

There's a shuffling static and then a heavy breath before Darragh says, 'Hullo?'

'Darragh?'

'Róisín? Róisín, you there?'

'Darragh,' she repeats. 'I'm here, yeah, what is it?'

'What do you mean, "what is it?" – you're the one called me.'

'You called me!' Róisín starts, then sighs. 'All right, I'm going.'

'Wait wait wait,' Darragh says. 'Lads, it's the sister, the one in America. Yes, very fancy. No, Niall, you can't speak to her. Róisín, here, wait a minute, I'm stepping out.'

She hugs her arms around herself for warmth. Her breath comes out as a stream of fog. It's so much colder here than it ever gets at home. She had expected some kind of in-between, a gradual transition from the hot haze of the smouldering summer to this. But no. So much can change in a matter of weeks. Against her ear, the background noise shifts and she can tell Darragh has moved from the pub to a busy street, conversation supplanted by passing cars.

'How's America?' Darragh says. 'Still shite?'

'Yeah,' Róisín says and smiles. 'It is a bit.'

'And have you gotten yourself a gun yet?'

'What are you on about?'

'A gun. They've loads of guns over there, or haven't you noticed?'

'No, I haven't got one.'

'Well, you'd better get on it,' Darragh says and coughs. 'The only thing stops a good guy with a gun is a bad guy with a gun, isn't that it? Or have I got it the other way around?'

'I don't know,' Róisín says. She imagines the pub Darragh is outside of and the voices inside of it, the warm bready smell of beer and the waterfall sounds of laughter.

'So you're having a shite time of it, then,' Darragh says.

'A bit. I suppose.'

'And you haven't even got a gun.'

'No, Darragh, I haven't even got a gun.'

'What about a fella?'

She isn't sure what to say.

'The silence speaks volumes,' Darragh says. 'So there is a fella. I suppose you won't be coming home any time soon, then? No point getting yourself banned from the country your fella lives in. That'd make it a bit complicated. And anyway, you'd be lucky not to be locked up on the way out, overstaying your visa.'

'I had a fella but I don't think I have him anymore,' she says.

'Good,' Darragh says. 'He probably wasn't good enough for you.'

'No,' she says and laughs. 'You're right. He wasn't.'

Darragh coughs. 'Well so, I know you didn't call me just to tell me how right I am.'

'I didn't call you, you called me.'

'Still,' Darragh says.

There's the crinkle of a packet and then the click of a lighter. Darragh breathes in and out. Somewhere on the other side of the call, thousands of miles away, a car beeps as it drives past a pub in Dublin.

'Tell me about your fella,' he says.

'He isn't my fella, I'm just after telling you that–'

'Your ex-fella, so.'

Róisín sighs. 'He's religious.'

'Fuck off,' Darragh says and laughs. 'What, like into Jesus and all that?'

'No,' she says. 'Not quite.'

'What's that mean? He's religious but he isn't into Jesus? What is he, a Mormon or something?'

'Mormons believe in Jesus.'

'What, a Jehovah's Witness, then?' Darragh says.

'No, they're well into all that Jesus shite as well.'

'Róisín, would you quit telling me what he isn't and tell me what he is, for feck's sake.'

'He's Jewish.'

'Oh,' Darragh says. He takes a deep inhale and exhale. She can all but smell the familiar smoke of her brother's cigarettes. 'Don't know anything about them, in fairness. Outside the obvious. So is he real religious or what?'

'He is, yeah.'

'And has the Jew got a name or have I just gotta go on calling him "the Jew" all the time?'

'We could just talk about something else instead.'

'We will to fuck,' Darragh says, then takes a deep drag from his cigarette. 'What's his name, so?'

'Aaron.'

'Aaron. See now, that's a surprisingly good, strong name for a cunt.'

'He brought me to a Jewish service a while ago. It was their New Year's.'

'Jesus,' Darragh says. 'I'd maybe leave that out of the report if you tell Mam and Da about him.'

'Why, have they got a problem with–'

'They haven't got a problem with any religion that they haven't got with every religion, you know that yourself.'

'True,' she says. She turns and glances into the café through the side door. It's not quite time to go back in yet.

'Have you talked to them lately?' Darragh asks.

'No.'

'Hm,' Darragh says. 'And so what was the service like, then? All Latin or something?'

'Hebrew.'

'Right.'

'Some man got up in front of the whole crowd and blew a horn. A shofar, I think it's called, pretty sure. It felt very tribal or something.'

She hears someone call out to Darragh and then the staticky bursts of conversation between them. The background noise quiets as he presses the phone back against his ear. 'I've got to head, Róisín, but give me a call another time soon, would you?'

'Yeah, all right.'

'Do me a favour and phone Mam and Da.'

'And Maeve?'

'I don't care about Maeve. She's got her hands full with the weans, and besides, she's hardly going to give me stick about this; she never talks to me. But Mam and Da will for sure.'

'I will.'

'They'll be on me non-fucking-stop if they find out I got a call and they didn't.'

'I will, I will.'

'I'm serious, Róisín, you've got to give them a ring or—'

'I said I will, so,' she says.

'Fine. Bye. Bye. Byebyebye,' he says as he pulls the phone away.

When she went home that night after services, she did some research online. One website told her that the sound of the shofar is meant as an alarm to wake people out of their 'spiritual slumber'. She liked the idea of people congregating for the purpose of waking themselves up even while being against the idea of those people congregating for religious reasons.

PLACEHOLDERS

Róisín grips the handle of the side door and prepares for the rest of her shift. Then she feels a sudden pang of nausea that fills her mouth with spit. She bends over the handrail to the steps and vomits into the bushes.

11

There are three distinct brands of Cheerios on the shelf. The yellow box promises to be 'heart healthy'. The brown box promises enough grams of fibre to fulfil the body's daily requirements. The red box has freeze-dried strawberries and promises only to be delicious. Beyond their colours, it is difficult for Aaron to understand how to differentiate the boxes in a meaningful way. He wants a healthy heart, sure, but should he prioritise it at the expense of his daily requisite fibre? And neither of these health advantages will have much effect if the cereal is too tasteless to enjoy; he'd be much more likely to simply settle for a slice of buttered toast. A fluorescent hum drips down on him from the lighting fixture above. Aaron takes a step back from the shelves and lets his eyes defocus. The boxes stare at him. There are literally hundreds of options to choose from.

A speaker crunches to life from somewhere overhead. 'Spill on aisle four, repeat, spill on aisle four.'

The walls and floors are unbearably white. There are squeaking sounds of shopping carts being pushed at meandering speeds from aisles beyond this one. Maybe the easiest thing to do would be to remember the box of cereal he and Jake usually buy and to purchase that particular box again. Aaron looks across the dizzying array of Kellogg's varieties and can't remember concrete details of any aspect of his life before he came into this grocery store.

He sent the first message at around eleven last night and the second this morning when he woke up. His manager responded by nine.

If you need to, take the day off as sick leave. :)

The implication of the message was clear, as was its emphasis on the word *need*. Aaron chose to read the message literally. He responded only with a thumbs-up emoji, silenced his work messaging notifications and went back to sleep. Or rather, he lay under his duvet in the dark and stayed very still as if he were asleep. The shower ran upstairs. The microwave beeped. Jake came down to the basement.

'Are you not coming to work again today?' he shouted.

Aaron opened his mouth to call back but the urge to cry came suddenly, thick in his throat like mucus. He bit the inside of his cheek to stave it off.

'Okay,' Jake said. 'I'll take that as a no. Again.'

He didn't hear Jake go back up the stairs. He imagined him standing there in hall, waiting, angry. Eventually, the front door of the house opened and closed and then, fainter, a car started up and drove away. Aaron was alone. He wondered what Róisín was doing right then; which exact part of her daily routine she was arriving at in that moment. Róisín at a sink, brushing her teeth. Róisín on a Red Line subway car. Róisín standing behind the counter of the café. In each, she was smiling.

He opened the messaging application on his cell phone and tapped buttons on the screen until the conversation thread with Róisín came up. He typed a message.

can we talk?

He deleted it, closed the application and tossed his cell phone onto the floor. Aaron had called out sick twice this week, two times last week and three times the week before. Company policy dictated that soon he'd have to manifest a doctor's note explaining his condition if he wished to keep taking sick days. He watched the clock on his bedside table make its rotations. It took another two hours until he was able to get out of bed. When he went to make a bowl of cereal, they were out. The box was not only empty, but missing, and, in a daze, Aaron stood blinking in the kitchen, wondering if they had ever eaten cereal for breakfast at all.

'Shoppers, are you looking for a wonderful surprise to bring home?' The pre-recorded voice is tinny and warbles through its message. There is a surplus of pepperoni freezer pizzas available in aisle nine. 'Be the hero of your family!' urges the voice.

Aaron chooses one of the boxes of Cheerios at random and it is only in the line for checkout that he remembers they usually eat Honey-Os, the supermarket off-brand alternative. He considers the cardboard box in his hands, the sharp edges of the lines of its logo, the vibrance of its colour. Aaron doesn't believe there is a meaningful enough difference between the flavour of Cheerios and Honey-Os for him or anyone else to have a preference. Really, what he's spending that extra money on is the cardboard box, and what a fine box it is. He imagines it perched on the kitchen table like some sort of exotic bird as he eats his breakfast and feels a terrific pride for buying the real deal. This is the American Dream realised, surely. Aaron is moving up in the world.

The person at the head of the line completes her purchase and the line grinds forward by one. He looks down again at the cereal box and feels an emptiness well up inside of him. The comfort is gone before he's even spent the money. For the first time in a long time, he wonders what the point of any of this is.

There's a tap on his shoulder. 'Aaron? Aaron, is that you?'

He doesn't recognise her. He nods and says, 'Yes, it is.'

The woman is wearing a sun hat, the kind people usually only wear in the summer. The brim of the hat flops over half of her face. She says something that Aaron doesn't hear. He leans forward and asks her to repeat herself.

'How are you, I said.'

'Good, yeah,' he says. 'All right. Fine. And you?'

'Better now. It's been a while.'

The next person completes their purchase. The line moves ahead by one. Something about how she smiles under the hat's brim trips a memory.

'Annabelle.'

'Next!' the cashier calls.

'I think that's you,' Annabelle says.

Aaron hands his cereal box to the cashier who asks him if he needs a hug.

'Excuse me?'

'A bag,' the cashier says cheerfully. 'Do you need a bag?'

Aaron says no on reflex and the box is handed back to him.

'Are you part of our loyalty programme?'

'No.'

'Would you like to join our loyalty programme?'

'No.'

'Our loyalty programme offers great discounts on many of our products in-store, and exclusive discounts for–'

'I really just came in here for the box of cereal,' Aaron says.

The cashier presses a few buttons. A price appears on the digital display. Aaron taps his credit card on the top bar of the payment-processing machine. He waits past the checkout line, holding his cereal box with two hands.

Annabelle moves through the line like she's dancing for an audience, smiling wide as the cashier makes a small joke and hands back her bottle of wine.

'I was meeting a friend for brunch around here. Do you live nearby?'

'I do.'

'It's been so long since I've seen you,' she says. 'I'm actually headed to a friend's thing back near campus now.'

'Oh,' he says.

She thumbs towards the door. 'You're welcome to join, you know. People from our class will be there. If you haven't got anything going on.'

'Okay,' he says.

'Yeah?' she asks. She seems surprised.

Aaron realises she was probably just asking to be polite. There surely exists some words that can be assembled in some order to extricate him from this situation.

She takes a step towards the exit. 'Should we go?' she asks.

He looks down to the box in his hands. Eating cereal at home doesn't seem like a valid excuse for anything, especially this. 'Sure,' he says.

The air of the subway station is hot and thick with the mouldy smell of underground tunnels and body odour. They wait for the Red Line outbound train. The platform is mostly empty.

Aaron leans against the wall. Annabelle stands on the pimpled yellow warning strip, facing Aaron. 'A bit of excitement,' she explains. 'It's funny, isn't it? They put up all of these barriers and restrictions to keep you from these little moments of feeling alive.'

Aaron wants to say that the MBTA's incentive to keep dreamers away from moving trains likely has more to do with their penchant for getting hit by them more than any conspiracy, but then the train comes in a gust of hot air and Annabelle's hair blows up all around her giggling face like autumn leaves and she clamps that stupid sun hat down on her head and even he has to admit that she looks like she's having fun. But that might be the point of Annabelle, to have fun. Or rather, to be seen having fun.

The doors of the train car open. Aaron sits across from her. He hasn't asked for any specifics as to where they're going or exactly why: which friend, how close to campus. It seems uncool somehow to ask for clarifying details about their itinerary. This is what people do, isn't it? This is surely some sort of normal life. Annabelle might be bringing him back to her house to have sex with him. The idea scares him more than anything else. He tries not to think about it. The cereal box has a crease in the middle of the logo where his thumb pressed into it. He considers the warped colours and lines.

Aaron would get a text around ten telling him to come over and then he would walk across campus to Annabelle's dorm. This was sometime after Moe. Their arrangement was simple: whenever they wanted to see each other, they would. No labels. No restrictions. Jake described it as Aaron having a 'reliable source of sex', as if sex were a natural resource like oil and Annabelle a deposit beneath the surface of the earth. After a few weeks, Annabelle told him she really liked him. Aaron wanted to tell her that food had lost its taste. Instead, he said they should stop seeing each other. She convinced him that what they were doing wasn't really dating, that he was free to see anyone else he wanted so long as he also saw her, so there wasn't really anything to end. It was an impossible argument. Aaron regularly drank two cans of beer before walking to her dorm and would sit on the edge of the bathtub when he got home with his head between his knees, breathing deeply. Jake told him that he was living the dream. And then Aaron got himself kicked out of school. That was over five years ago.

There's someone at the other end of the car with a baseball cap pulled over his eyes, arms crossed, slumped back into the seat. Annabelle stares at him intently, then turns to Aaron and waits until he catches her eye to shake her head.

'This city,' she says vaguely. 'They just don't care about the homeless.'

He wants to ask her why she thinks this man is homeless but then they arrive at their station. They walk up the stairs side by side and when they get to the top, Annabelle slips her hand into his and pulls him towards a café.

'Have you been here before?' she asks.

Aaron shakes his head. Her hand is soft and slight. It's like holding a bird. He gets the sudden urge to squeeze it as hard as he can, to feel the delicate bones crack and splinter in his grip. The violent impulse disgusts him. He lets go. She doesn't seem to notice.

'They have the best organic teas. Honestly, I don't know what I would do without them.'

'Do you live near here?' Aaron asks.

Annabelle nods. They enter the café. She explains in line that she's finishing her master's degree in nineteenth-century British literature.

'My thesis is going to be on the difference in how gender is used in the works of Jane Austen and the Brontë sisters, how that difference relates to the societal role of women at the time and how the authors' biographical lives may have informed their views.'

'Cool,' Aaron says.

After graduation, she worked as a teaching assistant for the university which led to her securing a spot in her current programme. 'My advisor is strongly recommending that I consider a PhD,' she says and lets out a long sigh. 'But I don't know if I have it in me.'

'Oh,' Aaron says. He clears his throat. 'And, uh, what does one do with a PhD in nineteenth-century British literature?'

Her mouth goes small. 'You mean, what does one do for money? One would be educated, isn't that enough to ask?'

'No, like, how would you pay your rent?'

She smiles and shakes her head like she knows something he doesn't. They arrive at the front of the line and she orders two peppermint teas. When the cashier asks for payment, she takes a step back. Aaron pays and they're handed the teas. They walk up a residential road towards campus. Aaron tucks his cereal box against his body with his elbow and sips from his tea while Annabelle tells him more about her life. She has a boyfriend, sort of, more of a partner, but they're not exclusive. They live together. He's in the same programme she is except his focus is on twentieth-century American literature and how it was informed by nineteenth-century British literature.

'We have a lot of friendly debates,' she says. 'Mostly friendly.'

What Aaron wants to do most right now is make an excuse to go home. He imagines telling the story to Jake when he gets back, the infuriated confusion on his face when Aaron gets to the part where he decides to go home and eat cereal instead of having complication-free sex in the middle of the day. There's a twittering of birds from somewhere above. Aaron can just make out the outline of a nest on the highest branch of a tree. His breath leaves a mark in the air.

They arrive at and walk along the perimeter of the campus in silence. Aaron looks through the chain-link fence at the

JAMES ROSEMAN

fields and the brick buildings. The grass is feathered with a thin layer of white frost.

'Is there anyone you're seeing at the moment?' she asks.

'No,' he says. 'Not really.'

There's a group of students congregated out front of one of the dining halls ahead. One of the students is standing on a picnic table with a megaphone. A few hold up signs.

'What's that?' Aaron asks.

Annabelle squints at the crowd and shakes her head. 'I don't know. Probably something to do with the labour union. They fired a lot of staff recently and then tried hiring them back at almost half their salary. It's really horrible, actually.'

As they get closer, Aaron can make out the writing on some of the signs. *Justice in the Middle East*, one reads.

'Oh,' Annabelle says.

There was that one morning freshman year that Aaron was woken up by a phone call from his mother.

'Stay inside,' she was telling him. 'Whatever you do, don't go to class.'

'Mom, it's eight in the morning,' he said.

'There's a rally against Jews. I can't believe they're allowing it. They might have a list. I bet they got it from Hillel. Who knows, the college probably gave it to them themselves.'

Aaron pulled his laptop onto his bed and typed a few words into the search bar of his web browser. 'That is not a hate group, Mom,' he told her. 'It's a group for justice in Palestine.'

His mother scoffed. 'You are so naïve.'

Annabelle looks from the protesting students to Aaron and back. They pass in silence. When they're far enough away that they can't hear the chanting anymore, she turns to him.

'What do you think of all that?' she asks.

Aaron shrugs. 'I remember people who went to things like that to meet girls.'

'But it's antisemitic, isn't it?'

He breathes in through his nose and out through his mouth. 'You think that it's antisemitic to support Palestine?'

'I think if there's a protest that antisemites would show up at, it's probably that one. It's a pretty convenient issue to hide strong feelings behind.'

'I don't think that anyone would describe anything about that situation as convenient.'

Annabelle sighs. 'This isn't coming out right.'

He looked it up after he got off the phone with his mother. This was the third or fourth such protest being held that semester. A student group was rallying once again to urge that the university divest from Israel, a boycott against the inhumane conditions in Gaza, the illegal settlement of homes in the West Bank, unanswered injustice and apartheid conditions. These causes solicited peripheral interest from Aaron, he believed in what they purported to believe in, but whenever he saw students with signs he felt like he was watching a performance. This was, after all, a campus where students treated political activism like an extracurricular activity. When Moe told the family he was volunteering for the IDF, Aaron thought that any ideological argument would only serve to create distance between them in a moment they needed closeness, so he swallowed his words. After Moe died, Aaron more regularly used the word 'Zionism' in heated conversations with his parents before they stopped speaking entirely. He stopped going to Shabbat services.

There exists an inextricable relationship between Judaism and Israel. By making the decision to take a personal stance on one, he is abandoned by the other. If there exists some way to reconcile the differences between these competing obligations,

Aaron can't see it. He is Jewish. He likes telling people that he's Jewish. He likes pastrami sandwiches and everything bagels. He'll never wear a Hugo Boss suit. He knows about Midrashim, even if he's never read any. He knows that Sandy Koufax sat out of the first game of the 1965 World Series. Aaron has collected trace amounts of culture from thousands of years of ritual and formed them, with clumsy hands, into the shaggy outline of a religious identity. This is the limit of what he is able to do.

The building is tall and skinny, squeezed between two modest houses. There are two front doors. One of them has been painted the same colour as the outside of the house, its doorknob removed. Annabelle skips up the steps and unlocks the other door, leaving it open behind her. Aaron stands on the porch. He takes a tentative step into the entryway.

'Ronnie!' Annabelle shouts. Her voice echoes through the hall and up the stairway.

This building was once a duplex. There's a subtle break in texture where the dividing wall was removed. There are framed photographs of Annabelle and a tall blonde man in front of mountains and churches and in museums. There's a coat rack overloaded with puffy jackets and scarves. The whole place stinks of incense. There's a table by the door with a bonsai tree and miniature buddha statue.

'Ronnie!' Annabelle calls out again.

Aaron follows her into the kitchen. The lights are off. Annabelle sets her bottle of wine on the kitchen counter.

'Do you want some of this?' she asks. 'I thought Ronnie was going to wait for me before going over, but it looks like maybe he went ahead.'

'I was thinking that I should head home, actually,' Aaron says.

Annabelle frowns. She takes the bottle of wine in her hands and uncorks it. 'We just got here. We'll have a glass and then head over. I'm sure there are some people who would love to see you.'

Aaron rubs the back of his neck. 'Yeah, I don't know.'

She takes two glasses down from a cabinet and fills one and then the other. She cuts the distance between them and forces one of the glasses into his hand. 'Just catch up with me for a minute.'

Something slips out of Aaron's arm and hits the floor with a slump. The cereal. He picks it up. The corner it fell on is crumpled inwards, the colours warped.

'I don't think I want this,' he says.

Annabelle takes a step towards Aaron and he takes a step back.

There's a bench on the edge of one of the athletic fields. A tree stands at the corner of the field, a thick trunk with mangled roots. Aaron can see his breath in the air. He remembers some plan in freshman year to remove the tree in order to extend the field which caused such an outrage the administration had to walk it back within the week. He looks up the trunk and then to the splits of its branches, those infinite fractals. The spiderweb structure looks like a cardiovascular system or a network of neurons or a streak of lightning. The thought that these things might be related, if only in structure, is a comforting one. Maybe the paths of his life, too, are sprawled out like these branches. There, that thick one towards the top of the trunk, that's him failing to convince Moe not to leave. Then, a few splits later, that's his decision to go over to Róisín's in the middle of the night. Maybe that small split at the end is Annabelle; the sprig on the right a decision to have sex with her, the left to refuse. And the split before that is him deciding not to leave the grocery store with her at all. It is impossible to see the consequences of his actions this close to them.

Life can only be understood backwards but it must be lived forwards. It's something his father used to tell him. He considers the tree and its branches, all the different versions of his life he could have lived and where each path might have led him. It's a useless thought. Still, he wonders, because wondering is all there's left to do.

12

The subway car stops and an automated voice informs the passengers of the train that they are entering Central Square. The car is thick with body heat. There is a crowd of people waiting on the platform to enter the car and, for a brief moment, Róisín thinks she sees Aaron standing among them through the grimy window. It's now been over a month since they last spoke. What started as 'time to think' has become too awkward a stretch of time to repair. Sometimes she thinks of the tender way he held her hand or kissed her, always tentative, always as if reassuring her that, if she pulled away, he would do nothing to stop her. These memories make her life today feel cheap and plastic by comparison. It is the same life as before, of course, except that now she has intimate knowledge of its beautiful alternative. If that isn't love, then maybe it's the closest thing there is.

The doors open and people flood into the car. A woman sits beside Róisín and hefts her bulky tote bag onto her lap and rummages through it, hitting Róisín multiple times with her elbow, her hand finally emerging clutching a thick hardcover book. A father sits to Róisín's left and helps his young son onto the seat next to him before adjusting the boy's hat and retying the laces of his boots. People filter into the aisle of the car and hold onto the overhead handrail. Every one of them woke up this morning and left some form of home and now they are here in silence, together but not together, inches away and miles apart. What colour is the front door of her childhood home? She can't remember.

The automated voice calls out, 'Stand clear of the closing doors, please.' There's a series of beeps and bells and then the car jolts forward, forcing Róisín into the woman with the tote, who shakes her head in annoyance. A man in a suit standing in front of Róisín looks from his phone to the woman and then to Róisín, rolling his eyes conspiratorially.

There are three stops and then the woman looks up at the framed subway map mounted on the wall behind her and then around the car. She taps Róisín on the shoulder and asks her which stop they've just left. Róisín tells her.

'Shit,' the woman says under her breath. 'Oh shit, shit, shit.'

The man in the suit glances up from his phone to the woman and then to Róisín. He rolls his eyes again. Róisín looks back down between her feet. The car slows as they arrive at the following station. The doors open. The woman hurries off the subway car. The man in the suit takes her place. The automated voice warns people to 'stand clear of the closing doors, please,' and then the car continues.

'Off to work?' the man in the suit asks.

Róisín nods.

'What is it you do?' the man asks.

There are two more stops until the café. Róisín removes her phone from the pocket of her coat and checks the time. She'll probably be half an hour late by now. There's a tap on her shoulder. The man in the suit smiles insistently.

'I asked you where you work,' he says. 'You must not have heard me.'

'A café,' Róisín says.

'Wow, a café! Awesome. Is that on the side or something? Are you a student?'

'No.'

The man in the suit continues looking at her even after she looks away. He taps his left foot. The clicking of his sole against the rubber floor of the car counts off like a metronome. There is one stop remaining on Róisín's journey to the café. She has at least three minutes left in the subway car.

'Aren't you going to ask me where I work?' he asks.

There is a prevalent belief among men that by exchanging courtesies they are indebted attention. Róisín wants to firmly correct this assumption. But even if she convinces this man, she'll never convince every man, and it is infinitely more difficult to fight the flow of moving water than to let it take her. 'Where do you work?' she asks.

'I work at a bank,' he says. 'One of the major ones.'

Róisín stares out of the window of the car. The father to her left coughs into his fist.

'You're really quite pretty,' the man in the suit says. 'I figured you for an actress or something, working in a café like that. Are you an actress? Or a model?'

'No.'

'Funny, I could see you as an actress. You're really quite pretty.'

The train slows as it approaches the next station, Róisín's station. She is twenty-five minutes late for her shift. The automated voice announces their arrival and she stands. She feels a hand close over her arm.

'Hey, wait a minute, I was going to ask for your number,' the man in the suit says.

Róisín shakes off his grip. There's a whooshing noise and then the doors open and then she hears the man say 'bitch' under his breath. She affords one last glance behind her before stepping off the train. The father of the young boy wears an expressionless face that has remained unchanged throughout this entire exchange. His son stares at the laces of his boots and swings his legs without concern. The man in the suit has already turned back to his phone.

She is a block away from the café when she sees the woman sleeping in the side-entranceway of a derelict office building. The woman is shivering and dirty and covered in a torn sleeping bag which has started coming apart at its seams. Róisín stops when she hears the woman crying. She approaches her cautiously and hovers a few feet away. 'Are you all right?' she asks.

The woman sits up. She shakes her head. 'He said he'd be back,' she says. 'He always comes back. He took my socks and he said he'd be back and he's not back yet.'

'Do you have somewhere to go?' Róisín asks. She looks around for help but she is alone.

'Please don't leave me,' the woman says.

It has started to snow. Róisín removes her phone from her pocket and types something into it. A list of search results for women's shelters appears. The closest is an eight-minute walk away. She turns the phone screen around towards the woman. 'I found somewhere we can go if you'd like. They'll have beds there. You'll be warm.'

The woman squints at the screen, shakes her head and tries squinting again. 'I can't read that,' she says quietly and looks down at her lap.

'The Reede Women's Center,' Róisín says. 'It's just under a ten-minute walk; I can go with you if you'd like.'

'No,' the woman says, shaking her head. 'I've been there before. I won't go back there. I can't go back there. He said he'll be back. I know he will be; he always comes back. He always does.'

They're soon surrounded by thick snowflakes which drift around them like moths; the fluttering bite of cold when they find exposed skin then the immediate melt.

'I can't leave you out here,' Róisín says.

'He'll be back,' the woman says. 'He always comes back.'

Róisín finds a receipt and a pen in her purse and writes out the address of the Reede Women's Center on the back of it as well as basic directions on how to get there. She opens her wallet. The woman watches her silently, her eyes fixed on the money inside. Róisín takes out ten dollars, changes her mind and takes out thirty instead. She folds the bills over the receipt with the directions and hands the fold of papers to the woman.

'Bless you.'

'Stay safe. Please, stay safe,' Róisín says.

The woman nods. Róisín is now over thirty minutes late. She continues her way down the street.

'Where is he?' the woman mutters behind her. 'He always comes back. He always does.'

Róisín stood hunched over the bathroom sink, watching the oval window of the pregnancy test as the lines appeared like ink staining white linen. This was three weeks ago. She knew it would be positive even before the lines fully set. The other four tests sat in a neat row, like fine dining cutlery. Maybe doing five tests was overkill. But it wasn't Róisín's fault the tests came in box sets. What was she expected to do when the first came back positive – save the other four?

Worse than finding out was the sudden silence that followed. She sat on her bed, staring at her bedroom wall, wishing she had someone to talk to. Sofia would try her best to be supportive in her own way, which would undoubtedly include phrases like 'be brave' and 'I'll go with you'. Family was out of the question, at least at first. She would have to tell Aaron, wouldn't she? At some point, she decided, but not now. Not until she better understood what she was planning to do.

She looked around her room at the cracked paint, the stained floorboards. She could see her front door from her bed. There was only one sensible option, of course, but then why was it so difficult to consider? Her life was being wasted on unfulfilled potential, or else was being lived to the fullest of its meagre constraints. She had long felt convinced that there was more to existing than what she had experienced so far. So there was only the one option, surely. Wasn't there?

When they've dealt with the backed-up morning rush and the café returns to some semblance of normalcy, Róisín takes her place behind the counter and Sofia at her favourite table, unfolding her laptop. Róisín makes her a flat white. She sets the cup next to Sofia. She removes the phone from her pocket and leans over the counter as she taps on its screen. She opens a messaging application and scrolls down the list of conversations until she finds one labelled *Aaron*. The last message was sent over a month ago. She exits this messaging thread and opens one with her brother. The most recent message is from today at two in the morning.

deal on flights in time for xmas... just sayin

The message is accompanied with a link which opens to a webpage where Róisín can purchase a nonstop flight from Boston to Dublin. There is a button at the bottom of the page which prompts her to add this flight to her cart and, just above it, a tooltip explaining that it is unusual for the flight to be this cheap. Róisín opens a web browser on her phone, which opens to the same page she had open last night and the night before that. The headline reads, 'Penalties for Overstaying

Tourist Visas (US)'. She reads the page even though she's memorised the information. She was granted a 90-day visa on arrival to Boston three years ago. According to this and many other webpages, the penalty for overstaying is an indefinite suspension of entry visas to the United States. It is unlikely, if she leaves the country, that she would ever be allowed to return.

She opens the messaging application again and reopens the thread with Aaron. She starts to type a message.

can you come by the cafe tonight to talk? i get off at 5.

She holds the delete key and watches it disappear, character by character. Biting the inside of her cheek, she types it again and presses send this time, breathing out and shoving her phone into her pocket.

'What are you doing over there?' Sofia asks.

'Nothing.'

'That doesn't look like nothing. That looks like an Aaron face.'

'It's not an Aaron face.'

'Sure,' Sofia says. She takes a sip of her coffee and sets the cup back down on its saucer. 'What's the deal with you two, anyway?'

'There's no deal,' Róisín says.

'Did you break up?'

The bell above the door rings. A man walks into the café. He stands at the counter and hugs himself as he reads the menu.

'What can I get for you?' Róisín asks him.

'Oh, uh, I don't know. I'm not sure yet,' he says.

Róisín feels her phone buzz in her pocket. The man taps his index finger against his lips and hums as he thinks. Róisín slides the top of the phone out of her pocket so that she can just make out the notification bar. It's a text from Aaron.

'All right,' the man says and smiles. 'I'll take a macchiato.'

When the drink is done and handed over, Róisín waits politely for the man to pay and leave. She takes the phone out of her pocket and unlocks it. Her thumb hovers over the icon for the messaging application.

'Now that is definitely an Aaron face,' Sofia says and laughs.

Róisín taps the icon and the messaging thread appears on her screen. There is a new message, added only moments ago.

i'll be there.

Three dots appear to indicate that the sender of this message is typing. Róisín waits. The animation disappears. There is no follow-up message.

'Well?' Sofia says.

'Nothing,' Róisín says and tucks the phone back into her pocket. 'My brother sent me some deals on flights back home for Christmas, is all.'

'Oh, that's fun. It's been forever since I got on a plane.'

Róisín sees Charlie approach the café through the glass just before he opens the front door. She busies herself polishing the metal plating of the espresso machine.

'Oh, Sofia,' he says.

'Hello.'

'I, uh, I didn't know you'd still be here.'

'I finished my shift.' Sofia says. 'It's okay to stick around, though, isn't it?'

'Yeah,' Charlie says. 'Yeah, of course. That's no problem at all.'

Róisín rubs the milk frother with a cloth. It is already clean. Charlie walks around the side of the counter and stops, turning around.

'Do you know what, though,' he says. 'There was an issue with your pay cheque from last week.'

'Was there?' Sofia asks.

'There was.'

'Well, that's no good.'

'No, it isn't,' Charlie says. 'I have the forms in the back room if you've got a second to sign them. But I wouldn't want to interrupt.'

Sofia tells Charlie that he isn't interrupting anything and that she has time now to sign the documents. She closes her laptop and leaves her things strewn across the table. Róisín has moved on to cleaning the chrome faceplate of the machine. When she hears the door to the back office close, she turns around and takes out her phone. She rereads Aaron's message, sucks on the inside of her cheek and types a response.

thank you.

Róisín looks up every time the bell rings for the rest of the day. She accidentally makes a latte instead of an americano and then, remaking the order, accidentally makes the latte again. On the third attempt, she finally makes the correct drink, which she hands over to an annoyed-looking man with long hair. Sofia closes her laptop at two and announces that she's hungry and that they should duck out for half an hour for lunch. During their walk, Sofia tells Róisín a story about Percy that she can't quite follow. Róisín nods when it seems appropriate to nod and says things like 'oh' and 'you're joking'. The gist seems to be that Sofia has broken things off with Percy so that when she lets him get back together with her, she'll get whatever it was he said no to in the first place. The story continues into lunch. Róisín puts forkfuls of salad into her mouth, chews and swallows.

'Do you love him?' Róisín asks.

Sofia looks confused. 'Percy?'

Róisín nods.

'I don't know,' she says. 'No. Almost certainly not, no.'

'Why are you with him?'

Sofia shrugs. 'It's nice being wanted, I guess.'

'Sure. And he gives you stuff.'

She laughs. 'Everything is transactional.'

'I don't know about that.'

'I do,' Sofia says.

Róisín thinks about the woman's sleeping bag coming apart at its seams. Charity isn't transactional, she wants to say. But then, didn't she feel that much better about herself when she handed over those bills? Soon Róisín's bowl of salad is empty and it's time to return to the café.

At four forty-five, Charlie comes out from the back office and tells Sofia he found one more document she needs to sign. She returns to the back office with him. Róisín leans on the counter and watches the clock. The café is empty. Soon it will be time to close and the day will have officially ended. She watches the door as if she can will Aaron to walk through it.

There's a dull thump and then the sound of breaking glass. Róisín follows the noise and stands at the door of the back office. She considers going back to the counter and pretending she didn't hear anything. Then she wraps her fingers round the handle and turns it.

'Wait—' someone says from behind the door.

She sees the framed photograph of his wife first. It sits in a dusting of broken glass. Charlie is up against the front of his desk with his hands outstretched to Róisín as if he can force time to go backwards. His legs are pale and hairy, his trousers bunched up around his ankles. And there's Sofia, kneeling on top of them, her eyes wide and staring.

'Oh, Jesus,' Róisín says and closes the door.

She walks back to the counter. There's a pressure in her head so immense that she can't see straight. Heat flushes her cheeks. There's a commotion from the back room. Charlie comes out first, then Sofia, wiping her mouth. Charlie is shouting at Róisín now. She can't quite make out the words through the waterfall of static that's rushing in her ears. She stares at the counter. Her breaths are shallow. She can't get enough air into her lungs.

'I'm talking to you, do you hear me?' Charlie says, louder now. He walks behind the counter and the constant rush of water breaks. She hears the ringing of a bell.

'Stop it!' Sofia says, crying.

Charlie grabs Róisín by her upper arm and pulls her close. 'If you mention this to anyone…' he starts.

'What do you think you're doing?' someone says. The voice is calm and measured.

Charlie lets go immediately. Róisín's arm throbs from where he grabbed her. Now someone is holding her by the shoulders and guiding her out from behind the counter. Not someone: Aaron.

'Get out!' Charlie is yelling. 'Get the fuck out! You're fired, do you hear me?'

Aaron doesn't respond. He keeps his arm over Róisín's shoulders and opens the door for her so they can step outside. The night air bites at the streaks of wetness on Róisín's cheeks.

'You didn't do anything wrong,' Aaron is saying. He takes off his canvas jacket and wraps it around her shoulders, pulling it tight.

'I have to tell you something,' Róisín says, sniffling.

'Later,' he says. 'You can tell me later.'

They get onto the subway and, when they sit, Róisín leans her head against Aaron's shoulder and cries. He doesn't tell her not to. He doesn't tell her anything. He just runs his fingers through her hair and kisses her forehead and the top of her head, stopping to ask if it's okay, continuing when she nods.

13

Aaron's father was an incredible home cook. Maybe he still is an incredible home cook, Aaron doesn't know; they haven't spoken in over five years. When he and Moe were children, they would stand on chairs and watch as their father took eggs from the carton and hit them against the flat surface of the countertop. They'd marvel as the shells came apart in perfect, even halves. Aaron hasn't thought about that in a long time. Here, in Róisín's kitchen, he cracks an egg the way his father taught him to. The egg fractures in a neat line. He pulls the top half from the bottom with his fingers and thumbs, emptying its contents into a bowl, then tosses the empty shell into the garbage. He cracks a second, then a third. The hum of morning traffic has just begun. The windows are fogged with condensation. The radiator in the hallway clangs to life and starts hissing. Aaron selects another egg from the carton and cracks it. Instead of splitting, it flattens under his palm into a mess that drips down the side of the cabinet and onto the floor tiles.

'Fuck,' he says under his breath.

He opens one drawer and another until he finds the rags. He mops up the egg from the floor and the cabinet and tosses the wet rag into the sink. He rifles through more drawers until he finds a fork and then whisks the eggs in the bowl until they're smooth. He knows that if he adds salt too soon, the protein in the eggs will break down and they'll go watery. Making scrambled eggs is one of few of his father's lessons that has stuck with him. He finds a pan and places it on the stovetop and then keeps whisking.

'What's this, then?' Róisín asks from the doorway. She's rubbing her eyes and blinking in the daylight.

'No, no,' Aaron says. He sets down the bowl and points to the doorway. 'Get yourself back in there, you're supposed to be asleep.'

'Am I?' she asks.

'You am,' he says. 'I'm waking you up with breakfast.'

'But I'm already awake.'

'You aren't awake, you're asleep. Because I'm waking you up with breakfast.'

They came up the stairs silently, step by step, and arrived on the landing. Róisín unlocked the front door. This was last night. Aaron stopped on the stairwell and looked into the apartment, all of those plants and framed photographs and empty cardboard boxes, and watched Róisín as she shuffled into her home and tossed her bag onto the table in the kitchen, her coat over a chair. She looked at him from the far side of the room.

'Aren't you coming in?' she asked.

'Sure. Yeah, of course.'

Aaron stood in the hallway and watched Róisín get settled. He wasn't sure what to do with his hands. He crossed his arms. She sat in one of the chairs and let out a sigh. He shoved his hands into his pockets.

'You're making me nervous; sit down.'

He sat across from her at the table. The oven beeped. A clatter of muffled footsteps came from the apartment above them.

'I'm sorry,' Aaron said.

Róisín looked through her bag and retrieved a packet of cigarettes. She opened the top flap and peered in, closed it, opened it again, folding it back and forth.

'For the last time I was here, I mean.' Aaron rubbed the back of his neck. 'And for not calling since.'

'I didn't call either,' Róisín said.

'Right.'

She took a cigarette from the packet and held it. The tip of it bounced impatiently between the knuckles of her fingers.

'You probably didn't feel like talking to me,' he said.

She looked through the window towards the fire escape. Maybe she didn't hear him. Maybe she heard him but she didn't care. She must be waiting for him to leave, grateful enough that he showed up in a moment of sudden crisis but now eager for him to go.

'I missed you,' Aaron said. 'That's all I mean.'

She continued to stare out the window. 'I can't believe I didn't see it,' she said.

'See what?'

'Sofia and Charlie. I can't believe I didn't see that they... It doesn't matter, I guess. I just feel like an idiot.'

He nodded. He wasn't sure what to say. When he'd arrived at the café, Charlie had had Róisín by the arm behind the counter while Sofia watched from a table, looking like a ghost. He was fixated on Charlie's hand and the impression its fingers were making on Róisín's arm. His vision blurred around the edges. There was a certain type of retributive absolution in the violence Aaron wanted then. But he kept calm. He wanted to be the person Róisín thought he was and, in that moment, he knew the only thing she needed was to get away.

'I'm sorry,' Aaron said.

Róisín looked down at the ends of her coat hanging from

the chair and dug a hand into one pocket, then the other.
She placed a lighter onto the table and her cigarette next to
it.

Aaron leant forward. 'Are you okay?'

She nodded towards the window. 'Will you help me with
this?'

It was stuck at its sides and took considerable effort for the
two of them to finally wrench it open. Róisín climbed out and
sat on the fire escape. Aaron sat back down at the table. He
passed through her cigarette and lighter. She lit it and took
a long inhale and then opened her mouth, letting the smoke
drift out. She made an indentation halfway up the cigarette
with her nail and then flicked away the ash. 'He groped me,'
she said finally.

'What? Who, your boss?'

Róisín nodded. Her head lolled to the right, facing the
building across the street. 'A while ago. He called me into the
back office for help with his computer or something. I was so
stupid. He told me to come around the back of his desk and
then, well.' She shrugged.

Aaron felt the blood pump through his body. 'And then
what?' he asked. His right arm felt stiff and it was only upon
looking down that he realised his hands were clenched.

'I think I got off easy, to be honest,' Róisín said. She
inspected the cigarette, looking from the cherry-red tip to the
indentation mark.

Aaron took a breath in through his nose and let it out
through his mouth. His hands relaxed. 'That sounds terrible. I
wish you had told me that.'

Róisín took another long drag and held it. Then her mouth
opened to let the smoke drift out. She looked down at her feet
and said, 'I've missed you too.'

Aaron rubbed his neck and smiled. He took another deep breath and then said, 'I think that I love you.'

'What?'

'I think that I love you,' he repeated.

Róisín held the half-finished cigarette with her thumb and finger and gently slid it between the metal slats of the fire escape by her shoes, then let go. The red dot fell towards the street below and, in an instant, it was gone.

'I shouldn't have said that,' Aaron said. He stood up and pushed in his chair.

She reached her hand through the open window and he took it. The kitchen felt smaller than it did before. They heaved the window shut together and then Róisín pointed to the latch at the top of it and Aaron locked it. They stood a foot apart. She smelled like cigarette smoke and perfume. Her cheeks were rosy with cold. Aaron's hands floated up and, before he could understand the mechanics of what his body was doing, he had Róisín wrapped in his arms and his lips pressed against hers. She didn't kiss him back. Her arms stayed at her sides.

'Sorry,' Aaron said, stepping back. 'I'm going to leave you alone now.'

Róisín considered him blankly. She didn't look upset or disgusted. She didn't look delighted or overwhelmed. Whether the words meant anything to her, whether she had even heard them, Aaron didn't know. He pulled one arm into a sleeve of his canvas jacket and then other. He walked towards the front door. Róisín said something behind him that he couldn't hear. He stopped.

She was leant over the table. Her face was wet. 'Don't go,' she was saying.

She wavered like the surf then crashed into him like a wave. She sniffled and cried and choked and pressed her face so hard into his chest that he was afraid she might suffocate against it. She grabbed fistfuls of his shirt and then pulled herself against him and pressed her mouth onto his. She didn't let go, not while they undressed in the warm darkness of her bedroom, not while he was inside of her and not after, when they lay there in a heap of tangled limbs. She held onto him like letting go would have her drift away forever.

He had his arm around her, tracing circles on her shoulder with the tips of his fingers.

'I don't feel like me,' she said. 'I feel like I'm looking out of the eyes of someone else.'

The room was dark and hot. Sleep nipped at their feet. Its tide rose quietly and quickly, then came a peaceful wave.

They eat at the kitchen table. Róisín stabs a clump of egg with her fork. Aaron takes measured bites and soon his plate is empty. She tilts her plate up towards him. He shakes his head. 'No, it's okay.'

The morning unfolds in relative silence. Aaron isn't sure what's supposed to happen next. He's confident that Róisín only let him stay because the alternative was to be alone. She needed someone for one night, a human-shaped supplier of steady body heat to keep her warm. It could have been anyone, surely. Even as he thinks it, he knows that it isn't true.

He clears his throat. 'I think I might head home.'

Róisín nods. She puts her fork next to her plate.

'I just thought…' he starts.

She looks out the window. *I just thought you would rather be alone*, he wants to say. She doesn't tell him to stay. She doesn't stop him when he gathers his things from the bedroom and brings them to the kitchen. He doesn't know why he expects her to. If he wants to stay, he should stay or, at the very least, say that he wants to stay. Instead, he ties his shoelaces.

Róisín stands and disappears into the bedroom. There's a clattering as dresser drawers are thrown open and closed, and then silence. Róisín takes tepid steps back to the table and sits. She opens her mouth, pauses, then closes it without speaking. She slides something across the table towards Aaron. He takes it autonomically. He's never seen a pregnancy test before. There is an ink legend on its side which explains that one vertical line indicates 'not pregnant' while two denotes the opposite. He holds the stick up to the light and squints. He looks at Róisín. She's staring out the window.

14

When Róisín and Darragh were growing up, they'd come home after school and the first thing they'd have was a cup of tea. Da would be watching the telly and bark out something like, 'It'd be awful nice to have a cup of tea,' and Mam would start the kettle and he'd act all surprised and grateful when she put a mug on the table in front of him. Just the four of them. Maeve considered herself too grown up for that sort of thing. She'd be up in her room, listening to her Walkman with the door closed. Mam would only ever pop back in with biscuits. Da loved a tea but he couldn't live without his biscuits. Mam would set out the tin and tell Darragh and Róisín they could have one each, but Da would nod towards it and make a shushing sign until they snuck an extra few while she wasn't looking.

Róisín is standing outside a café when she sees the familiar packaging through the dusty window of a convenience store. The café is called The Bald Man. She went in looking for a job and now she's out on the sidewalk, staring into the convenience store next door. Bourbon creams. They're not the ones she grew up with but they're close enough to hurt. The bell rings above her as she steps into the shop and she's met with the smell of bleach and turned fruit. The aisles are so narrow that she has to turn sideways to navigate through them. A television hanging over the register shows lottery numbers being chosen through a film of static. Róisín shoulders her way past shelves of shrink-wrapped ramen packages and bottles of cooking sauces to a shelf near the window displaying the tea biscuits. There's a printed-out, postcard-sized Union Flag pinned to the top of the shelf and a small label which reads, *From Across The Pond*. The lottery announcer calls out a new set of numbers and someone's life is changed forever.

Bourbon creams were always her favourite. Jammie Dodgers were a close second, to be fair, but Darragh claimed them as his when he was four and she didn't want to be thought of as a copycat. Beneath the shelf of biscuits is a shelf with boxes of *Authentic British Tea*. She thinks of the pitiful sachets of Lipton waiting in a jar at home and takes a box of Lyons.

Between the woman at the register and Róisín, there's a thick plastic dividing wall with a cut-out at the counter. Róisín sets down the biscuits and box of tea and slides them forward. The woman scans them.

'Lyons are Irish, by the way,' Róisín says.

'That'll be $12.65, please.'

The woman watches the television as Róisín puts the cash onto the counter. Without looking away from the screen, the woman taps on the plastic divider, drawing Róisín's attention to a sign that reads *Card Only*. Róisín slaps a card onto the counter, just far enough for the woman to have to reach for it.

The Bald Man was the fifth café Róisín had visited this week. Three weren't hiring. One only needed someone for a few hours a week. The Bald Man was a kind of Copenhagen-style café with plants everywhere and lo-fi music and six-dollar coffees. She eyed the shiny espresso machine behind the counter while the manager asked her questions and then asked when she was available to start.

'Right away,' she said.

The manager handed her the paperwork just as a customer approached. Róisín read the form, flipped the page, flipped back. All of those boxes asking for bank details and a Social Security number, all of those letters and numbers that she was unable to provide. She left the clipboard on the counter and snuck out while the manager was busy pulling a shot of espresso.

The payment-processing machine gives a resounding 'no' in the form of a beep and the woman holds the card up to the light.

'It's a prepaid card,' Róisín explains. 'A prepaid debit card.'

'What?' the woman asks.

'It's a prepaid debit card,' Róisín repeats.

The woman shakes her head and leans forward, holding a hand up to her ear.

'Prepaid. Debit,' Róisín says.

'I'm sorry, I can't understand what you're saying.'

The woman swipes the card through the machine and the payment is rejected again. She groans as she leans over to get something from beneath the counter and returns upright with a heavy-looking set of metal scissors. 'It says I'm supposed to cut it.'

'It's prepaid,' Róisín says. She taps on the plastic divider. 'It's a prepaid card, it's just out of money. I can run around the corner to fill it.'

The woman's eyebrows scrunch together and she shakes her head. 'I'm sorry, I just can't understand you,' she says. The scissors squeak as they cut the card in half. She sweeps the two halves into the trash and turns back to the television.

'Why don't you just come back home?' her mother asked her on the phone.

It was a simple question that Róisín had trouble answering.

'If you're dead-set on having it and that's not something we can talk you out of–'

'Sinéad,' her father started.

'All right,' her mother said. 'But I can make up the box room into a nursery, is all. You'd be home for Christmas. We would take care of you.'

'I don't know.' This quiet life. Her apartment had never felt so empty, so cold.

'Going to raise a baby in that kip all on your own, are you, Róisín?' her mother asked. 'Answer me when I'm talking to you.'

'Sinéad,' her father said again.

Her mother sighed. 'At least think about it, would you?'

'I will. I will think about it.'

'You can hardly raise a child on a coffee shop salary, Róisín. I don't think you've thought this through, is all,' her mother said.

'Unlike you, is that right? Having Maeve at seventeen, you really thought through that decision carefully, did you?' Róisín said.

'No,' her mother said. The line grew quiet. 'That was different,' she said finally.

'Different how?'

'Different because I had family around.'

Róisín sucked on the inside of her cheek.

'Your father and I have some savings we could put towards a ticket. Give me the word and you can be on the next flight home. Consider it, at least. There's no point in being proud.'

The walls of her bedroom were plain. There was a crack in the paint that ran like lightning alongside the doorframe. There was a radiator on the wall next to her bed and a blotch of discoloured paint above it from years of steam. Brown, like a malignant tumour, like the whole place was rotting from the inside.

'I will consider it, Mam,' Róisín said.

'You will?'

'I will,' she repeated.

'You ought to. I'm serious, now.'

'I will, I said I will, so.'

There is a convenience store on the corner of Róisín's street run by a father and a son. There is a room behind the counter and they often leave the door open so that the father can watch his son at the counter while he sits with his feet up. Sometimes, while she's shopping, she'll hear the father yell out and the son will emerge from behind the counter, stride to the freezer in the back and return with an orange cream popsicle. The father will say something else, something softer, while the son turns his attention back to his phone screen.

Róisín's first apartment had two bedrooms and five tenants. She shared a bed with a woman named Melissa for six months before finding her current place. It's further out and the estate agent asked her twice if she was sure she wanted to live in that neighbourhood but it is a space entirely her own. Since she moved in over two and a half years ago, she's been coming to this convenience store at least once a week. Neither the father nor the son show any signs of recognition when she walks through the door. She does not know either of their names. This is the closest thing she has to family here.

There is a wall of shelves where she usually finds the prepaid debit cards, below the unlocked SIM cards but above the dusty boxes of disposable mobile phones. Róisín doesn't have an American bank account, which means that she doesn't have an American bank card. She has an Irish bank card, which is associated with an Irish bank account. The first few weeks she found the balance was going up. Nothing major, obviously, the odd twenty here and there, a fifty on occasion. The deposits showed up on her monthly statements stamped with the address of the closest bank branch to her parents' house in Ireland. She never mentioned the deposits when they spoke on the phone. At the end of a call, her father would ask if she had enough for food and that, and she'd say yes, and he'd say something like, 'That's good,' and that would be the end of it. Then she told them that she wasn't coming home for Christmas. Then she told them that she wasn't coming home at all. The deposits stopped.

Money – as in physical, printed paper – turned out to be quite an inconvenient thing to manage. Most places didn't accept it, for one. So she's been coming here, to this convenience store, every week, to refill a prepaid debit card. That little piece of plastic was small enough to fit in her pocket and it unlocked the world. Utilities. Phone service. Online shopping. It was possible to live here so long as she had those raised numbers on that plastic card. Now, as she stands in the familiar space of this convenience store staring at an empty shelf, she feels that world of possibility close up around her.

'Do you have any of the cards left?' she asks at the counter.

The son is hunched over his stool. He doesn't hear her.

'Excuse me,' she says. 'Do you have any of the cards left? The prepaid ones?'

The father shouts something from the back room and the son looks up. He sets his phone down and rises from his stool. 'The what?'

Róisín points to where the prepaid cards are supposed to be stocked.

The son follows her finger and shakes his head. 'We had to take them off the shelves.'

'Why?'

The son hops back onto the stool and shrugs. 'I don't know. They changed the rules, I guess. It's a liability or something.'

The father laughs at the television. He looks up, catching Róisín's stare. She offers a smile. He unwraps a popsicle and turns back to the screen.

'Do you know where I can–' she starts to ask, but the son's already back on his phone.

She closes her eyes and focuses on the sound of her breath moving in and out of her body, like a tide advancing and receding, the whooshing noise the water makes as it scrapes against the sand. She removes the phone from her coat pocket and selects *Aaron* from a list of contacts. *Everything will be fine*, she tells herself. She presses the call button and holds the phone to her ear.

'Your call cannot be completed as dialled,' the automated voice says. 'Please hang up and try again.'

She steps out into the cold and waiting world. She shuts her eyes and focuses on her breath. She imagines a beach. *This is what being alive sounds like. Everything will be fine.* Her breathing goes ragged and the ocean churns, the waves crash onto the shore, spitting up fistfuls of spume like oceanic shrapnel. She dials Aaron again.

'Your call cannot be completed as dialled,' the voice says.

It urges her to give up before trying again.

15

H is mother is in the dirt when he walks up the front lawn of his childhood home, his bag heavy in his hands. Her knees are in the soil, her fingers wriggling in the earth. The taxi driver yells at Aaron from his window and honks his horn – all this racket because the driver was too fucking stupid to check that Aaron had any cash before they arrived and now that horn is all he's got.

'I'm planting table iris,' his mother says. She hasn't looked up once during this taxi driver exchange.

The cab grumbles back up the hill, leaving a familiar suburban silence. Now Aaron can only just hear the murmur of the nearby ocean waves and the twittering of the birds. It's hot for a late autumn day. He expected it to be colder, especially this close to the water, and can feel the sweat bead at the back of his neck. He sets the bag down beside him in the grass and waits for her to hug him, for her to tell him how long it's been since he's been home.

'Most people would think it's American bearded iris, but it's not,' she says over her shoulder, wiping her forehead on the sleeve of her shirt. 'Table iris is much harder to find.'

She continues digging. There's something ritualistic about the motion, like prayer. She wears her engagement rings from both marriages on her fingers and the sapphires and diamonds glint in the sunlight as she reaches into the sack of bulbs beside her. They look like small onions or desiccated eyeballs, tangled roots matted against them like optic nerves. She drops one into each of the three holes she's dug, fills them in and pats them flat.

'I didn't think I'd find you out here,' Aaron says finally.

His mother scoffs and wipes her forehead again. 'Where else would I be?'

She sits back on her heels and rests her hands in her lap. She looks to the right and Aaron follows her gaze to their neighbour's house. There's a flag fluttering in the ocean breeze. The black, white, green and red of the Palestinian flag. She tuts her tongue and says something under her breath and turns back to the dirt.

'What?'

'Nothing,' she says. 'I'm not going to start this with you again after all this time.'

When he was young, Aaron would plant bulbs with his mother. Some sunny day in spring, she'd drag him out front with a magnifying glass to see the wispy green tendrils reaching up, grasping for sunlight.

His mother holds onto the fingers of her right hand with her left and draws her hands into her stomach, bending forward.

'Do you need any help?' Aaron asks.

'No,' she says to the ground. 'You go on inside, I'll be in soon.'

'Are you sure?'

'I'm sure,' she says, softer now. She digs another hole and reaches for a bulb. 'I'll only be another minute.'

His mother would change something about the house every other week when he and Moe were growing up. A new toaster oven. A reorientation of the kitchen table. A framed photograph moved from a bedroom to the den, only to be returned a few days later. It's been over five years now and nothing's changed at all. It is exactly the same as when he left. The dishwasher hums below the sink. The kitchen smells like cold coffee and sawdust. Every surface is glossy wood. His mother loves wood grain. The first thing she did when they moved in was strip the paint from every surface and replace it with lacquer. There's a photograph from Aaron's high school graduation fixed to the cabinet door, where it's always been. The tape has gone yellow at the corners and the colours have warped a little. His graduation cap, once blue, is now on some spectrum between magnolia and violet. He's smiling with fat, ruddy cheeks. His eyes are clear and white. This is a face of blind optimism and undeserved hope. Aaron considers this younger version of himself like it's a different person, which it is. There are no flies on him.

Then he sees the picture of Moe below. It looks fresh, as if it were just tacked up. He's got a great big smile that glows against his tanned skin, the Mediterranean warmth radiating off the paper. The months following Moe's death were a blur. The funeral was over capacity. People filled their home for all seven days of shiva. And then after, when he hoped it was over, they were carted around from synagogue to synagogue like show ponies for months.

There was this congregation in Everett led by a young rabbi who was short and wore a pink bow tie. He had them come up to the bimah after the parshah reading and sit behind him for his sermon as though they were props.

'Hamas means violence,' he shouted into the microphone, gripping both sides of the podium with white-knuckled fists. 'Violence begets violence begets loss begets grief.'

Aaron was sat between his mother and father and stayed very still. The congregation looked at them with sad eyes and cheap smiles. His mother reached for his hand and he let her take it but he did not close his fingers around hers. How dare she let them be paraded around like this. His father too. How dare they allow Moe's corpse to be fashioned into a war drum and stand idly by while it was beaten by people who could never and would never understand the depth of their pain. There were children in the audience and, as Aaron looked over their faces, he wondered which of them, if any, would be inspired by this speech to be next in line. Israel. Canaan. The promised land. There was no limit to Aaron's anger. And there was nothing constructive for him to do with it.

'Look at what our enemy has taken from our community in the name of this violence. An eighteen-year-old boy whose sights were set on Harvard and becoming a doctor, who instead felt that calling to HaShem and volunteered to defend Israel from those who would do it harm. We are soon going to recite the Mourner's Kaddish. It is typical for me to ask that if anyone has suffered a loss, and if they feel comfortable doing so, they rise. Today, I will ask all who are able to rise, because we have all of us suffered a great loss to our people in defence of our nation. We have lost a hero.'

At the kiddush lunch, people kept coming up to Aaron saying how brave his brother was. Aaron wanted to tell these people that his brother was frightened almost every day of his service. He wanted to beat them with his fists and make them understand that most of his conversations with his brother involved counting down the days until they would be together again.

'Mino's,' Aaron used to say on the phone. Moe would groan.

'I would give my left nut for a super beef from Mino's right now. I would maybe even consider giving my right one too.'

'What would you give for one of their homemade root beers?'

And Moe would retch. 'I wouldn't give my left pinkie toe. I wouldn't give your left pinkie toe. That shit is rank.'

And so on, Aaron cycling through their standard orders

at their favourite North Shore joints, Moe responding with which body parts, if any, he would be willing to exchange for a regular order there. It was comforting remembering that sort of thing together over the phone, as if occupying the same mental space was a reasonable proxy for sharing a physical one.

Aaron once asked his brother if many Americans served. Moe told him there weren't many but that there were plenty of first-generation Israelis whose parents hailed from Brooklyn or Boston or Chicago and refused to talk about it, who wanted to learn all about their birth right culture from a bona fide American.

'It's a cultural exchange,' he said. 'They teach me Hebrew and I teach them about Babe Ruth and Big Papi. Making Sox fans outta sand and stone over here.'

When he was seventeen, Aaron went on a fully paid trip to Israel. They went to Jerusalem and Eilat and Tzfat, all around the country, really. They slept in tents with Bedouins and sunbathed on the beaches of the Mediterranean. On the second to last night of the trip, the adults did a spot check and found two bottles of rum in Aaron's suitcase. They didn't even have to look that hard, they just flipped open the lid and there were the bottles, perched on top of his clothes. He'd been attracted to that particular type of liquor because it had little flakes of gold in it which some kid from Marblehead named Ethan had promised would get them extremely drunk.

'It makes all these tiny cuts down your throat so the alcohol can get into your blood quicker,' he told them at the supermarket. 'My cousin said so.'

A few years later, Moe went on the same trip. When he came home, he started wearing a yarmulke and keeping kosher. He opted for the Orthodox Chabad synagogue over the Conservative one they'd always gone to, even though it was further away. Their parents were proud of their son's sudden piety. Then came Passover, when Rebbe Moe forced their mother to bin about fifty dollars' worth of chametz. Aaron watched her toss away the boxes of cereal, the plastic tub of pretzels, the breadcrumbs.

'When octopuses give birth...' she started to say.

'Mom,' Moe said. 'Let's focus.'

After a few months, he did stop wearing the yarmulke and going to Chabad but he kept going to the weekly minyan at their local synagogue. Then one weekend, when Aaron was home from college, Moe announced over dinner that his application to volunteer for the Israel Defense Forces had been accepted. He hadn't even told anyone he was applying.

There's a cough from the kitchen table.

'My son,' his father says. 'There you are.'

Aaron sets his bag down beside him on the hardwood floor and waits for his father to say something sharp, some criticism dressed as a compliment. It'll be a reference to how many years it's been since he's been home, surely. To his bag. His clothes. His job. But his father doesn't speak at all. The answering machine beeps. There's a message waiting to be heard.

'I didn't think I'd find you here,' Aaron says finally. It's too dark to see his face. He can only see the two frames of his father's glasses flash as he adjusts them on his face. His father turns slightly away and coughs into his fist.

'Is your mother out there?' he asks softly.

There's a window above the sink. The front lawn is empty.

'She must be coming around the back now.'

'Your mother is...' He trails off until he settles on the word. 'Perturbed.'

'By me?'

His father shakes his head. 'For once, no.'

Sweat rolls down Aaron's neck and soaks into his shirt collar. He wants to remove his heavy outer coat but feels somewhat self-conscious performing that action in front of his father. Removing his coat feels like the first concrete step in realising his plan to stay the night, even though that plan has already been communicated and agreed upon by all of the requisite parties. The room is hot and stuffy and all of its wood has Aaron thinking about coffins.

'Your mother told me not to bring it up to you.'

'What, the neighbour's flag?'

He cocks his eyebrow. 'So, you know what we're up against.'

'Because the first thing they'll do after getting themselves running water in Gaza is root out the Jews in Greater Boston, right?'

His father's hand comes down on the kitchen table in a whipcrack of lightning and Aaron stands in the stillness of its thunder. 'Don't do that,' his father says calmly. 'Don't minimise it.'

'I wasn't, I was joking.'

'How could you possibly still be this naïve after all this time? Do you really think everyone is rooting for one side instead of against the other? And where will they go, these people you're so keen on removing from their homes for the benefit of yet another Arab state?'

'I don't want to get into this,' Aaron says. 'Let's have a nice visit. I have something I wanted to–'

'You need to educate yourself, Aaron. I have quite a few books you can borrow on the topic. It's the least you could do. In the meantime, consider this. The UK gives a parcel of land to people who couldn't go back home. They won't tell you about the Kielce pogrom, about what happened to the Jews who went back.'

'Who's they? This was over seventy years ago, Dad. Let's drop it. I don't want to get into it.'

'And immediately those people were attacked on all sides,' his father continues. 'They defended themselves in '48, and again in '67, and on and on. We took the Golan Heights, it's ours!'

'We?'

'We, dammit!' he shouts, and his hand comes down onto the table again.

Aaron squints into the darkness to try and make out his father's face but he can only find the rough outline of his glasses, his white lenses shining. 'Dad…' he starts.

The door creaks open behind them. His mother shuffles into the room. She picks up a watering can on the counter and peers into the darkness, first at Aaron and then at the kitchen table. 'The bulbs are planted,' she says. The words go stale in the silence.

His father clears his throat. 'I was just telling Aaron to bring his things upstairs and get settled. What a wonderful surprise after all this time.'

'Yes, wonderful,' his mother says. She looks him over for the first time. 'Maybe a shower. There are fresh towels in the upstairs closet.'

'I know where they are,' Aaron says.

His mother considers him blankly. 'Of course you do.'

'Well,' his father says. He nods towards the duffel bag. This is Aaron's invitation to leave.

He lifts his bag and climbs the wooden staircase to his childhood bedroom. His mother whispers something to his father, who hisses something decisive back which ends the conversation. The back door opens and shuts and his mother returns outside to her garden. The answering machine beeps again. The message remains unheard.

The bedroom has been preserved like a living museum. There are headshots of the 2007 Boston Red Sox still pinned to the wall. That was the summer the *Boston Globe* included a new headshot each week and, every morning, Aaron and Moe would wake up early to try to get the newspaper before their father, in case he threw it out. Aaron didn't care much about baseball. He was always more interested in the completion of a collection than its contents. And, of course, Moe was happy enough being included in whatever Aaron did. Aaron sets his duffel on the bed and takes a deep breath in through his nose and lets it out through his mouth. He looks at the faces of Pedroia, Youkilis, Ramirez and finds that his hands are trembling. Even though nothing has changed, this feels like someone else's room. No man ever steps in the same river twice, for it is not the same river and he is not the same man. It's something his father used to tell them growing up.

The bathroom is an ensuite. Moe's bedroom is next door but growing up they both shared this one bathroom. He looks at it now and can't quite imagine how two people fit side by side at the sink every night, brushing their teeth. A few weeks before he died, Moe confessed to Aaron that he had started sleeping in bathtubs. There was something about a rocket blast, an entire family wiped out except the four-year-old who had curled up in the tub. When Moe got to talking like this, Aaron listened. The trick to their closeness was that he never once asked what his brother was hoping to accomplish over there.

'Me, I like to sleep with a pillow against my back,' Aaron said. 'So I totally get it.'

That made Moe laugh. When Moe laughed, he laughed with his whole body. It was impossible to hear it and not at least crack a smile. Aaron had forgotten that sound until just now, being in this room after five years. There are many things that Aaron purposely does not think about and it is reassuring, in a way, to know that these memories are only lying dormant and not forgotten. There are so many it is impossible to keep them all shut away all of the time. Life can only be understood backwards but it must be lived forwards. Aaron tries and fails to steady his hand. He unzips his backpack and removes the cell phone from its front pocket. There's a notification from Róisín. He taps a few buttons on the screen and pulls up their conversation. He bites his nail and types out a message.

i hate it here.

He holds the delete key until the message disappears and types a new one.

it's going well.

They had had a conversation about what to do next. Róisín told him she was moving back home. There were other things said, surely, but that's the only thing Aaron can remember about it now. This was no way to live, she was telling him.

'Do you want to go?' he asked.

'I can't stay.'

'But do you want to go?'

'I have nowhere to live,' she said. They were in his bedroom, sitting on the edge of his bed. She gestured at the walls. 'What am I going to do, move in here?'

'Why not?' Aaron asked.

'It's time,' she said. She picked at her nail. 'I don't want it to be, but maybe it is.'

'What if there was somewhere we could go?' he asked her.

Aaron locks his cell phone and returns it to the front pocket of his backpack. There was a way through this. He knew that if Róisín went home it would be difficult for her to get a visa back or something; the details weren't clear. And she had admitted that there was a version of him, Aaron at his best, who she could imagine being with. In theory. Meaning, of course, that, in reality, he was too fucked to consider. Aaron does not know if this theoretical version of himself exists, or if it ever existed outside of Róisín's hopes. And if it did, he is unsure whether or not it is possible for him to embody it again. He lies on the stiff bed and stares at the ceiling. It feels like someone else's room.

When Aaron comes downstairs, he finds on the kitchen counter two candles, a loaf of challah and a bottle of red wine. Standing around it, his parents recite the Shabbat prayers and he stumbles through the words with them, five years out of practice. Neither his mother nor his father ask why, after all this time, he's decided to come home. They would have discussed this, maybe even just before Aaron arrived: which tack to take to avoid driving him away. The candles are lit. His mother hands him a chunk of bread. Aaron takes a tepid bite and nods. The goblet of wine passes from his mother to his father to him. There is undoubtedly a jug of Kedem grape juice in the fridge, a constant of his father's breakfast routine. But to ask for it would be to call attention to the substitution, to invite questions about how bad his drinking must be that he wants to avoid it altogether. Aaron drains his half-glass in the name of HaShem. Róisín would understand. He told her he would cut back, but surely this is some kind of permissible exception.

They sit down to the dinner table and listen to the radio pump out grainy jazz. The lights in the kitchen are off. There are two candles on the table. Aaron only catches glimpses of his father's face in the flickers of the light. He arranges and rearranges the order of the words in his head. *Can Róisín and I move in with you?* No. *Wouldn't it be great if Róisín and I moved in with you?*

'Will you come to services tomorrow?' his mother asks.

The distance between thought and speech is infinite. They don't even know who Róisín is, so he'd have to begin with that bit of news.

'There's a new rabbi, you know,' she says. 'He's really quite good.'

'Is he?' Aaron asks between bites.

'He is,' his father says. 'He's traditional.'

'Yes,' his mother nods. 'We had one rabbi for a while, Rabbi Baruch, who was all about inclusivity. Towards the end, he had a full band playing services. We only did about half of the prayers in Hebrew.'

'We might as well have been at church.' His father shakes his head in disgust.

'Why do you say that?' Aaron asks, unable to help himself.

'Let's just have a nice dinner,' his mother says.

'There is a difference between inclusion and dilution,' he says. 'If that man had had his way, we'd have lost ours.'

'And where do you draw the line, Dad?'

'At church bands.'

'Please,' his mother says, setting down her fork. 'Let's change the topic.'

'No, I'd like to understand this. What are the core components you feel are essential to Judaism, Dad? Matrilineal descent?'

'In the Conservative practice, yes.'

'And what would you call a child raised with Jewish values to a Jewish father and a non-Jewish mother? Would you turn him away?'

'What a ridiculous question,' his father scoffs. He pokes a slice of brisket with his fork, raises it to his mouth then sets it back down. 'There are Reform organisations, Aaron. These people are welcome at–'

'These people?'

'These so-called Jewish people who–'

'So-called?'

His hand slams onto the table. Aaron's mother shrinks into her chair.

'Why is it,' Aaron asks, 'that someone can put a cross around their neck, never go to church and still be counted as a good Christian, but we can't even manage to accept the ones who want to be Jewish?'

'It's tradition,' his father says.

'It's blood purity.'

His father opens his mouth to bark something but his mother sets her hand on his arm and faces Aaron. She considers each word as she says it. 'My grandmother, your great-grandmother, immigrated to the United States when she was just a girl. That's how recently the pogroms happened. Someone who hid in a broom cupboard with her mother for two days without food or water, listening through the walls as everyone she'd ever known was gathered and shot, told me about her experience first-hand.'

'I know, but–'

'To be Jewish is to be handed a very small candle which has been burning for thousands of years. Rabbi said last week that there are only fourteen million Jews in the world. Without the Shoah, we would be three times as many. We have an obligation to everyone who came before us not to let that candle go out.' She squeezes his father's hand and they both return to their food.

His father picks peas from his plate. The fork clicks against the ceramic with every stab. He takes a long sip from his glass.

'My girlfriend is pregnant,' Aaron says.

His father spits out wine across the table. There's a moment of pause before his mother springs into action. She flips the light switch and rushes to get hand towels and cleaning fluid. Aaron sees his father's face for the first time. The left half is expressionless, drooping like putty. His right eye goes wide in shock and then he covers himself.

'Turn the light off, dammit!' he yells. He leans on the table with his right hand, his left one fixed to his face, and struggles to stand up. He flips the lights off as he limps out of the kitchen. His foot thumps off the steps as he pulls himself up the stairs.

His mother sets the rag and spray bottle on the kitchen counter and sits back down at the table. After a few minutes, she speaks. Two months ago, she came in from gardening and found Aaron's father motionless on the floor. At the hospital, the doctors told them it was a 'transient ischaemic attack' which can, in many cases, precede a catastrophic brain haemorrhage. During the precautionary brain scan, they found a tumour. It's small but growing and, due to its placement, completely inoperable.

'He doesn't want the fuss,' his mother says. What she means is that he's decided to die.

'What about you?' Aaron asks. 'He can't leave you alone.'

His mother scoffs and dots her eyes with the back of her hand. 'That's rich.'

'Mom—'

'You were gone more than five years, Aaron. I get a call out of the blue saying that you'd like to come home and stay the night. Do you know how excited your father was? You show up in a taxi that you don't have any money to pay for, expecting us to house you, which we will, because you need us. But it turns out it isn't even us you need. All you need is a place to stay, the house we happen to be living in. I wonder why it is never the parents who are allowed to need their children.'

Aaron reaches for his mother's hand. She pulls it away. Their faces are illuminated by candlelight.

'Losing one son and becoming a stranger to the other,' she says to herself, dotting her eyes. 'I don't know which is worse.'

16

The doorbell chime sounds out of an old movie. Róisín is in the kitchen searching for tea when she first hears it, elbow-deep in one of the many doors of what Aaron offhandedly referred to as 'the pantry'. She keeps finding faded, expired boxes and places them onto the kitchen table in the exact arrangement she finds them in, in the hope she can reassemble the shelves as they were, leaving no evidence that she has been through them. The house is empty – the only reason she's left the safety of Aaron's cramped childhood bedroom and come down here on her own. The doorbell rings again, the melody turning over itself. Róisín is holding a box of expired chewable calcium supplements. The cardboard is gluey. She sets the box down on the kitchen table and decides to open the front door.

The workman is wearing green overalls underneath a Detroit-style jacket – but a real one, one used for actual manual labour rather than the uber-hip imitation customers would wear in the café – and he's halfway back down the walkway when she calls out to him. He turns and considers her. The whole scene makes Róisín feel that she's looking at a painting instead of real life. His van out front. The bucolic patchwork of snow across the front lawn. The gulls, the hoarse wind carrying powdered white swirls across the lawn, the distant sound of waves crashing, the reeds of the marshland across the street, and the workman, who is in the moment of returning up the brick walkway to her.

'I was passing by and saw that tree there,' he says, through a thick Boston accent. He puts something into her hands and she takes it without reading it. He gestures to the tree on the front lawn. 'You see the branches there at the top?'

Róisín nods.

The man takes the cap off his head and scratches his forehead. 'All of that's well overdue for a trim. You don't want to mess around with that getting out of order. All my details are on the card, all right?' He puts the cap back on and squints at her, as if seeing her for the first time. 'Pass it along to your mother,' he says.

The card is thin plasticky paper. *O'Connell's Tree Service* is written in big block print at the top. There's a shamrock in place of a dot above the i in *Service*. The card goes on to list the litany of services the company performs, *including but not limited to*: grass clipping, gutter cleaning, tree removal and the aforementioned branch trimming, which is underlined twice. At the bottom is a name – Joe – and a phone number. The world still works in such a way that people come to your front door and offer to trim your tree for you. This world, she clarifies in her mind, this world of suburban houses that are three to four times larger than the terraced house she grew up in. Róisín turns the card over in her hands. She's smiling.

It's been a few days since she arrived 'to the boonies', as Aaron put it. She fit everything she cared about into two large suitcases and left everything else behind. What use was her budget furniture in an actual house? It was just stuff and any attachment she had to it had grown like mould in the absence of sunlight. She managed with extraordinary effort to get the suitcases and herself to North Station within ten minutes of her train's departure. She asked the ticket collector out front three times if she was getting onto the right train. She squeezed into a purple vinyl booth and looked out the grease-smudged window as the city evaporated behind her. The world looked distorted and yellow-tinted through the glass. Someone had scratched their initials in the corner. The scenery alternated between barren marshlands and dense, ugly downtowns and then it all cleared away. There was a screeching sound and the smell of burnt rubber as the train came to a sudden stop. The ticket collector threw open the door at the front of the carriage and told her they'd arrived.

Róisín heaved her bags onto the platform. The air was cold and fresh. The sunshine was stark and hot on her face. There was a house-like structure behind the station sign with red clapboard siding and a small wooden clocktower on its roof. The train started up behind her with enormous noise and then it passed a bend in the trees and there was sudden and complete silence. Her ears adjusted. She could make out distant cars, not in the overlapping noise of city traffic but as individual entities, the quaint sound of a squealing tyre as a singular car turned left. Aaron told her only that the town was small and near the ocean. And then there he was, waving at her from the parking lot below.

'So you didn't get lost, then?' he called up to her.

She gestured at her suitcases. 'What are you doing all the way down there while I'm all the way up here with these heavy bags? Here I thought you were the man in this relationship.'

Aaron came up the stairs two at a time. 'You were the one who wanted to look self-sufficient for some reason. How many times did I offer to drive down?'

'In your Dad's car.'

'Yes, in my Dad's car.'

'I think that's a bad first impression to be making with your parents. Speaking first-hand as the Irish barista you knocked up.'

'Not even a barista,' he said, climbing the last few steps. 'Unemployed, even.'

Then he was there, all teeth and smile lines, radiating warmth. He wrapped her in his arms and kissed her face and she pushed him off and pretended not to like it. He lifted her bags with ease, one in each hand. They descended the platform together and loaded the bags into the boot of a red sedan.

It all turned out to be more like a toy town than a real one, as if she and Aaron had been shrunk down to drive among intricately painted miniatures designed for display. She pointed out a brick building as they pulled out of the station parking lot.

'What is that – the fire house?' she asked.

'What, the one with all the fire trucks out front?' Aaron asked. 'Yep, that'd be the one.'

'Listen to how he mouths off to the mother of his child,' she said, which made him laugh.

The streets were lined with colonial houses. A thin layer of snow on the sidewalks. Aaron pointed out a tall wooden building on their right and told her it was an Orthodox synagogue. They stopped at a stop sign at the end of the street and Aaron smiled.

'You're going to like this.'

He turned the car right and then left onto the main road of the town and the ocean opened up into view in front of them. There was a boardwalk that wrapped along the shore and a few huddled clumps of people making their way up and down it. A wave crashed into the sea wall, spewing a great big cloud of mist above them all.

Róisín tapped on the glass of her window towards a woman in the distance. 'Is she eating an ice cream?'

Aaron laughed. 'She is, yeah.'

'That is mental,' Róisín said. 'You're all absolutely mad for an ice cream when it's freezing out, sure you are. What's that about?'

'Oh, we'll convert you. You'll see,' he said.

Róisín rolled down the passenger window and the car flooded with icy air, the sound of crashing waves and the smell of saltwater. She closed her eyes and took a deep breath in through her nose and out through her mouth and told herself that this was what the ocean smelled like, this was what it tasted like.

'It's like a movie,' she said.

They arrived at a stop light at an intersection of low shops and restaurants. A woman walked up to the crosswalk pushing an empty stroller, soon followed by a toddler wearing a puffy coat, hat and scarf, blocks of bright and beautifully clashing colours. His arms stuck straight out as he waddled behind her. The woman held onto his hand and pointed at the red sedan. Aaron genially waved them across the road. The woman waved back and mouthed, 'Thank you.'

After Róisín told Aaron she was pregnant, she told him that she was going to keep it.

'I don't expect anything from you,' she told him. 'But this is what I want.'

He kept looking around her kitchen, blinking, silent. He held the pregnancy test in his hands like a prayer book. He was silent even as he left. Róisín came to his apartment two days later and told him she was moving back home. She wanted to appear clinical about the decision. Final. The biggest mistake a woman could make was emotional honesty, she felt, because men would always point to the tone of their voice instead of the words they were saying and discount the message for its medium. But after she coldly told Aaron the facts – that she was leaving and it was unlikely she would ever be able to return – he opened his mouth and just said, 'Oh.' Tucked away in that single syllable was torrential heartbreak. His eyes were glossy. She opened her mouth to walk it back but broke down and cried. Then they embraced and he cried and, when all of that crying was just about finished and she felt dried out and used up, he tucked her into the sheets of his bed and brought her a mug of chamomile tea.

He sat on top of the duvet with his clothes on.

'Why aren't you getting under the covers?' she asked him.

'I didn't want you to think I was getting any ideas.'

When they had sex, he put an arm beneath the small of her back and stroked her face with his other hand, smiling and kissing her eyelids. His breath went ragged and he told her, almost apologetically, that he was close. She dug into his shoulders and told him to come inside of her, which he did, shuddering while she held him. She never said things like that. They laughed about it afterwards while she lay on his chest, a movie playing on his laptop in the background.

'I think it's a little late for caution,' she said, and he agreed.

He made her pancakes in the morning and they ate them in bed and she wondered if her heart had ever felt as full before. She felt a tinge of pity for everyone who was not her in that moment, who couldn't possibly ever feel the warmth of love she felt then. He made it easy to forget about the past. It was hard to reconcile this version of Aaron with the one who had arrived at her apartment in the middle of the night, coke-addled and bleeding.

She went back to her own apartment after that. She folded the pregnancy test boxes into quarters and took them to the recycling bin outside. She had nothing else to do then but sit on her bed and scroll endlessly through social media on her phone. A video popped up about parenting and it made her feel so suddenly and violently anxious that her vision shuddered and she closed the app, only to look from the bare walls of her bedroom down to her phone and open it again. Her apartment had never felt so empty and cold. She thought about calling Sofia and decided against it. They hadn't spoken since that night at the café. Eventually, she did phone her parents, and for the three hours that followed they talked through all of it again. They tried to convince her of various arguments: her mother, of how easy her pregnancy would be if she didn't live abroad; her father, of how easy her life would be if she were to become suddenly 'un-pregnant', as he put it.

'If you're asking my opinion…' her father began again.

'I'm not asking your opinion at all,' Róisín said with finality. 'This is what's happening and that's that. If we have a place to stay, we'll stay here, and if we don't, I'll come home.'

'Well, if that's that,' her father said.

They passed the town hall and Aaron did a loop around it so Róisín could see it from all sides. It was an old building designed to look much older, with Roman columns and a white dome roof. A bit ostentatious considering its purpose as a government building for a three-square-mile town, but equally adorable.

'And that's the library. I used to walk here when I was a kid,' Aaron was saying.

Róisín found it difficult to imagine Aaron as a child. She couldn't picture him waddling after his mother on the way to the library or playing in a field with other boys. She found it impossible to imagine Aaron any other way than he was right now. Reservedly vulnerable.

This was her first time seeing him drive. His eyes darted from car to car, to the side mirrors and back. His thumbnail was between his teeth. His eyebrows were scrunched together. If she asked him what could go wrong on the road right then, he would probably respond with a list of at least ten things. He was preparing himself for every possible outcome at all times, utterly focused on the task at hand. Róisín couldn't imagine Aaron before Moe died. Maybe that was it, really. The understanding that things could and would go wrong in an immediate and irreparable way at any moment was core to the Aaron she knew and it was difficult to imagine him with the innocent absence of that particular attribute. The worst part of him exploited this truth as an excuse to flirt with an inevitable oblivion. Now she could clearly see this better version of him who, in light of this knowledge, would fight to protect the things he cared about.

Space grew between the houses and the houses grew to fill the space. There were more trees and fewer shops. The closer they got to their destination, the slower Aaron drove. He stopped responding to her questions.

'Just down here,' he said, rubbing the back of his neck.

He turned right at the top of a hill and coasted down a street lined on either side with so many trees that they formed a canopy of branches above them, blocking out the sky. They arrived at the bottom of the hill. He pointed out a large white house with green shutters on their left.

'That's us,' he said.

'Fuck off,' Róisín said. She leant over Aaron to peer through his window. 'Fuck off, that is not your house.'

'It is so my house.'

Aaron stopped the car out front and cleared his throat. There was a pathway of brick and moss lazing up to the green front door.

'You are officially never allowed to see my family home. Like, ever,' she said. 'This looks like something out of a movie.'

'Like *Forrest Gump*?'

'I know you're teasing, but it does, it looks like the house from *Forrest Gump*, that's it exactly. Jesus, I can't believe you ever left.'

The house looked down on them from behind its manicured lawn and prim garden with flowers covered in snow, only blips of their vibrant petals visible, radiant and defiant life. A large bare tree bordered the sidewalk. One of the windows on the ground floor was illuminated. Inside, a silhouette moved from one side of the window frame to the other.

Aaron put his hand on the car key and then paused. 'Let's have a look at the beach before we go in,' he said.

Róisín sits at the kitchen table with a cup of microwaved Lipton tea, dry and watery and mildly irradiated. Aaron's family doesn't seem to see the purpose of milk or sugar or even a kettle. She's scrolling through social media on her phone, letting each square of content occupy the screen for a maximum of two seconds before jettisoning it away with her thumb to whatever intestinal destination digital content goes to once it's been consumed. Someone she knew in primary school got married this past weekend at an estate in County Mayo. Róisín had forgotten the girl existed. With a flick of her thumb, the former friend is returned to that same abyss.

She hears the back door unlock and then the volley of voices a moment before the door opens. Róisín feels panic rise and considers scurrying upstairs with her mug of tea. Worse than being caught sitting here is being caught fleeing, so she stays and watches them come in, first Aaron's mother, then his father and finally him, plastic shopping bags in each hand, a look of total exhaustion on his face.

Aaron's mother stops and puts a hand to her heart when she sees Róisín, shaking away the startle and giving a tight-lipped smile.

'Sorry, I didn't mean to frighten you,' Róisín says. It seems a diplomatic enough thing to say, even though she was just sitting there, existing, which to her seems a perfectly reasonable thing to have been doing.

Aaron's father walks through the kitchen to the sitting room without saying anything to anyone. Aaron sets the plastic bags down on the floor and returns outside to get more. Aaron's mother puts her hands on either side of the sink and lets out a deep sigh.

'Was it a good trip?' Róisín asks.

His mother purses her lips and swallows before speaking, looking through the kitchen window at the front garden. 'I wouldn't say good. Productive, yes, definitely productive.'

'That's good, then,' Róisín says. 'Or, good that it was productive.' She is excruciatingly aware of her hands. For lack of anything else to do with them, she points out the O'Connell's Tree Service card on the kitchen counter. 'Someone's left that for you,' she says.

His mother's face scrunches up. She takes the card and reads it, then tuts her tongue and shakes her head. 'These people,' she mutters. She tears the card into unnecessarily small pieces and throws them into the bin with force. 'Did he leave it through the letterbox?' she asks.

'No, he rang the bell and I answered the door,' Róisín says.

Aaron's mother gives another tight-lipped nod and then shakes her head. This was obviously the wrong thing to do.

Róisín has learned in the past few days that there are so many things she does instinctively which are, in fact, the wrong thing to do. When she cleans a plate, Aaron's mother takes it from her and cleans it again, things like that. His mother is relentlessly unyielding in what she must believe are the right ways to do things but, in reality, are just her preferences for how they are to be done. Not that Róisín would ever make that distinction clear to her.

Aaron comes back in with another few bags and sets them down. He looks from his mother to Róisín. 'All good?' he asks.

'Yes,' Róisín says and affects a smile. 'All good.'

17

Aaron grunts as he lifts another cardboard box from the asphalt and heaves it into the open trunk of his father's sedan.

'How many more?' he asks.

'Oh, a few,' his father says.

Aaron wipes his forehead with the sleeve of his jacket, leaving a swab of dark brown across the canvas fabric. 'How many is a few?'

'A few is a few,' his father says. He leans on the frame of the back door, breathing heavily and staring. 'Why don't you count them when they're loaded up? That's the only way to know for sure.'

Aaron's father doesn't cover his face anymore. He hasn't much since Róisín moved in. The half of his face which is paralysed hangs slack but, because his father is not an emotive man, it is only noticeable when he's scowling, giving his otherwise severe look a light-hearted quality of sarcastic reproach. They eat dinner with the lights on now. He's stopped wearing sunglasses indoors. It is unclear to Aaron whether this change in behaviour is a positive thing, a sign of acceptance that his life has changed, or else a very bad thing, an acquiescence that his life, no matter its form, will be over soon regardless.

Aaron fetches another box from the basement and brings it to the car. He hasn't asked his father about the contents of these boxes or why there is a sudden urgency to remove them immediately and all at once. As he sets the box into the trunk, the flap comes up, revealing baseball cards in plastic tubs. Aaron folds the cardboard edge back down and closes the trunk. There are three more boxes to load. They have to be stacked on the back row of seats. He feels his phone buzz in his pocket. A message from Jake.

how u settlin in? rudy's after work soon?

Aaron feels his face go hot. He hasn't spoken to Jake since he moved out. He scrolls up their messaging thread; there have been seven unanswered messages so far. It's unclear to Aaron what exactly is preventing him from responding but there's something. It feels like he's left that world behind. He archives the entire thread. He won't be notified of any new messages Jake sends.

'We'd better hurry,' his father says as he limps down the back steps of the house. 'It's nearly ten already.' He huffs as he comes around to the driver's side of the car and opens the door. He positions himself before letting his body fall backwards onto the seat with a grunt.

Aaron interlocks his fingers and breathes into the space beneath his palms, then rubs his hands together. His father starts the car.

'Do you need me to use GPS on my phone or anything?'

'We're only going to temple, Aaron,' his father says, then scoffs. 'GPS.'

'I'm only asking.'

'I had a stroke, not a lobotomy.'

The sign for the synagogue features a prominent Jewish star. A second sign hanging below the first reads *Song of the Sea*. Aaron's father stops the car to indicate left and points at it.

'Someone stuck stickers of Palestinian flags on there last month,' he says. 'They still don't know who did it.'

'I'd say high schoolers,' Aaron offers.

His father's eye goes wide. 'You really think so?' He shakes his head. 'Antisemitism is on the rise.'

'I'm not sure that quite qualifies,' Aaron says to the window.

'What?'

'Nothing.'

The car turns left and they descend towards the imposing brick structure covered in ivy. They drive around to the back of the building, to the parking lot, and Aaron's father chooses a space near the back door.

'All right,' he says, huffing. 'Okay, let's hurry up now.' There is a frenetic quality to his movements. He pushes the red button of his seat belt buckle and reaches for the door handle before the seat belt is free, getting tangled up in it and swearing at himself until he's outside the car, red-faced, pointing at the trunk. 'Let's hurry up now, go get the boxes.'

His father clears his throat before he knocks on the metal door. There's a moment of suburban silence while they wait for someone to answer, the sound of rustling branches, the smell of frigid air. Then the door opens. There stands a short bookish man with thick-framed glasses and an untidy beard. He's wearing a tan sports coat and a pale red tie. He smiles, first at Aaron and then at his father.

'Good morning,' his father says. 'Aaron, this is the rabbi. Rabbi, this is my son.'

'A genuine pleasure to meet you,' the rabbi says, holding out his hand. He hasn't stopped smiling.

Aaron shifts the heavy box onto his hip and removes one hand to give a quick handshake, shooting it back under the box before it topples.

'Right this way, gentlemen.'

Aaron's father walks beside the rabbi and Aaron follows behind. They've entered through the back of the sanctuary, by the ark. Aaron hasn't been here in over five years. The room is unfamiliar but holds a dreamlike recognition. To the left of the bimah stands an American flag. To its right, an Israeli one. They walk down the aisle between the rows of benches and through a door at the back, navigating suddenly cramped hallways until they arrive at a nondescript door.

'Here we are,' the rabbi says, and pushes it open.

The office is warm and smells of cinnamon. There's a record player in the corner, playing something crooning and sweet. The blinds are closed and the fabric glows with the gentle light of the outside world.

'Anywhere, really,' the rabbi says, nodding at Aaron's box and gesturing at the floor.

Aaron sees now that the office is full of cardboard boxes identical to the one in his arms. He bends his knees as he sets it on the floor carefully, next to a pile that is four boxes high.

'These aren't all from our house, are they?' Aaron asks his father.

The rabbi laughs. 'No, no, don't worry. We haven't pilfered your family heirlooms. The community has come together to aid the congregation. To great effect, I might add. This is the result of quite a few households emptying out the rooms within their homes which were in need of emptying. Tzedakah; you know this word?'

Aaron rubs the back of his neck and nods.

The rabbi smiles insistently. 'You know it, yes?'

'Yes,' Aaron says. 'Tzedakah. Charity.'

'I don't blame you; this is the translation we teach our children. You're imagining a little wooden box with Hebrew lettering painted on the front and a slot in the top for spare coins and the occasional bill, I'm guessing. Am I right?'

There was a box exactly like that at home once, one that Aaron and Moe fought over as children to see who had contributed more. Aaron nods.

'Tzedakah is related to two words in Hebrew, the first being *tzedeq* – meaning something like righteousness, fairness, justice, this kind of thing – and the second being *tzadik* – a similar word that means righteous but as an adjective, not as in the thing itself. And so tzedakah means righteousness but we often understand it to mean charity, as you pointed out. The problem with the word charity, as such, is that its American interpretation is something spontaneous and noble. If someone writes a cheque for a food bank or gives a dollar to someone who needs it, we think of these as acts of sudden, fortuitous goodwill. For us Jews, tzedakah is not a notable occurrence. It doesn't come from generosity but instead from obligation. To give and be applauded for giving is to transact, you understand? The giving becomes an exchange for praise. But Jews, we give because we give. You see?' He smiles.

Aaron's father shifts from one foot to the other. He points at a small folding chair propped against a wall. 'Do you mind if I sit, rabbi?' he asks.

The rabbi points to the large leather chair behind his desk. 'Take mine, it's much more comfortable than that one.'

'Where would you sit?'

'I'll stand,' the rabbi says.

'Well, if you don't mind standing, I don't mind standing,' Aaron's father says.

They go back and forth like this for a while, the rabbi insisting his father sit, his father insisting he'd prefer to stand, as if the interaction hadn't started with him asking for a place to sit. Eventually the rabbi wins, or else Aaron's father allows him to win, and he takes a seat in the leather chair with a sigh of relief.

'So,' the rabbi says, turning to face Aaron. He claps his hands together. 'The boxes.'

The second box is heavier than the first. Aaron sets it down on the concrete and looks through the crowded keychain his father gave him for a fob to the car. He presses the lock button twice and the car beeps in confirmation. A cold wind blows through the parking lot, cutting through his jacket and singeing the tips of his ears until they ring. The top flap of the cardboard box whips open. It's the box with the baseball cards. Aaron feels something jar loose inside of himself and he remembers that Moe used to play baseball. The Red Sox headshots hanging in his bedroom from the *Boston Globe* were for Moe, not Aaron. Those races to the front door to get the newspaper were because Aaron kept stealing them away, not their father. There is sudden sadness in the thought that something so significant could be forgotten, confused. Aaron opens the cardboard box completely now and pokes around its contents. He finds three large plastic tubs full of baseball cards. There's a David Ortiz figurine still in its plastic. At the bottom is a leather baseball glove. Aaron removes it from the box and holds it. He tries to squeeze his hand inside but it won't fit. The glove is meant for a child. There, in permanent marker on the inside label, reads, *Moe, Homeroom 204*. Aaron rubs his thumb over the carefree handwriting of his brother. He unlocks the car and tucks the glove under the passenger seat.

The back door to the synagogue is locked.

'Fuck,' Aaron says to himself.

He considers knocking, getting as far as placing the box by his feet and raising his arm, but he's struck with a sudden self-consciousness that won't allow his hand to hit the door. He lifts the box and walks it around to the front of the synagogue, through the entrance doors, past the lobby, in and out of the sanctuary and finally back into the office.

There's a whiskey bottle and two glasses on the desk between the men. Both look up like children caught mid-sentence in a dirty joke they shouldn't be telling.

'What'd you do, stop for coffee?' his father says.

'Locked myself out.'

The rabbi starts to speak and his voice catches. He coughs into his fist and motions towards the glass, eliciting a half-smile from Aaron's father. 'That was my fault,' the rabbi says. 'Here, set down that box and I'll prop the door open for you.'

Somewhere between the office and the back door, the rabbi puts a hand on Aaron's shoulder.

'If you ever want to talk, you know, my door is always open to you.'

'Uh, thanks,' Aaron says.

'Really. If there's ever anything.'

'Yeah, no. That's very kind.' Aaron stares at his shoes and keeps walking.

'I have a more progressive outlook on things than my digs might suggest,' the rabbi says. 'I found myself leafing through the *American Jewish Year Book* the other day. Do you know what that is?'

'No,' Aaron says.

'It's… Well, it's exactly what it sounds like, I suppose. It's a survey of the state of American Judaism. I find it fascinating. American Jews are, according to this census of sorts, growing on par with the rest of the American population. There's a supposition within the Conservative community – one you're undoubtedly familiar with, I suspect – a supposition that

American Judaism is eroding before our very eyes due to things like interfaith marriages. It's repeated to the point of being taken as fact. Everywhere I go, no matter the circle in which I swim, I encounter this supposed fact. Imagine my surprise, then, to discover that it isn't a fact at all, just a stubborn myth. Fascinating.'

They reach the back door. The rabbi pushes the bar in its centre and it swings open, cold air flooding in.

'Hold that, would you?'

Aaron holds the door open while the rabbi fiddles with a metal latch at the top. It seems to Aaron that it would make more sense for the rabbi to hold the door while he secured the latch, seeing as there's a good few inches of height between them. But it's too late now and it's unclear to Aaron how he could go about suggesting they swap roles without offending him. Aaron holds the door and shivers in the incoming wind.

'There's also a statistic in this year's edition concerning children raised in homes with at least one Jewish adult. If I'm remembering it correctly, families with at least one Jewish parent are five times more likely to raise their children with no religion than to bring them up any way other than Jewish. I suppose that's a comfort, in some ways, that interfaith families are preferring the absence of religion to an alternative religion. But these children are twelve times more likely to be brought up Jewish than not, which is a fact I am proud of. Now, for the sake of academic transparency, it's worth mentioning that this figure is pretty heavily distorted by non-interfaith families – when it refers to homes with one Jewish adult, the study doesn't seem to make a distinction between one- and two-parent Jewish households, but I find it fascinating nonetheless.'

'Right,' Aaron says. He's actively shivering now, his free hand tucked into his armpit.

'My point is just that… I don't know,' the rabbi says, sighing. 'My point is that I'm here if you ever want to talk. And that all are welcome here.'

When the rest of the boxes are delivered and they're back in the car, Aaron asks his father why he's decided to give away all of Moe's old stuff. His father looks at him blankly, confused, and then asks him to repeat himself.

'I saw the baseball cards,' Aaron says.

His father shakes his head. 'And did you see the room we were removing those boxes from?'

'You don't even care that these are his memories, do you?' Aaron says.

His father turns to him. 'You haven't been home in five years, Aaron. You don't get a say in what we're allowed to do with your brother's things. Yes, I donated his baseball cards, a tiny fraction of the binders upon binders that I kept. It is just like you to see the things that are gone and not the things that are left.'

'Still,' Aaron says. 'Why couldn't we have left them? What's so important about the basement you need it empty?'

'Son,' his father says, suddenly calm. 'I need you to tell me something and I need you to be honest about it. Can you do that for me?'

Aaron nods.

'Think about it before you agree. I'm going to ask you something and, when you answer, I want it to be the truth. That's all I'm asking for, the truth.'

'Okay.'

His father clears his throat. 'Is this real?' he asks.

'What?'

'This… girl. This whole mishegoss. Is it real between you two?'

'Dad,' Aaron says. 'How can you–'

'You cut us out of your life and show up on our doorstep with some Irish shiksa as if we've been sitting in the dark for the better part of a decade. Your mother and I have our own lives. We are willing to help you because you are our son. She would set herself on fire if it kept you warm. But me, I need to know for her sake, before she lights the match, is this real?'

Aaron stares at his shoes. He can hear the blood rushing in his ears.

'Look at me,' his father says. 'Good. Now, is this real?'

Aaron nods. 'Yes, Dad, it's real.'

'Then you'll need a nursery, don't you think?'

'What?'

'The basement. The boxes. As if you and the girl and an infant are going to share your bedroom and a twin-sized mattress.' His father starts the car. He puts a hand on the shoulder of Aaron's seat and turns to look behind himself as he backs out of the parking space.

'Oh,' Aaron says.

'Yeah, that's right, "oh". Pisher.'

They drive back to the house without speaking. His father brings the car to a stop in the driveway and removes the key from the ignition. He reaches for the door handle and then stops, turning back to face his son.

'Róisín.'

'Yeah?'

'Róisín, like that?'

Aaron nods, confused. 'Yeah.'

'I pronounced it right, I mean?'

Aaron nods again. 'Yeah, Dad, you pronounced it right.'

'Hm,' his father says and opens the door. 'I had to look it up on the internet to be sure.'

He heaves himself out of the car and slams the door behind him. Aaron watches his father limp up the back steps and unlock the door to the house, disappearing inside, leaving it open behind him for his son to follow through.

18

Róisín pinches the corner of the duvet between her thumb and index finger and turns it over, then over again. Aaron is roughly drying his hair with a towel. The room is cold. Steam lifts off his skin, backlit by the bathroom light. He's looking at her with a quizzical expression as he tilts his head upright and wraps the towel around his waist.

'What?' he asks.

'Nothing,' she says.

'Are you mad at me about something?'

She holds the corner of the duvet still. 'No,' she says.

'He started it, you know he started it,' Aaron says, walking into the bathroom, closing the door behind him.

An argument broke out over dinner. This wasn't unusual. The meal would start in silence, then Aaron would say something provocative that could be taken one of two ways and his father would respond to the worse of the two. They'd go at it like that, each saying things without saying them, the back-and-forth amplifying like feedback until the speaker blew and one of them – usually Aaron – would stand up and storm out.

Tonight, Aaron's father asked Róisín a fairly innocent question about the difference between Irish and American politics. Specifically, he understood the word 'republican' to have a completely different meaning in the two countries and wanted to better understand the difference. Róisín's response included the phrase 'British occupation'. After she said it, there was a beat of silence in which everyone chewed. Then Aaron opened his mouth.

'They essentially came in and just decided it was their land, didn't they?' Aaron asked her.

'Basically,' Róisín said. She looked from Aaron's mother to his father, both of whom were looking squarely at the food on their plates. This might have been the wrong answer. 'I suppose it depends who you ask,' she offered.

'Most people in Northern Ireland would agree, though, wouldn't you say? They'd want their land back from the occupying forces, right?'

'I haven't seen the census results,' Róisín said.

'It must be more than half, though. Of people who want their country back, I mean.'

'I don't know.'

'There was some sort of ancient history they dredged up to justify it,' Aaron said. 'You told me that once, didn't you?'

Aaron's father took a sharp breath in through his nostrils and sighed. It was obvious then that Aaron wasn't talking about Northern Ireland at all, that he was using it as a proxy to talk about Palestine, which was itself, whether he knew it or not, a proxy to talk about Moe.

'Then there was a war, isn't that right?' Aaron's father asked. 'And after the war, there was a treaty, an agreement between the sides? There hasn't been much violence or resentment since.'

Róisín ignored the comment. Pointing his attention to the Troubles-shaped hole in his argument felt too much like taking Aaron's side, giving him the ammunition needed to win.

Aaron set down his fork and chewed over his words before spitting them out. 'I suppose, when people are civil, you can do things like that. It's a bit harder to get over, say, someone rolling a flaming barrel of oil down your street to kick you out of your homes.'

'I don't think anyone would use the word "civil" to describe what the British did to—'

'Because that's what they did,' Aaron said, waving his fork. 'They rolled barrels of flaming oil down residential streets in 1947. Róisín, did you know that? In Israel, I mean.'

She did, in fact, know that. Aaron had brought it up three nights prior during a similar argument-by-proxy which had started out as a conversation about an invasive species of plants.

'What's your point, Aaron, that extremist violence is bad? You won't find many on the other side of that argument.'

They chewed. The food was tasteless in Róisín's mouth. She was accustomed to family squabbles over dinner, she certainly hadn't been raised in a quiet household, but her family arguments were always more direct and actionable. Mam would find a dirty sock on the stairs that Darragh had thrown down and chew him out, asking whether he'd confused her for his butler or something. When Aaron fought with his father, they did so under the guise of intellectual debate even though each of them spent the entire conversation essentially talking to themselves and convincing no one of their point. It was at times like these that Róisín struggled to understand how she fit into this family dynamic. There was a seemingly insurmountable distance that existed between her and the people of this home. She could not yet understand how a child would change this in any significant way.

Aaron's father looked Róisín in the eye. 'It's important to understand the context of these things. It's equally important to appreciate that any atomic action can be seen as right or wrong; it is the molecule of context which has the most import. What do you call the infantryman who comes home to a broken country and uses the political tools at his disposal to raise that country to the mightiest state in its history? A hero? A revolutionary?' He smiled and cocked his eyebrow, waiting for an answer to his rhetorical question.

Róisín knew he was going to say Hitler. 'I don't know, what do you call him?'

'Hitler,' he said, smirking.

'Hitler was a lance corporal, not that it matters,' Aaron said as he chewed. He threw his fork onto the table and said, 'It's a struggle for some Jewish people to have a constructive conversation about Israel without invoking the Holocaust.'

'You can't have a conversation about Israel without invoking the Holocaust. It's like having a conversation about the Big Bang without mentioning physics. One is the lifeblood of the other.'

'The Zionist movement began when Hitler was eight years old. They're almost completely unrelated,' Aaron said.

'Bullshit, what utter bullshit.'

'Theodor Herzl published *Der Judenstaat* in 1896 and—'

Now they were both shouting, reciting facts they'd memorised, their sentences overlapping so that Róisín couldn't understand what either of them was saying. The noise enveloped her like silence. Aaron's mother carried on eating.

Aaron's father slapped his hand on the table. 'You've made your position clear, Aaron, we're all very impressed. I'm convinced, let's round up all of the Jews in Israel.'

'They're living on stolen land. That's all I'm saying. It's an apartheid state.'

'Gifted land, Aaron, that the United Nations proposed be split into two countries. A proposal rejected by one of the two sides, by the way, I'll let you guess which was—'

'A plan that left them barely any arable land, I really wonder why they would reject–'

'So then we fought and we died and we won, Aaron. And we have continued to protect it since the moment of the country's inception. That is how geopolitics works. That is how the world works. Citizens get to live without war because soldiers die to ensure their freedom to do so.'

'Israeli citizens get to live without war, you mean. Not so much Palestinians who–'

'Enough!'

'This is the exact same brand of bullshit that you fed Moe and me growing up and how did all of that propaganda work out?' Aaron said.

Then there was silence. Aaron's father opened his mouth to say something, then closed it instead. He dotted his mouth with his napkin, stood with great difficulty and left the kitchen.

Róisín is sitting on the bed when Aaron comes back out of the bathroom and sits beside her. He rubs the back of his neck. She can smell the wine on his breath.

'I acted like an asshole, didn't I?'

She puts her hand on his leg and sighs. 'I never understand what you hope to gain from conversations like that.'

'It's important to talk about, isn't it?'

'I don't know,' she says. His shoulder is warm against her lips. She closes her eyes and imagines them on a beach somewhere far away. 'You turn into a different person around them.'

'It must be important to talk about,' he says softly.

'And then I wonder which is the real you; maybe that's really you and the Aaron I know is the mask. Then,' she starts to say, quieter, 'I doubt the drinking helps.'

Aaron's eyebrows furrow. His cheeks grow hot. 'I hardly had a glass.'

'You had three.'

'I'm allowed to have some wine with dinner, aren't I? It's not as if I have a problem with it.'

'All I'm saying is that you promised me, do you remember that? Before we moved out here, you promised me that you would keep it all under control. This is me telling you that it doesn't feel in control. It makes me uncomfortable.'

Aaron slapped his leg and sighed irritably. 'I'm not doing drugs. I'm not getting into fights. I'm not in any real sense of trouble, am I? I'm just having some wine with dinner.'

'It's not the wine you should be worried about,' Róisín says. 'I'm uncomfortable. That's what you should be thinking about right now. Forget it.'

Aaron looks down at the floor now, contemplative. 'Do you remember our first date?'

'You left me waiting for an hour, it's a hard thing to forget.'

He winces. 'Our second date, then.'

Róisín nods. There's a beat of silence between them as they each remember. She wonders what specific details are coming to him, what made it come to mind. He misses how easy those days were, maybe, how free he was, surely. Finding them somewhere to live so she wouldn't move away was the noble thing to do but, faced with the reality of the situation, he probably regrets it. Most of the time that Róisín is around Aaron's family, or specifically around this family-influenced version of Aaron, she regrets it too. She imagines sitting around the dinner table at home, her real home, a place she hasn't been in so long. Mam probably wouldn't let her lift a finger, she could be so accommodating it was annoying. And Darragh, with his comments. She could perfectly imagine Maeve balancing the weans on her arms, saying something like, 'You'll miss being pregnant once he's here.' Then she realises that Maeve's children are nearly four now; she's imagining everything as it was before she left.

Róisín feels anger and restlessness and for a moment she doesn't know where it's coming from and then she knows exactly. She hasn't been homesick for so long she's forgotten what it feels like, or else she's purposely left the feeling unnamed within herself, afraid or unwilling to call it what it is. To give something its proper name is to acknowledge its existence. The cure for homesickness is, she knows, to go home. In a way, it's not the place but the time she misses. She could move back in with her parents, get her job back at the old café if it's still around, and, even then, her life would barely resemble what it was. She didn't have much then, but she sees now, only retrospectively, that she had more in some ways than she has now. She grew a tree from a sapling and left it to rot on the wrong side of the Atlantic. A life isn't something built, it's something grown, and everything that grows wastes away when left unattended. Take your eye off it for a second and it dies.

'You don't have all the time in the world with them, you know,' she says.

'No,' Aaron says, frowning. 'No, I don't.'

Róisín puts her arm around his chest and presses her cheek to his back. She feels a twinge of pain from somewhere above her pelvis and a dull thump when it passes. Whenever they discuss the pregnancy, it's always in the abstract – wondering what the baby will look like, whose mannerisms it will affect more. These conversations usually happen in bed, surrounded by the growing whispers of sleep, Aaron's voice all light and breathy as he talks about alleles and eye colour. For him, a child is speculative. It must be prepared for, of course, but that preparation is intentional, the work full of purpose and responsibility. Róisín's relationship to their child-to-be is entirely physical: there is a foetus inside of her which grows every day. Her back hurts. She feels the sudden urge to pee at the least convenient moments. She's starting to show. Sometimes there are unfamiliar pains which she hesitates to mention, afraid Aaron will get worked up and think that it's serious, more afraid that he will turn out to be right. Now the pain passes and, once gone, it's frighteningly easy to forget.

Aaron looks up at her now and touches her face, kisses her forehead, smiles. 'I hear you and I know that I can do better. On all of it. You're right.'

She would give up almost anything to have him make her feel this way forever. 'I'm always right,' she says, which makes him smile.

19

They start with the primer layer. Rather, Aaron starts with the primer layer while his father watches him from a chair he had Aaron bring down from the kitchen. Every once in a while, his father tilts the fan drying the wall towards Aaron for 'air circulation' and the cold breeze hits him full in the chest.

'We're doing this for you,' his father keeps saying.

Once the primer layer is finished, Aaron paints three colour options on pieces of plywood and waits for them to dry. He brings them upstairs and stands behind the bedroom door trying to determine if Róisín is asleep or not. The strip of space beneath the door is black. There aren't any lights on. He presses his ear to the door and hears a soft, indecipherable noise. He knocks twice.

'Yeah?' a voice calls out. 'You can come in.'

He opens the door slowly. Róisín is lying in the dark with her phone inches away from her eyes. It's been like this all week.

Róisín told him that she was uncomfortable with his drinking. It was true that he'd agreed to cut back before they moved but, honestly, he didn't think he was doing anything unreasonable. She pointed out that it was her discomfort he should be primarily concerned with, not the logic informing that feeling. He asked his father for an old pair of running shoes and sweatpants. He started setting an alarm on his cell phone and slipping out from beneath the covers of the bed while Róisín was still asleep. He'd dress in the dark and watch her sleeping for a minute before sneaking out the door. She always looked more peaceful lying there without him.

The running wasn't enjoyable. He could last about a block before he felt the stitch in his side open up and no amount of perseverance seemed to make a difference on that front. He pushed through as long as he could, the frigid air tearing through his nostrils with every breath. Then he'd come into the kitchen, the sudden warmth stifling, and find that he was covered in sweat. He was surprised each time by how long he'd been out for. It only took a few days for the soreness in his legs to become something he looked forward to. A morning run before his father drove him to work. As it turned out, a person could become addicted to anything. He had excised beer and wine from his diet entirely and his parents had stopped putting out a bottle with the meals. It was as if they knew, even without any communication, exactly what was happening.

Aaron steps into the bedroom. 'I have some colour swatches for you to look at,' he says.

Róisín looks up from her phone.

'For the room,' he says. 'The baby's room.'

'Oh.' Róisín looks back down at her phone. 'Whatever you think is nicest.'

He sits on the bed and fans out the pieces of plywood on the bedside table. He runs his fingers through her hair. She keeps on scrolling. It's more like petting a well-trained house cat than anything else, an animal entirely ambivalent to the show of affection it is receiving. He stops after a minute.

'Can I turn on the light?'

'Sure,' Róisín says.

Her fingers stop moving and the phone slips out from them and drops onto the mattress. She stares at the bedside table while he leans forward to turn on the lamp. The room fills with a dull yellow glow. The floor is covered in scattered piles of clothing and torn cardboard packaging.

'Can you see them better?' he asks, and she nods. He points to one on the far right. 'Do you like this one?'

Róisín blinks. She shrugs. 'Yeah, that one is nice.'

'It is, it is nice. Would you prefer this one instead, though?'

She shrugs again. 'I don't know. What do you think?'

They're all nice, Aaron wants to say, *but we're supposed to be doing this together.* He doesn't say this, because he knows how unfair it is to say, and then he feels guilty for even thinking it. He stands and pats Róisín's head and turns the light back off.

'I'll do what I think is best, okay?'

'Sure,' Róisín says.

'You just rest.'

She lifts the phone from the mattress and unlocks it with her thumb. The vacant expression on her face is illuminated in different, shifting shades of blue and white. Her eyes are glossy. Suddenly, she looks up at him. 'Do you love me any less?' she asks.

'No,' he's quick to say. 'Of course not.'

She bites her lip. 'But do you love me any differently?'

'Differently compared to what?'

'Than before we moved in, before I told you I was pregnant.'

Aaron rubs the back of his neck. 'Where's this coming from, then?'

'I think that you do,' Róisín says. Her voice is flat and lifeless. 'I think that I love you differently too. You're not the same person I met.'

'Oh,' he says.

For the past week or so, for at least as long as his morning runs, Róisín has been getting pains. She'll be in the middle of a sentence and then her eyes will clench shut and her hand will move towards her stomach and stop there, then she'll finish the sentence as if nothing has happened. Aaron always plays along, pretending not to notice. It seems important to her that he doesn't notice.

He watches her use an index finger to scroll through the stream of endless content. Pictures and videos of other people's lives, people Aaron has never met before. The escape she's after is freedom, he sees that now. She's agreed to the idea of living together, of transitioning from a couple to a family, but, now that the practicalities are in place, she must regret it. They've never talked about marriage, for instance. Not that Aaron has any money for a ring or a ceremony. He looks at Róisín's vacant stare and it feels like his heart is being dragged through his stomach. The words exist, he's sure, that, when put in some combination, will make her feel herself again. But he can't find them. He wants to sit beside her and kiss her neck until she smiles. He wants to take that phone out of her hand and throw it as hard as he can against the wall.

Róisín reaches out absently for Aaron's hand and puts it on her stomach, then lifts the covers and her pyjama top and presses it against her skin. Her skin feels hot against his hand. She winces when it makes contact.

'Am I the same person you met?' she asks.

'You make everything better. Occupying the same space as you makes me happy.'

'That's the answer to a different question,' she says. She pulls his hand out from under her shirt and kisses it on the knuckles before turning back to her phone.

Aaron closes the door softly behind him so that the tongue of the lock just barely clicks as it shifts back into place. He stands outside of the bedroom door, overwhelmed by a complete sense of failure. His throat feels thick. He feels like crying. He swallows hard instead, burying the feeling.

'She likes this one,' he says from the basement stairs, picking one of the pieces of wood at random.

'She's the boss,' his father says.

The next few hours pass in relative silence. Every few strokes, Aaron's father tells him to redo a section to avoid drips or gives pointers on how to hold the paint roller to get smoother layers. Aaron is covered in sweat. His T-shirt sticks to him like a second skin. When the first coat is finished, he sits on a stool and his father hands him an open bottle of root beer. This used to be something of a childhood ritual, Aaron remembers suddenly. His father with a real beer, he and Moe with sodas.

'You've earned this,' his father says. He clinks the bottom of his bottle off Aaron's, then takes a long pull.

Aaron rests the heel of his bottle against the back of his neck. The glass is refreshing on his hot skin.

'You know,' his father says, and sighs. 'It's nice. You being here. Doing this together.'

'It is nice,' Aaron agrees.

The soda is prickly and sweet in his mouth and, when he swallows, he feels its coldness dissipate inside of him. He places the bottle on the floor next to one of the stool legs.

'What?' his father says.

Aaron squints, confused. 'I didn't say anything.'

'No, but you're thinking something. Nudnik, out with it. You look constipated.'

'I wasn't thinking anything.'

'You were,' his father says, annoyed. 'We can make this bottle last an hour and then you can tell me, or you can just cut the shit and tell me what's on your mind now.'

'I don't know what to tell you, I don't–'

'Out with it!'

'How do I know that I'm ready for this?' Aaron blurts out. He takes a measured breath. 'How do I know that I have what it takes to do this right, I mean, I guess… I don't know what I mean.'

His father considers the question carefully. He leans forward and shrugs. 'You don't.'

'Then how do I know that I'm doing the right thing?'

'I was about your age when your mother got pregnant for the first time. Did you know that? She miscarried four times before we had you. Four. The first and second were devastating but within a month or two we were talking baby names again. The third was when it became a medical concern. We saw specialists, all sorts of doctors. "These things happen," that's what they tell you. I wonder who tells doctors to tell their patients things like that, because it isn't helpful. It took a year before we were ready to try again. She was three months pregnant the fourth time it happened. I could see it in her eyes, something just broke. And then she became pregnant with you. We held out hope. Days became weeks, weeks became months, then there you were. Our little miracle. Blinking eyes, grasping hands, existing in the wide, waiting world.'

Aaron shuffles his feet on the dusty concrete floor. 'And you didn't regret it?'

'Sometimes,' his father says. 'If I'm honest. At its hardest points.'

'Like now?' Aaron asks the floor.

'I wouldn't call it easy. You were an asshole when you were a teenager, thought you knew everything, but that's everyone's kid at that age. It was certainly me. Maybe we get the kids we were as kids, some kind of parental karma at work.'

Aaron looks up at his father, who looks back at him.

'It never lasted long,' his father says. 'The regret, I mean. It was always a fleeting thing.'

Aaron takes a sip from his bottle and sets it down. His father shifts in his seat like he might get up, but stays still.

'When Róisín told me she was pregnant,' Aaron finds himself saying, 'all that I could think was that I don't know how to be a father. I didn't have – I don't have – the skillset for it, I guess? The knowledge? And then I came home and the whole cab ride here I was just thinking about how maybe you'd teach me how to do it.'

His father nods. 'Sure,' he says.

'And now you're... I don't know...' Aaron starts to say, before the words catch. He takes another sip from his bottle and clears his throat.

'What? Now I'm what?'

Aaron feels his eyes well up the moment before they do. He looks up at his father, blinking. 'I don't know how I'm going to do this without you.'

'Oh,' his father says. He looks down at the empty bottle in his hands, tearing the corner of the label. He laughs to himself. 'You know, for a minute there, I forgot that I was dying.'

They sit for a moment in silence and then he scoots his chair closer to his son's and reaches forward. They embrace in an awkward hug. Aaron cries and his father pats his back. They stay leant forwards for some time, like the outer angles of some structure whose stability depends entirely on an even pressure from each of its walls. Without one, the other will fall. They stay like that for a beautiful moment. And then the moment passes.

20

There is a stabbing pain, like a corkscrew being twisted, in the base of Róisín's stomach and then the overwhelming urge to pee. Aaron snores beside her. There was a period of time when he woke up before she did and now their roles have reversed. It's become rare for her to sleep through the night. She flips on the light to the ensuite and closes the door behind her. The porcelain toilet seat is like ice against her bare skin. Her urine comes out in a stream and she sighs in relief. The stream ends. An aching remnant of the corkscrew pain remains. Her jacket hangs on a hook attached to the wall mirror. A corner of her cigarette packet is visible poking out of its pocket. She's quick to remove it and jams it deep into the pocket of her pyjama pants.

Róisín yawns as she comes down the kitchen steps. The windows are fogged and pinkish, illuminated by the glow of the morning's first light. Aaron's father is kneeling by the cupboards, taking out pans and boxes and setting them gingerly on the floor.

'Good morning, Mr Cohen,' Róisín whispers to him.

'Michael,' he says from inside of the cupboard.

'Sorry?'

'Enough of this mister-missus business,' he says. 'Call me Michael. Call her Annette. There's coffee, by the way.'

The family has an American-style coffee pot with a massive glass carafe that sits on a hot plate. She was amazed the first time she saw it. Hot coffee on demand, instantly, waiting for her to want it. Róisín takes a mug down from the shelf and fills it. She sits at the kitchen table and watches the continued extrication of kitchen equipment from the bottom cabinets.

'Are you looking for something?'

It's a stupid question she regrets asking. She blows on her mug. The coffee is hot and bitter in her mouth. She grimaces as she swallows.

He's sitting up now, watching her, a bemused look on his face. 'Strong stuff,' he says.

Róisín nods. 'Maybe a bit harsher than I'm used to, is all.'

'Everybody drinks tea over there, isn't that right?'

'Tea, exactly. Breakfast tea.'

'We might have some… Lipton or something,' he offers, waving his hand towards the pantry doors behind her.

'Coffee is fine,' she says.

Michael pulls himself out of the cabinet and then stands up against the kitchen counter. He is an intimidating man in stature and tone but, in these moments of physical frailty, Róisín finds herself looking away from him. He picks up a small white cardboard box on the kitchen counter and brings it over to her, placing it on the table.

'It's one of those Italian things. For coffee. I never could figure out how to use it. You might like it more than the sludge.'

'A moka,' Róisín says, and smiles. She holds the box in her hand, turning it over. 'A nice one, actually.'

'Moka. Right.'

Róisín undoes the latch in the cardboard packaging and removes the metal water reservoir, the grounds basket, the percolator, laying the parts out on the table like a mechanic. 'The water goes in here,' she explains. She sets the basket in the open hole. 'Then the grounds.' The percolator screws on tight after a few twists. 'Then the whole thing goes on the burner.'

Michael groans as he sits down across the table from Róisín. 'And what, the water evaporates up that spout?'

'Exactly, yeah.'

'It always just spat at me. I don't know what I was doing wrong.'

Róisín holds the thing in her hands, unsure of what to say. This is the longest conversation she's had with either of Aaron's parents. 'Have you got grounds?' she asks.

Michael nods and points to the cabinet closest to the back door. 'Just in there,' he says.

Róisín moves to stand and stops. 'May I?' she asks, holding up the moka.

He nods. She finds the espresso grounds in the back of the cabinet. She carefully fills the water reservoir to the line and places it beside the stove. She tips over the bag of grounds carefully and taps on it until a small pile forms in the centre of the basket. With her pinkie, she evens out the grounds to form a loose puck.

'There are teaspoons in that drawer,' Michael says. He's been watching her perform this set of actions with interest. 'What do you call that, again? When you press it down?'

'Tamping,' Róisín says absent-mindedly. 'But you don't tamp moka.'

'You do,' he says.

'You don't.'

He grunts but doesn't argue any further. Róisín screws the percolator onto the moka pot and places the whole thing onto the burner. She turns the knob and the burner hisses and clicks and bursts into a small flame.

'Gas,' she says under her breath.

'What's that?'

'You have gas burners. I only just noticed. It must be nice to cook with.'

For the first time, Róisín sees him smile with half of his face, the other limp and unchanging.

'If you think that's good…' he starts. He stands with considerable effort and shuffles past Róisín and through the back door to the mud room. He returns wearing fleece-lined rubber slippers and tosses another pair onto the floor by her feet. 'Try those on,' he says.

They're massive on her. The heels flap up and down as she walks. Michael grunts as he pushes the kitchen table out of the way and opens a door which leads out onto a deck. The floodlights come on automatically. The sky is now some colour on a spectrum between grey and periwinkle. The wind is strong and cold. The branches of the trees in the back garden rustle. Michael pulls a black cover off something large and stands back.

'This is my baby,' he says proudly.

Róisín reaches out and touches the shiny red exterior. 'What is it, a grill?'

'A grill, a smoker, a barbecue, a rotisserie. I've got an attachment to make it a pizza oven, even.'

'A pizza oven?'

Michael nods. He pats the side of it, dull thumps resonating from inside. 'Do you cook much?' he asks.

'I like to cook. There weren't many opportunities to do it, though.'

'Why not?'

'Small house. Big family. Irish tastebuds.'

Michael lifts the cover back over the grill and Róisín helps him pull it across and secure the buckle straps at the sides. 'I'm not sure I understand what that means,' he says.

'Just that they're picky eaters,' Róisín says.

'Ah, like Aaron.'

'Is he? I never knew that.'

Michael gives a tight-lipped half-smile and nods. 'Big time. It used to drive me up the wall. Gross. Nasty. Weird. The operative words of his rejection for nearly ten years.'

He holds the kitchen door open for Róisín and locks it behind them. The air is thick with comfortable warmth. The moka pot sputters on the stovetop. Róisín hurries to turn it off, the heels of her oversized shoes slapping against the floor.

'Did it work?' he asks.

Róisín flips open the lid of the pot with her thumb. The percolator is full of rich brown liquid. The centre stem burps out thimbles of almond-coloured crema.

'No tamp,' Michael says.

'No, no tamp,' Róisín repeats.

Michael squints out the window, now a very light orange. 'I usually watch the sunrise this time of morning,' he says. 'Why don't you come with me?'

She agrees and he retrieves two of his long, puffy jackets from the closet. Her hands don't reach the ends of the sleeves. He zips her up so only the top half of her face pokes through the hood. She watches him dump the contents of the moka pot into two heatproof flasks and put one in each of the oversized pockets on the outside of his coat.

They walk to the beach in silence. There are no cars this early, no noise of any kind. They are alone. Róisín feels the soles of her shoes squeak as they bite into the snow-packed roads. They pass through the entrance to the beach. The plastic boards of the walkway creak under their feet. They clamber to the top of a moderate hill. The ocean is still and dark against the sky, which has turned a sort of blueish orange. Michael hands her a flask and she takes it. They unscrew them together and watch as the sun breaches the horizon. All at once, the ocean breaks golden and the sky turns red. Róisín takes a long, satisfied sip from her flask. The sunlight hits in a wave of sudden, radiant warmth. She closes her eyes and takes a deep breath in through her nose and out through her mouth. *This is what home smells like,* she thinks, *this is what it tastes like.* It feels like she's pretending. She forces away this last thought and concentrates on the view in front of her.

'We used to bring Aaron here when he was a baby,' Michael says. 'He was a terrible sleeper. He'd cry right through dinner and pass out around ten, up a few hours later, back to sleep, and up for good just before sunrise. He was our little rooster.' He takes a deep breath in and out, a jet of steam in the cold air. 'I can imagine it,' he says.

'Imagine what?' Róisín asks.

'Another one. Running down the beach.' He takes a long, contemplative sip from his flask.

Róisín pats her pockets then pulls up the side of her coat to take something from her pyjamas. She holds up the packet of cigarettes. 'Do you mind?' she asks.

He shakes his head.

'Apparently it's worse for the baby if I quit cold turkey,' she says. She removes a cigarette and makes an indentation three-quarters of the way up. 'So now I do this.'

Michael nods. 'Coffee and a cigarette.'

'Do you want one?'

He doesn't say yes, but he doesn't say no either, and she sees for the first time how similar he is to his son. What he wants to do and what he should do are at odds. The indecision plays out in the expression on his face. She takes out another cigarette and hands it to him, forcing the active choice to be giving it back instead of accepting it.

'I suppose it won't kill me,' he says. He half-smiles and nods. 'Thank you.'

The house is fully illuminated when they return to it. The sky has folded into a brilliant blue. Birds chirp. The wind howls. A car passes slowly beside them on the road, stops, and someone shouts out to Michael, who waves and shouts back. The car continues on.

'That's the rabbi,' he explains to Róisín. 'Lives just around the corner.'

The world still works in such a way that people stop to say hello. This world out here, she thinks, this one I'm becoming a part of. There is a part of her that feels she will never be a part of this community, not really. It's inextricably linked to a hereditary history she does not share. Matrilineal descent means something that is passed down by mothers. Aaron explained it to her once. To him, the explanation was academic. To her, it was instructive. She forces away the thought.

Annette is at the kitchen sink, cleaning out the moka pot with soap and water. Róisín knows this is bad for the device, that, counterintuitively, one should only clean it with water, but she sees no reason to talk herself into an unnecessary argument.

'Was something wrong with the coffee this morning?' Annette asks them when they get in.

Róisín's cheeks flush in the sudden warmth. She unzips the puffy coat and emerges from her downy cocoon. Her clothes are soaked in sweat and stuck to her skin. The kitchen smells like wood grain. The heating has kicked in.

'Rosh here was just helping me figure something out with the pot,' he says.

Annette shushes him. 'You're too loud,' she hisses. 'Aaron is still asleep.'

'He should be out for his run by now,' Michael says.

'It's hardly seven.'

'If we wait for that pisher to wake up, we'll spend half the day silent,' he says. He wraps his arms around his wife and kisses her cheek.

She's quick to shrug him off and nods towards Róisín. 'What do you think you're doing?' she whispers.

'She's pregnant. I don't think she's going to be offended by a kiss.' He removes one flask from the pocket of his coat and then the other, setting them on the stretch of kitchen counter bordering the sink.

Annette lifts the flask to her nose and sniffs. 'Is this espresso?' she asks.

Michael nods as he unzips his coat.

'She's pregnant.'

He stares blankly.

'Pregnant as in no caffeine,' she says, hitting him lightly on the chest.

'Oh,' he says.

'Pregnant as in no caffeine at all, especially not a Thermos full of espresso. Hello?'

'I hear you, I do.'

'Well?' she asks, holding up the flask.

'No more espresso,' he says.

Róisín slinks up the staircase to the bedroom. Neither Aaron's mother nor father acknowledge her presence or subsequent departure. Halfway up the steps, she feels the corkscrew pain again, stronger this time, and then the corkscrew twists and it feels like she's being carved open with a rake. She lets out a dull gasp and hobbles up the final few stairs, through the bedroom door, into the ensuite bathroom, locking the door behind her.

'Róisín?' Aaron's voice calls from the bed.

It's like her head has filled with helium. The world gains a shimmering afterimage that she cannot discern from its source, so everything blurs together in an indistinguishable mess. She blinks and something runs down her cheeks. She touches her face and holds her fingertips up to her eyeline before she can confirm that what she's feeling are tears. She reaches out with two hands to steady herself against the bathroom sink. There are three gentle knocks on the door.

'Róisín?' Aaron says quietly. 'You okay in there?'

The pain is immaculate. She thinks of burning forests, searing flesh, carved meat. She wants to respond but finds it impossible. There are three more knocks, louder this time.

'I'm fine,' Róisín blurts out. She is unsure why she says this. Perhaps she hopes that if she says she's fine, it will become fine, as if the things she says are prescriptive instead of descriptive. Her knuckles go white where they wrap around the sink basin. The pain remains. There's blood between her legs and she sees now that it's soaked through the crotch of her pyjama bottoms.

'Okay,' Aaron says through the door. 'Let me know if you need anything.'

There's a clammy feeling of sickly lightness and Róisín pulls on the shower door until it opens. Blood drips in tiny dots onto the tile floor from the hem of her pyjamas. She'll have to clean that up now, she thinks. She steps into the shower and the glass door swings shut behind her. Shaking, she peels the cotton from her body like the skin from an orange. Her underwear is a deep red. She feels faint and eases herself down onto the tile floor of the shower. She reaches upwards for the faucet and grazes the edge of it with her fingertips. Another wave of pain hits and she clutches onto herself. Taking a breath, she tries again to turn on the shower and succeeds. She's met with a blast of freezing water that sputters before it streams and slowly warms. She peels the rest of her clothes from her skin and forms a pile of soaked cotton in the far corner of the shower. Now she is naked, her pale and freckly legs splayed out. Blood weeps from between her legs and drains into the hole in the centre of the shower. She watches, disinterested, and wonders vaguely if she'll continue bleeding forever, if she'll empty out completely and soon there will be nothing left, and if whatever remains will simply slip through the drain. It's a comforting notion. Then bits of crimson mucus come out in clumps like half-formed cells and catch on the tiles, too large to wash away. Panic echoes in the back of her mind. She does not know what is happening to her body.

'Aaron,' she finds herself saying. It comes out as a whisper. Nothing changes. The world remains as it was before she spoke. She puts an arm against the shower door to push it open and finds the action impossible to complete.

'Aaron,' she shouts.

The bathroom door opens a crack. Finally, he appears.

When Róisín opens her eyes, she's in a hospital bed. They're there, all of them, this surrogate family. Annette sits in the chair closest to the bed with her legs crossed, a newspaper unfolded on her lap. Róisín's hand floats towards her, as if autonomically, and Annette takes it in her own.

'I'm so sorry,' Róisín says, crying.

'Sorry?' she says. She folds the newspaper along its creases and sets it on top of Róisín's bedcovers. 'Sorry for what?'

'I didn't know about the coffee.'

'The coffee?' Annette shakes her head. 'Oh, this isn't because of that.'

'No?' Róisín asks softly.

'No, dear.' She holds Róisín's hand firmly in her own. 'This has nothing to do with anything you did.'

'All right,' Róisín says.

She blinks, her eyes heavy, and when she opens them, she finds that she is alone. The hospital is decorated for Christmas. A doctor whips open the privacy curtain and pulls it closed behind him as he sits down and reads through a clipboard. He has a felt peppermint candy cane stitched onto the breast of his scrubs. She wonders what day it is. Her mother would have surely put up the decorations by now. They'd have their Christmas tree sorted, the customary proposal of using a plastic one rejected, its practicalities discounted yet again in the name of tradition. The doctor is telling her something she can't follow. She's had something called a 'threatened miscarriage'. She cannot remember if the front door of her parents' house is green or purple.

'Is the baby all right?' she asks.

The doctor nods as he reads from his clipboard.

'And the clumps?'

'We're doing tests and we'll have to do some more, but it's not cause for concern just yet,' he tells her. 'These things happen.' The doctor stands and opens the curtain.

'My family…' she starts.

'They're in the waiting room,' he says, not unkindly, and closes the curtain behind him.

She imagines Mam and Da and Darragh and even Maeve

with her kids, all piled up in the sterile white room, sitting on chairs. The doctor means Aaron's family, of course, not her own, but, as she drifts back to sleep, she finds it difficult to differentiate members of the two.

21

The decision is made that Aaron will quit his job and start taking the requisite classes at the local community college in order to complete his degree in computer science. It would be inaccurate to say that this choice is made for Aaron, but it would be equally inaccurate to say that it is his idea entirely. It is, as so many things have become in the past few weeks, a family decision.

'You're coasting,' his father tells him over dinner.

Evidently, there exists a threshold which has been unknowingly crossed over and now, on the other side of it, Aaron's choices are no longer his own. Róisín has started to show more prominently. The baby has moved from a state of speculative existence to one of physical evidence. Of course, the baby had always been real; maybe it is only Aaron's perception of the situation that has changed. His mother taps on the screen of her phone and Aaron immediately thinks back to a night, only months ago, when he might have snorted something off of it. That is a before memory, he realises, and he is living in the after. Jake, Percy, nights out, Rudy's, the old apartment, these are all things that once existed in such surplus as to be tiresome but have become permanently inaccessible to him now. He wonders if he misses it.

'I'll take you into the office tomorrow, as usual,' his father says between bites of lemon-crusted salmon that Róisín helped him prepare. 'It's better to do this kind of thing in person.'

The lemon breadcrumb crust was her idea.

'What will I say?' Aaron asks.

'You tell them you're leaving, that's all,' his mother says.

Róisín helps him fill out the online forms for the community college that night. His mother has his high school and university transcripts stored in her filing cabinet.

'A for Aaron,' she says to herself as she removes the printed pages from a folder.

Two hours later, Aaron is sent an automatically generated letter of acceptance by email for the spring term starting in January. His mother helps him fill out the financial details.

'Don't be ridiculous,' she tells him. That's all.

Life has begun to move at an incredible pace.

Aaron stops at his cubicle with an empty cardboard box and looks for personal effects to fill it with. The whiteboard held up with Blu Tack. The corporate bobblehead. The document inbox. The phone. It is, all of it, company property. He leaves the cardboard box on his keyboard. It all looks so small now, so insignificant. Five years spent typing letters and numbers onto a screen. His contributions are part of something larger, surely, but from down here Aaron cannot see how they relate to anything he could call progress. He hears a quiet weeping. He peeks above the dividing wall of his cubicle and sees Marge bent over her trash receptacle with a box of tissues in her hand.

'Hey, Marge,' Aaron says softly. She doesn't respond. He comes around to the side of the wall and knocks lightly on it, leaning his head through the entrance of her cubicle. 'How are we this morning?'

Marge looks up, sniffling, trying and failing to maintain a forced smile. 'We are good,' she says.

'Is everything okay?'

Marge nods and then pauses. Her smile wavers and falls and then she shakes her head. 'We're supposed to be a family,' she sniffles. 'But families don't treat each other like this, do they?'

Aaron isn't sure what he's supposed to say. Work is a thing that happens outside of real life. He's been operating under the assumption that everybody knows this. Now he understands that, for Marge, work is the whole and everything else is what happens in the interim. He takes a tentative step into her cubicle and places a hand on her shoulder. This seems to be the right thing to do.

'Things will get better, won't they?' she asks him.

He considers the question. He nods slowly. 'Yes, Marge, things will get better. That's what things tend to do.'

The elevator door closes as he jogs towards it.

'Could you hold that for me?' Aaron calls out.

The doors shut. There's a ding and then they open again. Standing there, one hand in his pocket and the other on the elevator's buttons, is Jake. He looks at Aaron with total indifference.

'You heading to lunch?' Jake asks.

Aaron shakes his head. 'No, I, uh…' He takes a deep breath. 'I kind of just quit.'

'Oh,' Jake says.

They ride in silence for two floors.

'How've you been?' Aaron asks.

'How've I been?' Jake shakes his head. 'Fuck me, man. Radio silence for how long? Fine. I've been fine.'

'I'm sorry I've been a little hard to reach since moving out.'

'I get it, sure,' Jake says. 'Living clean. Real suburban man. I guess, I don't know. Percy, I get. There's no hope seeing him without it turning into a whole thing, I know that more than anyone. I just thought...'

'What?' Aaron asks.

'Like, we lived together. For, like, a seriously decent chunk of time. It's kind of disappointing finding out that someone you thought was a close friend lumps you into the same bucket as an empty-headed fucking banker coke-fiend. I get that there were things you couldn't talk about or whatever, that you didn't feel comfortable talking about with me. But I really thought that, underneath it all... I don't know. Fuck it, I guess.'

'It's not like that,' Aaron starts. He takes another deep breath. 'I never told you this, but my brother—'

'Yeah, I know all about that. Do you know how I know? Fucking Percy told me. Said you freaked after a bump on a night out ages ago, crash-landed the mood in a fucking heartbeat. I had to find out from Percy, of all people. After everything we've been through, nothing, but you felt fine opening up to him at one of his banker bars.' He shakes his head. 'I bet the drinks were, like, fifty bucks a pop or something.'

'I don't know,' Aaron says. 'Percy—'

'Percy paid for it. Is that what you're about to say?' Jake laughs, shaking his head.

The elevator reaches the ground floor. There's a ding just before the doors open. Jake exits first.

'It really didn't happen like that. I didn't mean to—'

Jake holds up a hand and shrugs. 'It doesn't matter. It is what it is. Good luck with whatever,' he says.

Jake's right, of course, and as Aaron watches him disappear down the hallway, he becomes aware only in retrospect of the transactional light in which he's viewed their relationship. Since college, Jake was always the 'cool' one to provide guidance or score beer. Maybe Aaron's never seen him as a real person. Not in a fundamental way, not in the way that it turns out Jake has seen Aaron for as long as they've known one another. *It doesn't matter*, Aaron tells himself. *Let the old life die. There's a new one waiting at home.* But there's something else deep inside himself, something injured and sore. The pulsating pain of an old wound.

Aaron sits in the passenger seat of his father's red sedan. They drive back to the house from the business park in silence. Then Michael takes a left instead of a right and Aaron asks where they're going.

'I think you should come with me,' he says.

'For acupuncture?'

'Sure, why not.'

Thursdays are the day Michael now goes to the Malden Eastern Healing Center for acupuncture and incense treatments. He told Annette about it last week over dinner and she half-frowned, chewing on a salad.

'That's my Mahjong night.'

'That's okay, I can go alone.'

She kept chewing, her eyes wide and unblinking. 'Are you sure?'

'I'll be fine.'

Now Aaron shifts uncomfortably in his seat. 'I don't have to get poked with needles or anything, though, right? I can just, like, loiter in the lobby or something.'

Michael laughs and shakes his head. 'No, you don't have to get poked with needles.'

He takes a left and a right through a densely residential neighbourhood. He stops the car.

'I thought we were going to Malden,' Aaron says.

His father grunts as he gets out of the car and waves at Aaron to follow him up the walkway of one of the houses. He opens the front door without knocking. 'Hide the contraband! My son's here!' he shouts, and a raucous cheer explodes from the kitchen.

There's the rabbi at the head of the table, the cantor beside him. Aaron recognises a few of the other faces sitting around the table. Some have glasses of whiskey in front of them, others have cigars hanging from the corners of their mouths.

'Busted,' the rabbi says, grinning.

'Acupuncture and incense,' Aaron says.

'For me, I tell my wife it's a Talmudic study group,' the rabbi says.

The cantor shrugs. 'Singing lessons.'

'I'm learning German,' someone says.

Michael withdraws his wallet from the inside pocket of his coat and removes two twenties, tossing them onto the table. He sits with a groan and pats the empty seat beside him. Someone starts counting out piles of chips.

'Now, just because he's my son doesn't mean you need to take it easy on him, okay? The boy's got to learn.'

'I'll take his money,' the cantor says. 'You don't have to tell me twice.'

Someone passes the rabbi a deck of cards and a cigar cutter.

'Tonight's parshah,' he says as he shuffles, 'is no-limit Texas Hold 'Em.'

22

The only consequential change to the daily routine of the house during the eight nights of Hanukkah is that, for ten minutes, they gather before dinner to light another candle on the menorah. Aaron drives Róisín to the small cluster of shops by the ocean boardwalk after the first night, where she picks out an omelette spatula and a small, decorative book on exotic flowers from around the world. She hands out the gifts to Aaron's parents. Michael smiles politely and nods. Annette turns the book over and over again in her hands as if she's unsure what to do with it. She looks up at Róisín with an expression not dissimilar to anger.

'I didn't get you anything,' she says.

It is initially Annette who proposes going to Shabbat services as a family after the final night of Hanukkah. Aaron makes a face but Róisín, seeing her opportunity, immediately agrees.

'I'm pregnant,' she says to him. 'What I say goes.'

Now, sitting in a synagogue that is very different from the one in Boston all those weeks ago, she is unsure whether or not the reward of his mother's favour is worth the cost. It is nine in the morning and she is dressed in the only nice clothes that she owns. Aaron tugs on the collar of his button-down shirt beside her and yawns. The sanctuary smells like mothballs and canned air freshener. Everything is beige carpet and maroon felt seating. The congregation consists of, as expected, mostly old people. Róisín feels the corkscrew tighten and loosen inside of her. She squirms in her seat, hoping her pad is doing enough damage control to prevent her from bleeding all over this nice fabric. Only on the third try did she get through to the doctor on the house phone, and he told her in a curt but professional tone that light bleeding was to be expected and nothing to be worried about. 'These things happen.' Or, in other words, to stop bothering him.

Annette sits straight beside her, leant slightly forward, a prayer book splayed out on her lap.

'Now they're going to take out the Torah,' she whispers to Róisín. 'Do you know what the Torah is?'

She's been doing this throughout every minute action of the service. She is calmer when she explains things. Róisín nods.

'It's like our Bible, I suppose. I'm not sure what the Catholic equivalent is.'

'I was brought up Protestant, if anything.' This is not the first time she's said this.

Annette holds a finger to her lips and turns her attention back to the front. A woman with grey hair uses a silver pointer to trace along the unrolled scroll, chanting in Hebrew. Aaron yawns again. Róisín nudges him with her elbow.

'What?' he asks.

Michael leans over Róisín and says something to Aaron in a hushed whisper.

'What?' Aaron says. He jerks upright, staring at the bimah.

The rabbi is watching him, smiling, gesturing towards the steps. Aaron shakes his head.

'You have to,' Michael says.

'I don't.'

'It's the first aliyah, Aaron. It's either you or me.'

Aaron stands and makes his way onto the stage. He bites at his nails and rubs the back of his neck. The rabbi nods him forward and the grey-haired Torah reader makes room. Aaron clears his throat. He starts to read Hebrew from a laminated piece of paper, stumbles, clears his throat and starts again. Annette mouths along silently beside Róisín, her eyes fixed on Aaron, who is quite actively not returning the gaze. His face has turned a deep shade of red.

'The first aliyah is reserved for a Kohen,' Michael whispers to Róisín. 'The namesake is passed down from father to son.'

'Will your grandchild be a Kohen, then?'

'No,' Michael is quick to say. Then he sees Róisín's expression and shakes his head. 'I mean, maybe.'

'If they're even Jewish,' Annette snorts. 'Maybe we should worry about that first.'

'Annette,' Michael says.

Eventually, Aaron gets through the reading, the rabbi shakes his hand and Aaron steps to the side of the bimah. The Torah reader resumes. Róisín smiles at Aaron. He looks away. He's invited back to read once more before he's released. He walks briskly back to their pew and slumps into his seat with his arms crossed.

'Yasher koach,' Michael says.

'Fuck off,' Aaron says, quietly enough that only Róisín can make it out.

When the Hebrew reading is all done, the rabbi steps up to the microphone at the podium and clears his throat. He adjusts the tallis around his shoulders and smiles at the congregation.

'Shabbat shalom, everybody,' he says.

'Shabbat shalom,' the congregation responds.

He holds a hand up to his ear. 'I didn't quite catch that, let's try it again. I said, Shabbat shalom, everybody!'

'Shabbat shalom!' the congregation calls back, louder this time.

'Our parshah this week concerns Joseph, beginning and ending with his dreams. Joseph is famous for his dreams, of course – specifically, his ability to read them as prophecies – and for being an icon of family comeuppance. Who among us doesn't dream of our families begging for food at the feet of Pharaoh, only to find us standing beside his throne?'

There is muted chuckling. Someone in the back row coughs loudly.

'The dreams Joseph is famous for include those of the cupbearer and the baker and, eventually, the Pharaoh himself. These do not interest me. No, what interests me instead is Joseph's first dream. Let me set the scene. Joseph is toiling in the field alongside his half-brothers when he tells them of a dream he had the night before. Context may be helpful: it's worth remembering that this is the favourite child we're talking about here, favoured by their father to the point of having special clothing made for only him. It would be fair, if not understating things, to describe his half-brothers as envious of Joseph. Still, he tells them one day that, in his dream, they were out binding sheaves – meaning, stacking hay, typical farmhand terminology I'm sure all of us are familiar with – and his brother's sheaves bow to him. Then another dream: the stars and the moon bow to him. Joseph's brothers envy him and the parshah is clear that it is these dreams that tip their envy into bloodlust.'

The rabbi pauses, unscrewing the cap from a plastic water bottle and taking a sip. He adjusts the shoulders of his tallis and clears his throat before continuing.

'My question is this: why? If I were Joseph and I had dreams like this, aware as I must be of my brother's feelings, I would keep them to myself. Perhaps Joseph is proud; he truly believes his dreams to be so important they must be shared. Perhaps he is simply young, blurting things out without reflecting on how they will make people feel. There is little in the scripture to inform us how Joseph feels about his dreams, only that he has them. If we suspect pride, we must also allow equal suspicion of shame. An alienated child wants nothing more than to fit in. Perhaps Joseph's flaw is simply naïveté. He reports his dreams as if to explain his favour is of divine origin, out of his hands. If this is his plan, then it is short-sighted, but forgive him. He's only seventeen.

'It is important for us to remember that it is Joseph's decision to share his dreams that is the catalyst for everything which follows. His brothers sell him as a slave out of jealousy. He is propositioned by his master's wife and subsequently imprisoned. There, in the cell, is where his story truly begins. That which got him into the cell – his ability to decipher dreams – is also what gets him out. Of course, anyone can decipher dreams, can't they? If knelt before the Pharaoh and asked to foretell his future, who among us wouldn't say the words we thought he'd want to hear? We should admire Joseph's commitment to the truth. And what is a commitment to the truth but an obligation? Perhaps this, above all, is what we can learn from Joseph. Our strength can be our weakness. Our uninformed choices can lead to our worst defeats and to our greatest triumphs and, sometimes, there is very little difference between the two. With so much beyond the horizon of what is visible to us, we ought to follow Joseph's footsteps. Follow our truths. Fulfil our obligations. Amen.'

The congregation nods and repeats, 'Amen.'

There's a hushed murmur as everyone turns to their neighbours and nods or shakes their head in agreement or disagreement with the quality of the sermon.

It is clear to Róisín that life is not some karmic recycler where good deeds are transformed into good fortune. Life is a question without an answer. This hasn't stopped generations of all sorts of people – mostly men, come to think of it – from trying to find one, or else invent one that best serves their purpose. People find an answer in religion under the guise of unity when it seems clear to Róisín that it only provides an unnecessary and arbitrary differentiation that encourages people to hate each other for absolutely no reason.

Annette shifts in her seat, turning towards her. 'Really gives you food for thought, doesn't it?'

Róisín nods and offers a smile. 'It does, sure.'

'What did you think of his sermon?'

'Good, yeah,' Róisín says. 'Very interesting. Did you like it?'

'I don't know if I would say I liked it. I did find it interesting. He's great. We had a rabbi before him who was all over the place, frankly, so it's nice having someone… Ugh, would you wake him up, please?'

Aaron snores beside Róisín. She digs her elbow into his ribs and he jolts awake, looking around. 'What?' he says.

His mother glares at him and shakes her head. 'Honestly, Aaron.'

Perhaps it is because Róisín has never had this type of religion in her life that she doesn't anticipate the warmth of its community. It's less shouty than she expected, for one. It's singularly focused on rote repetition, which, in fairness, is exactly how Aaron described it to her all those months ago, that Judaism is closer to an ethnic subculture than a religion in the traditional sense. He told her that half of Jews were atheists. She didn't understand that – she still doesn't. All these people sitting here listening to what they know to be nonsense for the sole reason that generations of people before them did the same. She can't shake the feeling that this is purposeless, that people should have better things to do with their Saturdays, but the feeling is muted. She doesn't mind this.

Annette is explaining the story of Joseph and his tunic, which Róisín knows as his 'Technicolor Dreamcoat', though she's not going to mention it. Aaron nudges her gently with his shoulder.

'You okay?' he mouths.

Róisín smiles and nods. She puts her hand in his and his fingers close around it. She takes a breath in through her nose and out through her mouth. *This is what community smells like*, she thinks, *this is what it feels like*. And though she also feels distinct from this community, she sees for the first time the possibility of an entrance into it. Something that is not home but close enough to serve the same purpose. If this is the shape she must contort herself into, if that is the price of admission, then so be it. Maybe this is something she can bear.

'It's almost over,' he says and kisses her cheek.

There are a few more prayers in Hebrew and then the rabbi announces something called the Mourner's Kaddish. Aaron watches his father struggle to stand and then his mother rises. He whispers something to his mother and she says something back that sounds like 'yahrzeit'. The temperature drops a few degrees as Aaron looks to his mother and then his father and then stands. Róisín doesn't know what to do, so she stands. All but a few in the sanctuary are seated.

יִתְגַּדַּל וְיִתְקַדַּשׁ שְׁמֵהּ רַבָּא

And the congregation responds, with one voice, 'Amen.'

As the prayer continues, Aaron puts his hand over Róisín's, but soon sniffles and withdraws it to wipe his cheek. It is then she sees that he is crying. Annette looks sharply in his direction and then her face softens immediately. She puts her hand on Aaron's shoulder. His father pats his back awkwardly. The prayer ends. They sit down.

Aaron clears his throat and tries to smile. 'I'm fine,' he says.

Róisín holds his hand and squeezes it. He squeezes back.

Lunch is served after the service and the congregation dissipates into clumps around the table of food in the centre. Annette helps Róisín assemble a bagel with lox.

'Schmear,' she says, pointing at the cream cheese.

'Schmear,' Róisín repeats.

'It's Yiddish. It means "to spread" but you can also use it as a noun to describe the thing you're spreading.'

Róisín nods intently. 'And is it always like this after the service?'

'How do you mean?'

'Everyone just hanging around and talking?'

Annette nods. 'Schmooze,' she says.

Róisín repeats the word.

'It's Yiddish.'

'What does it mean?' Róisín asks.

'This,' Annette says, gesturing vaguely at the room. 'Hanging around and talking.'

Róisín finds Aaron and his father sitting at a table at the back of the room with the rabbi and sits next to them. The rabbi has a bemused look on his face. Michael looks annoyed.

'The Reform movement has been around much longer than the Conservative one,' Aaron is saying. 'In 1800s Germany, most Jews had Christmas trees.'

'How did that turn out for them?' Michael asks.

The rabbi laughs and shakes his head. 'I'm not debating the history with you, Aaron, I'm sure you're right, but I don't think that the congregation would approve of one in the lobby.'

'Nor would your mother approve of one in our home,' Michael says. 'I hope that goes without saying.'

Aaron squints and opens his mouth to say something. Róisín kicks his foot under the table. His mouth closes.

'Is that something you two have discussed yet?' the rabbi asks. 'We have many interfaith families in the congregation and they all handle the holiday season differently, it seems.'

'No, we haven't had a chance,' Róisín says.

'I think it could be confusing for a child to grow up Jewish but have a Christmas tree,' Michael says.

They were in bed the other night when Aaron made a comment referencing their baby's bar mitzvah. It wasn't even the focus of what he was saying, more of an afterthought to the main point. Róisín went quiet, thinking. It took Aaron a few moments to notice.

'What is it? What did I say?'

'No, nothing,' she said.

'It's not nothing,' Aaron whispered.

'I didn't know you wanted to raise them with religion.'

'Oh,' Aaron said.

'It's never been a big part of my life,' she said.

'Right.'

The bedroom was dark and cold but they were warm beneath the duvet. Aaron traced his fingers along her shoulder, a gentle motion that hesitated before continuing.

'Would we celebrate Christmas, at least?' she asked.

'German Jews saw it as a symbol of integration,' Aaron says now at the table. 'A reclamation of what would otherwise be a purely Christian symbol.'

'But it is a Christian symbol,' his father says. 'Christ's Mass.'

'It was adapted from the pagan celebration of the winter solstice to get more Christians. That's how Christianity spread so quickly as a religion: it was always adapting. Something we could learn from.'

Michael shakes his head.

Róisín excuses herself from the table, asking where the bathrooms are, and the rabbi points her down the hall and to the left. She gently removes Aaron's arm from the crook of her own. She checks her phone in the hallway. She has one new notification, a message from her mother. It's a picture of Sinéad holding up five hand-knitted stockings complete with stitched names – one for her, one for Aaron, two for his parents and one for 'Baby'.

Send me their address!!!

Róisín zooms in on the background of the photograph. Red-and-green bunting is stapled to the wall. Christmas trinkets occupy every available counter space – a model train beside the radio, elves resting on the windowsill. Her father sits at the kitchen table with a pint glass and an empty green bottle, looking up at the camera in surprise. Darragh must be the one taking the picture. Róisín feels the warmth of that room, of those people, and feels an enormous emptiness well up inside of her.

23

The car shudders as Aaron slows down and then jerks forward as he presses his foot down on the gas.

'Sorry,' he says.

Róisín doesn't notice, or else notices but doesn't say anything. She's in the reclined passenger seat, her forehead leant against the fogged window. She has one hand resting on her stomach and the other propped up beneath her jaw.

Aaron clears his throat. 'Sorry,' he repeats.

'It's fine,' Róisín says to the window.

He turns a dial on the centre console two clicks clockwise and the hot breath from the vents gets stronger. Róisín leans forward to slide the vent in front of her seat closed.

'Oh,' Aaron says, turning the dial back to where it was. 'I thought you might be cold.'

'It's fine,' she says.

'Only another hour,' he says, even though it's closer to two.

Róisín nods. Her eyes are open, listlessly gazing out over the endless, barren highway landscape. Everything is white snow or black road, or else some intermediary grey sludge piled into enormous frozen waves on either side of the road.

'It's not much to look at,' Aaron says.

He checks the clock on the console and does the mental math. They'll likely arrive too late for sunset after all. He found the vacation cabin online. Outdoor hot tub. Beautiful view of the lake. Snow-capped trees. The cabin is on an inlet, surrounded on all sides by a wide lake. Every picture in the photo gallery had some hint of purplish sky, the red sun sinking into the water. Aaron had opened another tab in the web browser to check his bank account balance and then navigated back to the rental website to reserve it for one night. What he'd forgotten to account for was distance, as in the four hours it would take them to drive up to the backfuck of nowhere, Maine. But the pictures were beautiful.

The past few days have all unfolded in the same way. Aaron wakes up alone, Róisín and his father long since gone for their sunrise walk. He dresses for his morning run and comes home to find that Róisín is already back in bed for her morning nap. He helps his father around the house while Róisín lies in bed, scrolling through social media on her phone. She's been doing a lot of that lately. The activity is an empty salve. It doesn't seem to restore any energy to her. She is no more relaxed nor communicative at the end of a binge than at its start. Sometimes Aaron will stand at the end of the bed and say something and have to repeat it two or three times before Róisín acknowledges him. He'll ask if she wants to join him downstairs and she'll shake her head and turn back to her phone. The basement is a nursery now. Róisín hasn't come down to see it yet. They have things in online shopping carts like cribs and baby toys and clothes that are sized in months. Aaron is learning how to change a diaper.

Róisín coughs into her fist and nuzzles against the glass of the window. Aaron reaches out and puts a hand on her shoulder. She nods towards the windshield and tells him to watch the road. He returns both hands to the steering wheel.

It's not so much that Róisín explicitly says that she's hungry, but that Aaron notices her staring at the lit-up golden arches of the

McDonald's sign while he fills the gas tank. The sky is blue with tawny streaks. Róisín looks like a ghost through the car window, an afterimage imprinted beneath the distorted reflection of sky. He'd envisioned them in the outdoor hot tub watching the sky break apart into fiery colours as the sun sank into the lake, his arm around her, things exactly the same as they used to be. He watches the numbers on the pump go up. Róisín is still staring at the McDonald's sign. When the tank is full, he swipes his credit card and plops back into the driver's seat.

'I'm really hungry,' he says.

Róisín tilts her head. 'Do you want to get something to eat?'

'Yeah,' he says. 'Is that all right?'

'Sure, of course.'

Now they're sitting across from one another at a plastic table, the only ones in the place except for the teenagers behind the counter. There's a red tray in the space between them, complete with burgers, fries and two large cokes. Róisín chews on the end of a fry.

'Do you remember when we went to that state fair?' Aaron asks.

He wants her to think back to it and be surprised by the warmth of the memory. He wants to see her smile and watch all this distance between them collapse.

She only nods. 'What about it?'

'Nothing,' Aaron says.

They eat in silence. When he finishes his burger, he folds the wrapper into neat squares. He leans back in his chair and watches Róisín pick at her food. She looks tired. No, she looks exhausted. Since the moment she told him about the pregnancy, Aaron has fixated on the state of their lives once the baby arrives. The after. Any comfort he's provided her has always been within the context of that future. A crib. A nursery.

Maybe he's ignored the space between now and then and, in doing so, has lost track of the love they share, that real and beating heart at the centre of their universe. Róisín finishes her food and looks around the restaurant with a vacant stare.

I know that you are more than our future, Aaron wants to tell her. *I know that you exist.* Aaron feels a pain in his chest, acutely aware that something fundamental has changed here. He moves to stand and jerks his head towards the car outside. The sky is dark. The sun has set.

'Ready to go?' he asks.

She comes out to the hot tub eventually, after spending the better part of an hour horizontal on the couch. Aaron watches her through the cabin's side window as she stands up and walks towards the door, hurrying to look away as she steps outside.

'It's freezing out here,' Róisín says.

'Get in, you'll keep warm.'

Róisín squints in the dark, clutching her elbows. 'Is it on the list?'

'Shit,' Aaron says.

There's a computer printout taped to the refrigerator in the kitchen at home with a list of activities and foods that are prohibited during pregnancy. It appeared there a few days after Róisín's visit to the hospital. Neither Aaron's mother nor father have mentioned the list, which precludes Aaron from commenting on it. It is the exact breed of parental passive aggression he's come to expect, that he's had to decipher for Róisín to understand. The first item on the list read, in neat, even handwriting, *Absolutely no coffee.* It was underlined twice.

'What about your feet?' Aaron offers.

Róisín tiptoes across the porch to the raised steps and clambers up until she's sitting on the edge of the hot tub, then swings her legs over and into the water. She smiles for the first time all day. 'That's really nice,' she says.

'Isn't it?'

There are lights on the bottom of the tub. Róisín's face is illuminated in shimmering blue light. It reminds Aaron of the first time he saw her in that nightclub, a lifetime ago. They sit in silence for a while and then Aaron pulls himself out of the water, his skin steaming in the sudden cold, and sits beside Róisín. He offers her his hand and she takes it.

Aaron has a dream about the ocean and then finds himself being rocked awake. He's so tired that his eyes are stuck together. When he peels them open, he sees Róisín standing over him, pulling gently on his arm.

'Come on,' she's saying. 'You don't want to miss this.'

He stands and yawns. She hands him a mug of coffee. He follows her out of the bedroom, through the living room and onto the deck. The air is immediate and cold. It's so bright he's squinting now, looking from his feet to Róisín's back, following the oblique shape of her silhouette. She sits him down in a wooden Adirondack chair beside her. She tells him to close his eyes fully, so he does.

'Now start to open them really slowly, so the light just comes through your eyelids. It'll make it easier to adjust.'

The colours go from black to blotchy purple, then white.

'Now open your eyes fully,' Róisín says.

The sky is shattered in a million different shades of vibrant colours. Deep blue slips into hazy greens, reds and yellows towards the horizon. The lake is rich with the colours from the sky.

'Nice, isn't it?' she asks and Aaron nods.

He takes a long sip from his mug. The coffee is hot and bitter in his mouth and it warms him as he swallows. Róisín lifts her mug from the arm of her chair and holds it with both hands in her lap. Water and lemon. Her recent favourite substitute for a morning cup. The steam rises thick and quickly dissipates into the fresh lake air. Róisín smiles as she looks out over the water.

24

Róisín lies in the dark, blinking, listening to Aaron snore beside her. She is nauseous in the half-light and the whiplash of sudden semiconsciousness. Aaron's index finger is hooked into the pocket of her pyjamas. He often grasps for bits of fabric to touch in the last moments before they fall asleep. She shimmies the pocket from under his finger and holds her breath as she extends her foot to the hardwood floor, anticipating cold, finding instead something soft and slight. A slipper. Aaron must have laid them out for her before going to sleep. She creeps out of the bed. He rolls over into the space she's left vacant and tucks one of her pillows into his chest. He looks so peaceful sleeping alone.

The kitchen air is warm and thick with the smell of dried fruit and cloves and roasted coffee. The moka pot is on the stovetop. Róisín taps the side of it; it's hot. The percolator is full. The kitchen windows are black and dewy with condensation. The oven offers a low beep. Michael yawns into the room and yelps when he sees Róisín standing there.

'Jesus,' he says. He leans against a chair with his hand on his chest. 'You scared me. Good morning.'

'Good morning,' she says, taking her usual spot at the kitchen table.

'I've got something for you, actually,' Michael says. He rifles through the cupboard closest to the door. 'Okay, now close your eyes and hold out your hands,' he commands, and she does.

Something light is placed onto her outstretched palms.
'Open.'

It's a pouch of decaffeinated espresso beans. The resealable slit at the top has been cut. The bag is open. She looks to the moka pot on the stove.

'That's very kind of you,' she says.

'I figure you miss the taste of coffee under the harsh no-caffeine regime of the commandant.'

Róisín smiles, reading the bag. 'You didn't have to do this,' she says.

Michael looks at her, confused. 'It's Christmas, isn't it?'

She checks the clock on the wall and does the simple mental maths while Michael tells her something about a record amount of snow that's coming down. It's after eleven back home. The family is probably on some spectrum between still-asleep and drunk by now. Her phone is upstairs. She resists the urge to make an excuse to fetch it.

Michael asks if she wants to join him on a morning walk to the beach while all that snow's still untouched and she says yes. He gets two pairs of snow boots from the closet and tells Róisín to sit down so he can put them on her. She lets him. Then she stands and holds out her arms so he can zip her into a long, puffy coat. As always, only her nose to her forehead is visible from under the massive hood.

'What's in the oven?' she asks.

'A surprise,' he says. 'A Christmas miracle.'

Michael empties the contents of the moka pot into two heatproof flasks and tucks them into the outside pockets of his coat.

There's three inches of snow on the ground already and it's still coming down. They walk along the road in the spotlight circles of the street lamps, the soles of their boots squeaking as they chew into the snow. Róisín's never seen so much white. The world is muffled around them. Flakes gather like moths beneath the street lamp bulbs, heavy shadows fluttering against the light. Michael hums to himself as they walk. He stops suddenly. Róisín doesn't notice at first, she keeps walking, only registering his absence in her periphery a good few metres down the road. She turns left, right, completely around to find him standing aimlessly in the centre of the street behind her. The image of the woman with the toddler Róisín and Aaron saw on the drive back from the station the first day she arrived here comes to mind.

'You all right?' she calls out.

He looks around, nodding.

'Will we go home?'

A switch flips inside of him and he's back. He puts a hand on the shoulder of her puffy coat. The lenses of his glasses are covered in snow. He takes them off, folds them and tucks them into the inside pocket of his coat.

'I always wanted a daughter,' he says.

They arrive at the crest of the sand hill ten minutes before dawn. They sit on the lip of their usual rock and Michael removes the flasks from his pockets and hands one to Róisín. The waves crash violently against the sand, spewing foam into the air. The brackish waters churn but, in the distance, there is an illusion of a still-calm ocean. The air is crisp and refreshing. The sand is constant and frozen. Róisín breathes out fog. Dawn breaks. The ocean burns. The world wakes up.

'It all feels so permanent,' Róisín says.

Michael takes a long sip from his flask and nods, gazing at the horizon.

'This,' she says, touching her stomach. 'This feels so permanent that I have to get it right. All of it.'

'Hm.' He nods.

'It seems impossible, though, casting someone to be there for the rest of my life. Do people know these things for sure?'

'I think that love is a problem people tend to solve in reverse,' Michael says. 'They approach the situation academically, prepared with some list of desired attributes ranked by how willing they are to compromise. I don't know.' He takes a long pull from his flask and lets out a contented sigh. 'I believe that anyone can find a certain type of shallow love if they look hard enough for it. Finding the right person, though, that's transformative. If you get it right, it can turn you into the very best version of yourself. That love, true love, I don't know if you find it by looking for it. I think it's something that catches you unaware at the least convenient moment. Maybe it's something you can only see after it happens, in retrospect, and it's impossible to identify while experiencing it.'

'Life can only be understood backwards but it must be lived forwards,' Róisín recites. 'Aaron says it all the time.'

Michael smiles, bemused. 'It's nice to know he listens sometimes.'

Róisín stares at the ocean and watches it advance and retreat, the violence of its arrival, the meditation of its exit, on and on like that in an endless cycle. Life can only be understood backwards but it must be lived forwards.

'Did you know that Rosh is a word in Hebrew?' Michael asks.

'What's it mean?'

'Rosh Hashanah, the new year. Rosh Chodesh, the first day of the month. Head? Leader? I don't know exactly, I'm not sure.'

'I like that,' Róisín says.

'I thought you might.'

Michael removes the pie from the oven and sets it onto the kitchen table along with plates and forks. He cuts a hefty slice for each of them and then sits down across from Róisín. This thing in front of her is supposedly a mincemeat pie. Michael did some research and found an 'authentic' recipe, as close to its thirteenth-century origins as he could get. She brings a forkful to her mouth. The pie is probably ten times larger than it ought to be, but it smells right. It tastes right too, at least at first. Then she chews and tastes something else among the spice and fruit. She swallows.

'It's funny, the way we have different words for the same things,' Michael says. He sticks a fork into the contents of his slice and brings it to his mouth. He chews. His lip trembles as he swallows with a grimace. 'Hm,' he says.

'Like what?' Róisín asks.

'Boot instead of trunk,' he says. 'Courgette instead of zucchini. Minced beef instead of ground beef.'

Róisín looks from her fork to her plate. 'Did you put mince in this?'

He nods, confused. 'Was I not supposed to?'

Michael goes into the basement to look for 'another Christmas surprise to make up for the last Christmas surprise' and Róisín retrieves her phone and turns it on at the kitchen table. At first nothing happens. *This is finally the year they forgot me,* she thinks. Then the phone buzzes to life, vibrating the table, again and again, until she's forced to move it onto her lap to wait for the stream of notifications from her messaging application to peter out. The bulk of these new messages are from a conversation thread which includes Róisín, Maeve, Darragh and their parents, labelled 'Grá'. She opens the attached images and videos one at a time, slowly, savouring the content as she consumes it, letting the videos play three or four times before moving on. There's Maeve and her twins, Eoin and Claire. In one video, they struggle to unwrap presents that are taller than they are. The last time she saw them in person, they were only babies. She's watched them grow up in digital images and videos on her phone screen. There are her parents, Sinéad and Henry, sitting back on the couch in matching Christmas jumpers, mugs of steaming tea in their laps. Some of the videos show Darragh with his wild hair and bloodshot eyes. The ones of Maeve are shakier, presumably filmed by Darragh. Maeve is prim and neatly dressed, all bleached teeth and fake tan.

This makes four Christmas holidays since Róisín has been home. She'd brought her then-boyfriend Brian and spent the entire morning ensuring he was happy, a fruitless task that entailed remaking his tea twice and fussing over his plate of food. Every time he glanced at an errant piece of wrapping paper, she was quick to snatch it up and stuff it into an expanding bin bag until Henry finally swiped it out of her hands and ordered her to 'sit down, for feck's sake, running around like a chicken with its feckin' head cut off'. Róisín wishes she'd enjoyed the day more. Maeve was pregnant and they hadn't known it would be twins yet. Everyone got her things for the baby and then, a few months later, had to run out and get doubles of everything they'd bought. Maeve's husband hadn't left her yet. That was the first Christmas he missed and Maeve was pretending to not be bothered by it. She kept making excuses about how busy he was at work and how badly he'd wanted to come. It's funny how inevitable even the most surprising of life's twists become in retrospect, when given the time and distance to see them properly for what they are.

Róisín taps on her family group chat and navigates to a screen which lists its members. She taps on Darragh's face and her phone screen goes black for a moment and then displays his face in full screen, stretched and distorted. She holds the phone to her ear and listens to the dial tone until eventually she hears three beeps indicating that the receiver of her call has failed to answer it. She tries Darragh again and when he doesn't answer a second time, she taps her mother's face instead, who picks up the call immediately.

'Merry Christmas, Róisín!' her mother coos.

'Merry Christmas, Mam,' she says.

Sinéad takes her around the room, handing the phone first to Henry ('How're ya gettin' on, Róisín? Be sure you're minding yourself, won't you?') then to Darragh ('Still shite then, is it?') then to Maeve ('Hang on, just a second – Claire, don't play with that!'). Sinéad keeps Róisín on the line while she asks the room who wants a cup of tea. She hears a chorus of voices say yes. The shuffling noise a box of Lyon's makes as teabags are dug out of it by the handful. The hiss of the kettle. The homely clanging of plates and cutlery. Sugar being spooned out of its paper packaging. It's not until the tea-making business is done and Sinéad is back on the line that Róisín feels a tickle run down her cheek and realises that she's crying.

'How are you, Róisín?' her mother asks.

'Good, yeah. All good.'

This kitchen is empty and cold. The windows are fogged and have started turning pink. A light flicks on at the top of the staircase and then there's the sound of running water. The bathroom door swings shut and the noise is muffled.

'G'wan, tell me, what's it like at their big house for Christmas?' her mother asks. 'Have they got a tree?'

'Yes,' she lies.

'A great big one, I'd bet.'

Róisín wipes her eyes with her sleeves. 'Exactly.'

Sinéad yells into the other room that Aaron's house has got a great big tree and Darragh yells back asking if he can expect his cup of tea by New Year's or if he should just fuck off to the neighbour's, then. Sinéad yells back that he's blessed with two legs and two arms and that if he's got a problem with the speed at which tea is being delivered in her house then he can do them all a favour and get the feck out of it and take his bad attitude with him, as if he'd ever made a cup of tea in his life. Róisín closes her eyes and listens and it's like she's there, it's like she's home. She wants to ask her mother to leave the phone on the mantle for the rest of the day and let her listen, just like that.

'Well,' she says instead, 'I'd best be off, so.'

'I'm up to my neck but you'll call us later, won't you?' her mother says.

'I will, yeah.'

'You promise?'

'I promise you, Mam, I promise.'

'A great big tree! Isn't that wonderful? You'll call me later, so.'

'I will. Bye. Bye. Byebyebye.'

Róisín stares at her phone feeling the hole in heart tear open that much wider. She taps the icon that opens a web browser on her phone. It takes her to the most recently visited page, titled 'Penalties for Overstaying Tourist Visas (US)'. She reads the information again, hoping that the government may have amended their stance on amnesty for unlawful residents in the twenty-four hours since she last checked the page. The information is, of course, the same. If she goes home, she should be prepared to stay there and never return.

Michael emerges from the basement steps, dusty and smiling, his arms full of boxes featuring faded pictures of twinkling LED light strips. 'I knew we had them somewhere,' he says.

Róisín affects a smile. 'What are those for?' she asks.

'We haven't got a tree inside, but we do have quite a few trees outside. Better late than never, isn't it?'

'That's kind of you,' Róisín says.

'What do you say?'

Róisín gives a tight-lipped smile and shrugs. She doesn't want to cry in front of him. 'I think I might like to go back to bed for a while, if that's all right with you.'

Michael sets the boxes on the kitchen table. 'Of course.'

She stands, walking towards the stairs.

'Rosh,' he says. He clears his throat. 'I uh, I didn't do anything to upset you, did I?'

She shakes her head. 'No, not at all.'

'Okay,' he says, giving a sad half-smile. 'Just checking.'

The door to the ensuite bathroom is still closed. She sits on the edge of the bed and scrolls through social media. Someone she knew as a teenager is back home from London. Her best friend from when she was eight got engaged; there she is holding out her ring towards the camera, surrounded by presents. One of her uncles has made a social media post about Christmas and the failing government, specifically in reference to the drug abuse crisis and the housing crisis and how one crisis has informed the other, although it is unclear from his phrasing which crisis he believes is the root cause of the other or how either relate to the holiday.

She feels a familiar anger and restlessness. She wants to be back in Aaron's old apartment; that's a version of home. She wants to be back in her own apartment; that's a version of home too. She wants to be back in Ireland, where her home is no longer her home, where her life would only imitate the life she once had. She understands only in retrospect that the time and effort and love she expended to build her previous life has done nothing to sustain it since leaving it behind. When she decided to stay in America, she thought that she would have two homes. Instead, she has none.

The bathroom door opens and there's Aaron in a cloud of steam, backlit, drying his hair with a towel.

'I've decided that I'm going to introduce you to the world of Chinese food and movies,' he says, smiling. 'How does that sound?'

Róisín nods. 'Sure.'

'I couldn't help myself. I heard my dad working away on that pie, and I'm sorry, but I couldn't bring myself to stand in his way. Was it disgusting?' Aaron rifles through a paper bag on the floor and removes a small box from inside. He stands and flips on the bedroom light and stops.

'What?' she asks. She touches her cheek. It's wet.

'You've been crying,' he says softly, sitting beside her.

'I haven't,' she says stupidly.

He rubs her cheek with his thumb. 'Okay, you haven't,' he says quietly. 'It's just been raining.'

She swallows hard and nods. 'Exactly.'

'Just a bit of rain, is all.'

She nods again.

Aaron rubs the back of his neck. 'Do you wish you were home?'

Róisín shrugs.

'You won't hurt my feelings if you say that you do.'

'I wish that I was home.'

'And I suppose these don't make much of a difference?' he says.

There's a box in his hands and he places it on her lap. Mincemeat pies, the real ones, wrapped in foil and topped with a powdered sugar star. She smiles despite herself and sniffles. 'These are a nice touch,' she says.

There's a thump as something heavy hits the kitchen floor.

'What was that?' Aaron asks, standing up from the bed.

25

I t's after four by the time Aaron's father is situated. The doctor meets with the rest of them in the waiting room.

'I'm afraid I don't have good news,' he says.

Everything after that is static. Aaron tucks his head between his knees and tries not to throw up. Róisín cries.

'He said it was unusual,' his mother keeps repeating to herself.

Aaron has expected this day since that first night home. What surprises him most is how surprising it is. They had arrived at a kind of rhythm, some prolonged limbo, and sustained it so well these past few weeks that he'd tricked himself into thinking it could go on like that forever. There was an end approaching, he knew that in the strictly academic sense of facts and schedules, but, on a deeper level, Aaron had tricked himself into believing time would stretch infinitely on its journey there. They might spend the rest of their lives preparing the house for a baby that would never arrive, for a funeral that would never be held, living in a time without time. He stares at the bleached white tiles on the floor and thinks about supermarkets.

'This isn't happening,' he hears himself say. 'This cannot be happening.'

The body of his father was sprawled across the kitchen floor, that's how Aaron found him. That's what he thought at the time too, not that those arms and legs bent at awkward angles belonged to his father but that they were part of his father's body, which was itself a distinct and meaningless entity. His father was a stern, serious man who presented thoughts with poise. This useless heap carelessly slumped on the hardwood was just meat and bone and cotton. Then his mother came in, screaming. Aaron called the emergency services on the landline phone. They asked him if his father was alive or dead and he told them he didn't know. They told him to take his father's pulse and he said, 'Okay.' He set the phone down on the kitchen counter and rushed to his father's side and poked at his neck before realising he had no fucking idea what he was feeling around for, and then he heard a gurgle followed by a hollow breath. That's what he told the man on the phone.

'Will he be all right?' Aaron asked, knowing the man did not have the answer.

When the ambulance arrived, Aaron told the paramedics that his father had an untreated tumour in his brain called a glioblastoma and the paramedics told Aaron to get the fuck out of the way so that they could do their jobs. Aaron's mother got into the passenger seat of the red sedan. Róisín got into the back. Aaron drove. This arrangement was decided without speaking. Aaron tailed the ambulance to the hospital, wondering the entire drive if he should have told the paramedics about the stroke instead of the tumour, if they were in the process of wasting valuable time of his father's life by treating the wrong cause. There was such a rush to get there but then, once they arrived, there was nothing to do but wait.

It's another hour before the doctor returns to the waiting room. They are permitted to visit but they should know that he isn't conscious and sustained some minor injuries from his fall.

'We've bandaged the cuts but there is some light bruising on the face which may look alarming, but I assure you that they are strictly superficial injuries.'

'All right,' Aaron's mother says, standing. 'Let's go.'

Róisín puts her hand in Aaron's. 'Will I come with you?' she asks.

'Do you want to?' he asks.

She opens her mouth as if to say something then slowly nods instead.

'Are you sure?'

'Only if you want me to be there,' she says.

'Come if you want to come,' Aaron says, standing.

'I don't want to intrude,' she says.

'It's just this way,' the doctor says, motioning towards a set of swing doors.

Aaron and his mother follow the doctor. Róisín stays behind. They wind through endless hallways, endless other doors, so many other people. Then they arrive. The doctor enters the room first, then Aaron's mother and finally Aaron. There is a narrow hallway past a bathroom that opens into the small room. There's a television mounted to the wall. It smells like bleach and lilacs and there's a window with the blinds closed. There's a gentle hum of electronic equipment. Aaron's father is perfectly still. His face is blotched with purple clouds, the largest of which is located on his forehead and extends like an oblong galaxy beneath the surface of his skin. Aaron watches his mother approaching, crying, sitting beside him, putting her hand in his. The doctor is telling Aaron something involving numbers that he can't understand.

'Is he...' Aaron starts.

The doctor waits for him to finish his question. Aaron leaves the words out there, unsure what information he specifically wants to know. His father isn't dead, obviously, and yet it is difficult to see him like this and not think that he must be. There is a disconnect between what he knows and what he's seeing.

'Is this normal?' he decides to ask.

'Normal,' the doctor repeats. 'How do you mean?'

Aaron decides he doesn't know what he means. He can't look away from his father's face. There's a cut above his eyebrow that's started to scab over. There are two white strips attached to the skin at either side of it, holding it closed. Eventually, the doctor looks down at his beeper and leaves. Aaron watches his mother weep at the side of his father's hospital bed. He finds himself unable to take a step forward. He is only now struck by the realisation that these two people are more than their relationship to him, that being father and mother are parts – significant parts, surely – but parts and not the whole, all the same. They have lived for the past five years on their own, having birthed and raised two sons that were inaccessible to them. They were children once. They fell in love. The depth of their lives is only now evident to Aaron. It crushes him with the weight of its significance.

Life can only be understood backwards but it must be lived forwards. Aaron used to hate his father for saying things like that. There was the time in high school when the family computer conked out the night before a paper was due. He asked his father to fix it, who just replied, 'Problem solving, Aaron, problem solving.' He wanted his father to be like all of the other fathers, to step in, to fix the issue, to save the day. It was only in reading manuals online that he discovered a love for taking computers apart and putting them back together, the reason he applied to study computer science. It was true that now he felt invincible, as if any unsolved problem could be dissected into its basest parts and solved. No man ever steps in the same river twice, for it is not the same river and he is not the same man. He and Moe would roll their eyes as teenagers when their father said things like that, blind to all the gifts he was giving them.

One of the machines beeps particularly loudly and then goes silent. Aaron holds his breath. His mother doesn't appear to have noticed. Then the machine beeps again, softer this time, and all seems well.

It's another hour before a nurse comes in for a routine check. 'You should go home and rest,' she says.

'I need to be here,' Annette is quick to say.

The nurse doesn't argue. Aaron asks what the beeps mean and she just looks at him.

'That one, that one there,' he says, pointing.

The nurse looks at the screen and shakes her head. 'These things happen,' she says.

They return to the house in silence. There are boxes of string lights on the kitchen table. One is tipped over, dripping wires down the side of the table and onto the floor. Róisín gasps when she sees them. Aaron grabs a handful and wraps them around his wrist and places the coil back into the box, interweaving the cardboard flaps at its top to close it. There's three-quarters of a pie sitting on a heatproof cork pad on the countertop, cold to the touch. Annette paces around the kitchen.

'I should call,' she says. 'There's so much to do.'

Aaron guides his mother up the staircase to the master bedroom. He helps unclasp her shoes and then she lies down on top of the duvet.

'Wait,' she says, sitting up. 'I have to–'

'There will be time,' Aaron says. 'You need to rest. That's the best thing you can do right now. Might be the only thing any of us can do.'

She swallows hard and nods. 'Yes. All right.'

Aaron turns off the lamp on the bedside table. There's a well-worn paperback book on his father's side. In the inside cover is a receipt from a convenience store with a recipe for mincemeat pie written in pen on the back. His father's messy scrawl reminds Aaron of the writing on Moe's baseball glove. He realises he never took the glove out of his father's car, that it must still be there, tucked underneath the passenger seat. He hears his mother's ragged breath and sees that she's asleep.

Róisín is at the kitchen table when he comes in. He sets his father's book on the counter and sits down next to her. For a little while, neither of them says anything and they sit in the silence together, listening to the answering machine beep. There's a message waiting to be heard.

'He'll get better,' Róisín says.

Aaron nods and gives a tight-lipped smile. It is unclear to him whose benefit she says this for. It's something people say, sure, but it's not necessarily true. His father might get better this time the same way he did last time and, if he does, then he'll return home changed or the same and they'll spend the next few weeks waiting for it to happen again. If it doesn't, then they'll forget it can until the next time it does. There is no cure. They will continue to withstand a series of escalating incidents until one of them is final. Things can and will only get worse.

Aaron opens the book, a paperback edition of *Walden* by Henry David Thoreau. There is a quote written in pencil on the inside cover, underlined twice:

I went to the woods because I wished to live deliberately, to front only the essential facts of life, and see if I could not learn what it had to teach, and not, when I came to die, discover that I had not lived.

Aaron wants it to apply to his life in a direct and actionable way. He wants it to be a metaphor for something, a key to a lock he's been lugging around half his life. He wants his father to be okay. When they went to Shabbat services as a family and his father insisted he go up to the bimah to fulfil that ancient obligation of the kohanim, Aaron had hated him. He'd even told him to fuck off, hadn't he, albeit under his breath. Maybe his father had heard him and pretended not to. With the grace of even a small amount of time, Aaron was able to see what his father was trying to give him. The rabbi's poker game. The aliyah. A community to take care of him. And, like all the other times Aaron received a gift from his father, he threw it on the ground and spat on his face.

They sit at the kitchen table in silence and then Róisín leads Aaron up to bed. She holds him beneath the warmth of the duvet, clutching him. He feels a distance between them even though she's right there, running her fingers through his hair. They slip wordlessly from a sitting position to a lying one and soon Róisín is asleep. Aaron stares at the ceiling of his bedroom. He tries to remember what the ceiling of the hospital room looks like but is unable to do so. All of that time spent there and he never once looked up. Róisín murmurs something in her sleep, rolls over and pulls the covers up over her shoulder.

26

It's the tapping that wakes her, or else the tapping is the first thing she notices once awake, those low rhythmic thumps. She reaches out in bed and finds herself alone.

'Aaron?' she whispers.

There is no response. She opens the bathroom door slowly; it's empty. She takes timid steps down the staircase into the kitchen. The table has been cleared, the string light boxes all put away. Róisín feels like crying or screaming, something to do with all that guilt and grief churning in her stomach like hot oil. She checks her phone. There's a text message from Sofia.

i've been thinking about you a lot lately and wanted to say–

Róisín swipes the notification away. She closes her eyes and thinks about ocean waves. There it is again. Tap. Tap. Tap. She finally finds Aaron in the basement, his face scrunched up in concentration, nails sticking out of the corner of his mouth. He doesn't notice her come in.

There's a crib against the far wall. A pram still in its box. Everything has been painted an inoffensive shade of blue. She remembers Aaron bringing her the colour swatches while she lay in bed, how badly she wanted to tell him then how she was feeling: like there was a piece of her missing in the shape of a home, that she wasn't sure if she could do this after all. But admitting that fact was tantamount to taking away a life ahead of Aaron, a life he was so clearly excited for. Some amount of discomfort and pain could be exchanged in order to solve his want. It was that simple. Now, standing in the nursery she's refused to visit, she sees the impossibility of the path ahead. She puts a hand on Aaron's shoulder and he jerks back, seeing her.

'I didn't mean to scare you,' she says.

'Why are you whispering?'

'It's late, I don't know.'

'Right,' Aaron says. He takes the nails out from his mouth and holds them in his hand.

'What are you doing?' she asks.

Aaron rubs the back of his neck and makes an off-hand gesture towards the wall. There's a wooden bracket hanging by one nail and another matching bracket on the floor. The rest of the shelf sits in pieces.

'He wanted me to put it together and I kept saying I'd do it another time. I want it to be up for when he comes home,' Aaron says.

Róisín pulls him towards her and wraps him in her arms, pressing him tightly against her as if, through sheer will, she can absorb him, or at least absorb his pain. He sniffles and, when Róisín releases him, he's quick to wipe his face and erase any evidence of tears that may have existed.

In the waiting room, when the doctor asked if anyone wanted to see Michael, Aaron asked Róisín if she wanted to go. Annette flinched when he asked it, only for a second, but it was visible. Róisín was not welcome in that room and, as she sat back down and watched the two follow the doctor out of the waiting room, she felt embarrassed to have thought she would have been.

When they moved into the house, Róisín felt like a stranger. Her presence was an unwelcome intrusion. It took time for her to feel comfortable even coming down the stairs on her own without explicitly asking Aaron if it was allowed, or to grab a fork when she needed one, or a mug for coffee. Eventually, Michael was the one who made her feel at ease; her time with him convinced her that the feelings of otherness she had were unwarranted. He called her his 'future daughter-in-law' once, as an off-handed explanation of their relationship to someone outside the family. *I am home*, she had convinced herself. So she would have assumed she could come with the doctor to see him. It was the question that gave her pause, the sudden revelation that she was still an outsider who needed to be asked. And then his mother's flinch. She sat back down and waited, alone. Her stomach felt like it was folding inside out.

'I didn't do anything to upset you, did I?'

When she closed her eyes, she saw Michael's face in the moment of asking that question. Even with the muted expression of his half-frown, he had managed to convey utter hopeless sorrow that he might have done something wrong. He only wanted her to feel at home, she realised in the waiting room. Any arguments were between him and his son. That relationship was incidental to the one growing between the two of them. He always wanted a daughter, he'd told her that, hadn't he? The plastic seat dug into her. The longer she sat, the more she imagined an edge to his voice even in these tenderest of moments.

'I didn't do anything to upset you, did I?'

As in, you have no right to be upset. As in, any perceived slight against you should be measured carefully against the favours done on your behalf. Perhaps what Róisín was imagining, if anything, was that there ever existed a heart in his words. She was never welcome here. Aaron told her once about something called tzedakah after running an errand with his father. He said that charity for praise was performative, a transaction with good deeds on one side and applause on the other. Tzedakah meant the Jewish obligation to do the right thing. At the time, she'd seen this lesson as an effort of inclusion. Only looking back, she saw that what he was trying to tell her was that she was an obligation, a responsibility, a burden. He and his family would take care of her because they had to, that was all. She stood up and stretched. A dull ache had set into the muscles of her legs. She removed the phone from her pocket and checked the time. Only thirty minutes had passed. They felt like hours.

Now, in the basement of the house, Róisín takes Aaron's hand in hers and they look at one another. Aaron opened a locked door inside of himself once and Róisín thought the world of the simple action of letting her in. Now he has nothing left to confide. She has nothing more to comfort him with. He squeezes her hand twice and then lets go, nodding towards the wall. She feels the distance grow between them, the coldness of standing on the outside of a door that is locked once more.

Aaron brings a nail to the wall and steadies it between his index finger and thumb. He raises the hammer in his other hand and, just before he can strike, the phone upstairs unleashes a ring. They stand there and dumbly look at one another in the momentary silence that follows. Then it rings again. Aaron runs up the stairs and Róisín follows him. He picks up the landline in the kitchen. Róisín watches his face. There's the staticky buzz of a voice on the other end. Aaron nods. The buzz continues.

'Yes, okay,' he says. 'All right.'

There's a clattering of footsteps above, Annette waking up, maybe, coming down the stairs. Róisín sits at the kitchen table.

Aaron nods again. His voice is gummy when he says, 'okay.'

'What is it?' his mother asks.

'What happens now?' Aaron says into the phone.

His mother looks at Róisín for a moment, seemingly considering her presence, then refocuses on her son. 'What is it?' she repeats.

'Okay,' Aaron says. His voice is wet, his eyes glossy. 'Right.'

Róisín stands from the table as Aaron hangs up the phone. He looks at his mother and opens his mouth to say something, but there's only a dry pop. Annette rubs his back, coaxing out the words.

'He's gone,' Aaron says.

Róisín holds onto the chair at the table head for balance and watches Aaron weep onto his mother's shoulder, crying as she holds him. This is the end of something utter and complete. Róisín feels a voyeuristic compulsion to watch the grief unfold and forces herself instead to stare at the floor between her feet. The world blurs and rights itself as tears gather in her eyes and fall away.

27

Traffic starts up half a mile out from their exit. Aaron holds onto the steering wheel with both of his hands and stares at the back of the car in front of them. Two talk radio hosts argue about football. The audio is so riddled with static it is impossible to understand what they are saying.

'What?' Róisín asks.

'I didn't say anything.'

'Oh, I thought you said something.'

'I didn't,' Aaron says.

Róisín tucks her hand against her cheek and rests her head against the passenger window. They sit in silence. Breaks form in the line in front of them and soon it is their time to move forward a few hundred feet. The breaks close and they slow to a standstill again.

Aaron finds himself glancing at the lanes on the other side of the highway divider. There is no traffic in the other direction. The ride back home will be uninterrupted. Róisín leans towards the centre console and turns the radio volume down.

'I'm getting a headache,' she says.

'I can turn it off if you want.'

'No, that's all right.'

'I'm not even really listening to it,' he says.

'I prefer it on.'

Space appears in front of them as the traffic crawls. Aaron takes his foot off the brake and they roll forward to catch up with the car ahead then stop again. It'll take an extra hour to get there at this time of day, but they've afforded an extra two, just in case.

'Sorry,' Róisín says.

He taps a button on the centre console and the radio cuts out. Now there is only the dull, muted sounds of moving vehicles from the other side of the highway.

'Leave it,' Róisín says, turning the radio back on. 'I said I didn't mind.'

Aaron rubs the back of his neck as he flips through the stations. Talk radio, music, advertisements. Each surface through the depths for a brief moment before he turns the dial and they return to the static. He circles the stations twice before turning the radio off again.

'There's nothing on anyway,' he says.

In Judaism, it comes in waves. That's what the rabbi told him. Grief, like anything else in this faith, has well-established steps to be followed. His father was dressed in white muslin clothes and buried with his tallis in a plain pine box less than twenty-four hours after dying. Aaron pushed a shovelful of dirt on his father's casket and left the shovel in the ground for the next person to pick up instead of handing it to them, lest death be contagious. Everything was followed according to custom.

The morning after shiva ended, Aaron and Róisín woke in silence and dressed in the dark, walking to the beach without saying a word. He put his gloved hand in hers and they waited for the sky to lighten and the sun to appear. And then she said what she needed to say.

'When?' he asked, and she told him.

He turned back to the ocean and nodded. It felt like suffocating. It felt like drowning. His face was calm and placid.

He was shutting her out already. Soon, he'd feel nothing at all, only that familiar and comfortable numbness.

'It's time,' she said. 'I'm just taking up space.'

'You aren't.'

'I am. You know that I am.'

Aaron forced himself to look at the shore. There was something growing in his throat that he struggled to swallow. He blinked a few times before he could ask the question. 'Was it something I did?'

Róisín smiled sadly. 'No,' she said.

'It must have been.'

She shook her head. 'It wasn't anything you did.'

'What do you want me to do, move?'

'No,' she said. 'I don't expect you to move.'

'What, then? Tell me what you want me to do and I'll do it.'

'I don't want anything from you.'

'Great,' he said.

'I don't mean it like that, you know I don't mean it like that. I only mean that I have no expectations.'

'I'm his father,' Aaron said. The words felt cheap and plastic in his mouth.

'You are,' Róisín said, then added, 'Or hers.'

'Will you come back?' he asked.

She didn't answer.

The sun broke the horizon and the ocean burned golden. It was beautiful and it was fleeting and soon it was gone. The sky became plain, leaving only the smouldering memory of its passing vibrance.

Aaron heaves her bags from the trunk of the red sedan and sets them on the sidewalk in front of the terminal. He's decided not to park and walk with her to the gate. She didn't object. Better to be done with it. If she's going to leave, then let her leave. They are surrounded by cars, all in the process of entering and leaving tight parking spaces, meandering in and speeding away.

Róisín hugs him. Aaron hugs her back. He can't keep himself from crying now. He buries his face in her shoulder and she holds him, squeezing him tighter. *Please don't go*, he thinks.

'I'll give you this love on loan,' she whispers in his ear. 'And you'll hold it for me.'

Aaron tries and fails to steady his breath.

'It'll tide you over until someday, whenever someday is.'

He nods. There is so much he wants to say but his mouth refuses to form the words, his lungs won't produce the requisite air. 'Okay,' he says. This is all he manages.

He watches Róisín pull her bags behind her as she walks to the entrance of the terminal. The doors slide open automatically and then she turns the corner and disappears into the crowd. His heart feels full and pure and he thinks for a moment that maybe she is right, maybe this is a feeling that can sustain him until they see each other again. Then the moment passes. Love is not a thing to be banked and dispersed as needed, he knows this. It is a living thing that breathes and bleeds and dies when you let it alone. Aaron stands by the car for another moment, not sure what it is he's waiting for, and then someone honks and he's quick to get in and drive away.

He chews on the inside of his cheek until he tastes blood. He glances at the line of cars on the other side of the highway as he drives back home, all of them still stuck in traffic on the way to the airport. They had so much time, and only now that it's gone does he realise how little he made of it. He could have made a joke. They could have laughed together. He looks at the empty passenger seat and it hits him for the first time that she is gone, really gone, and she is not going to come back.

It's some day in spring when his mother yells up to him to come with her out to the lawn. Aaron yawns as he descends the stairs and looks through the kitchen window. She's already out front.

Her knees are in a flowerbed. Aaron recognises this as the place he saw her planting bulbs when he first returned home. She's leant over the dirt and waves at him to come to where she is so that he can see better. There, interspersed in the soil, are little specks of green, fingertips emerging to reach towards the sun.

'Table iris,' Aaron says, and his mother nods and smiles.

'They're perennials,' she says. 'They'll come back every year.'

Aaron's hand sinks into the dirt as he kneels next to his mother. Small changes like these are happening all the time, all around them. Soon there will be a flower here, vibrant and rebellious, and then the petals will wither and the flower will die. How pitiful a life, and yet how beautiful.

'As opposed to annuals,' his mother continues. 'Those only come the once.'

Aaron stands, brushing away the wet clumps of dirt stuck to his knees.

'It can be difficult, sometimes, to tell the difference by only looking at the bulb; sometimes the only way to tell is by waiting,' she says.

She does this often, saying things without saying them. He looks down, considering her, feeling an enormous swell of gratitude and sorrow. He offers her a hand and she takes it, groaning as she stands. She smiles and pats her son's shoulder.

The remainder of this day will play out like the one that came before it, like the one that will follow.

This life, Aaron thinks. *There is so much of it.*

There comes the distant sound of the ocean tumbling into sand then sucking back out into the surf. The twittering of birds. The mechanical roar of an airplane engine, quieted by enormous distance, from somewhere far beyond.

Acknowledgements

Thank you to my friends who read early drafts of this manuscript: Tarlach; Scott; Hannah; and Larissa. Thank you to Maitiú, whose friendship and guidance led to the start of my literary career.

Thank you to my agent, Edwina de Charnace, for your confidence. Thank you to my editor, Jenna Gordon, who has made this a better book and myself a better writer.

Thank you to Stuart Nadler and Alice Mattison, who taught me how to write.

Thank you to my parents, who taught me how to read.

Every step of this incredible journey has been made possible only by the support of Sarah Conn. The debt I owe you is incalculable, and I will spend a lifetime trying to repay it. I love you.

About the Author

James Roseman is an American author born in Cheyenne, Wyoming, and raised outside of Boston. He's lived in Dublin, Ireland, since 2019. He received his MFA in Creative Writing and Literature from the Bennington Writing Seminars at Bennington College, Vermont. *Placeholders* is his debut novel.

jamesroseman.com

Book Club Questions

1. Do you think Aaron and Róisín have real feelings for each other? Or do they merely fill a void in each other's lives?

2. Why do you think Róisín decided to remain in Boston? Do you understand why she fears returning to Dublin despite her immense homesickness?

3. Does Aaron intentionally keep Jake and Percy at a distance? Do you think some of the judgements he makes about them are unfair or hypocritical? How similar, or different, is Aaron to them?

4. Róisín's boss at the coffee shop exploits her lack of visa. Why does she continue to work there? Do you think it's right or fair of her to end contact with Sofia towards the end of the novel?

5. Consider how interpersonal dynamics change when Aaron and Róisín move to the suburbs, within their own relationship and with other characters.

6. To what extent do Aaron's political and religious debates with his father function as indirect discussions of their grief about Moe's death? Why might they struggle to talk about their emotions more openly?

7. Do you think the lack of clarity around what happened to Moe, and the absence of a clear person or event to blame, prevents Aaron and his family moving forward from their grief?

8. Consider religion as a means of community in the novel. Does returning to his family home solve Aaron's loneliness at all? Does Róisín's atheism contribute to her loneliness in the suburbs?

9. How does the relationship Róisín has with Michael compare with the one she has with Annette? Despite their conservative views, how open are they to welcoming Róisín into their home and family?

10. Did you feel Aaron and Róisín's relationship was doomed from the start? Do you think Róisín made the right decision to leave in the end? Is there a chance of reconciliation for the pair?